A Country Music Christmas

A Country Music Christmas

B. J. Swanson

Lifetime Writings

2019

2024 Edition

ISBN 978-164669280-4

Lifetime Writings
Murrells Inlet, South Carolina, 29576

www.bevswansonbooks.com

Dedication

To Swanie

Thank you for your support and patience.

Titles by B. J. Swanson

Misguided Loyalties

Contingent Loyalties

Betrayed Loyalties

From This Day Forward

For Love of the Story

The Blue Tractor

Secrets & Lies

I Believe in You

As Waves on the Sand

In the Fullness of Time

Taproom

A Rose in the Marsh

8

Chapter 1

With her cell phone to her ear, Jenna Atherton faced the windows of her management office in Nashville, and laughed at her best friend Scout's comments.

"If only I were coming to see you for Christmas," Jenna sighed, "It has been way too long since I spent a holiday with family. Do they still serve hot cocoa and cider in the shops on the square?"

"Of course," Scout told her, "but I have to go. I'm back at work. I'll tell everyone you send your love."

"Thanks," Jenna said, "I'll call you from Lexington. Bye"

Jenna swung her chair back around to her desk. She put down her phone, and sent her fingers back to her keyboard as she worked to finish the details of her first quarter assessment since becoming the Sales Manager of Benton Corporation. She was the youngest sales associate to make manager and the only female in an all-male management team. She had worked hard for this position and wanted her first presentation to be perfect. Jenna loved her new office with windows overlooking Nashville, the city she moved to after college graduation. Benton Corp was her first and only job in the energetic city with the country music vibe. It was the place she now called home. The river was slightly in view between the two buildings across the street, but she rarely took time to notice. When her assistant Deborah entered her office, Jenna's cell phone rang. She looked and saw the handsome face connected to the caller and sighed.

"Hi, Brad," she answered on speaker as she waved Deborah into the office.

"Hi darling, are you on your way home?"

"Brad, it's only 4:35. I have a pile of work to get done before I can leave since I'm taking two days off."

"I thought we talked about maybe leaving this evening for my parents' house. It will be so good for you to get away from work for a while and just relax."

"Only you talked about that Brad; you know I can't leave today. It's only Thursday, and Christmas isn't until next Tuesday. I have a job that requires I work long hours. My first presentation is tomorrow. I can't miss that," she sighed.

Deborah waited as Jenna continued her conversation with Brad. "But Jenna . . ." he began.

"I told you I can't leave tonight," she said as she rolled her eyes at Deborah. "Listen, why don't you just go ahead and enjoy your family. I'll be there sometime this weekend. Christmas Eve is not until Monday."

Jenna impatiently listened to Brad's reasoning for about 30 seconds and then interrupted him to say, "Brad, I have work to do. Just go see your family. I'll call you tonight when I get home."

When the call ended, she reached up to take the papers from Deborah.

"You may be my boss and my friend," Deborah said, "but I have to say I think you're too hard on him. I wonder why he puts up with you."

"What about why I put up with him," Jenna said as she signed the papers she had been handed.

"Maybe because he's perfect," Deborah sighed, "handsome, sweet, patient, smart, romantic, caring."

Jenna looked up at her assistant. "Maybe you should be dating him."

"You know he's a nice guy," Deborah reminded her, "You've been dating him for two years and yet sometimes you speak to him as though he's a ten-year-old."

"Sometimes he acts like a ten-year-old."

"Why, because he wants you all to himself for a few days?"

Jenna looked up at Deborah and softened. "You're right," she said, "He is a nice guy, but it's not even like we'd be all by ourselves. We will be in the middle of his extended family. Anyway, I only talk to him that way when he whines."

"I think it's kind of cute—its sweet that he wishes you didn't work 24/7."

Jenna handed the papers back to Deborah. "He's a teacher. He gets two weeks at Christmas, a week in the spring, and two months off in the summer. It's a conversation Brad and I have had before. He doesn't understand my job."

"Well, I think he's sweet and I'm sure his students love him and think he's smart. What's not to like?" she mumbled as she exited Jenna's office.

Jenna leaned back in her chair and swiveled to face the big window again. Deborah was right about Brad. He was smart and good with the kids. He's probably being sweet when he pesters her to not work so hard, but it's the only way Jenna knows how to work. She did not get to a management position in the company by taking all her vacation days to hang out with friends and family. If it weren't for Brad, she probably wouldn't have taken a vacation day in the last two years—maybe not since her divorce four years ago. Even then she had taken vacation days only when she was told to.

Had it really been four years already? Jenna thought back to her short 2 ½ year marriage and how Drake, handsome and charming as he could be, told her what to do and how to do it concerning everything. He never asked; always told; commanded, from Jenna's point of view. The day she walked out she had vowed no one was going to boss her around again. That was what had attracted her to Brad when they were first set up on a blind date; he was so nice and laidback, nothing like Drake. Deborah was wrong about one thing. Brad was not perfect; and as far as Jenna could tell, no man was.

Jenna swung her chair back around as her cell phone rang. Expecting it to be Brad again, Jenna was surprised to see Scout's picture on her phone again.

"What's up?" she smiled into her cell.

"Oh, Jen," Scout sobbed.

Jenna sat up straight in her chair. "What's wrong? What happened?" she asked.

"It's my mom," Scout sniffled, "There was an accident. She's in a comma, Jenna. My mama may be dying. Oooohhh, Jenna. I need you!"

"I'll leave tonight," Jenna told her. "I'll have to delegate some work here and then go home and pack. I probably can't get there until midnight, but I'll be there. Is Jack with you?"

"Yes. He's here and my brother, Carson, is on his way. He was coming anyway for Christmas. We were all going to be together for Christmas," she sobbed, "and now mama . . ."

"I'm so sorry, Scout," Jenna felt the tears on her own cheeks.

Suddenly she was talking to Jack. "Can you come, Jenna?" he asked. "She is really upset. We all are."

"I'll be there as soon as I can, Jack," she said. "It will be late tonight before I can get there."

"I'll be up. Everyone is just devastated."

"I'm so sorry, Jack."

"Drive carefully, Jenna. If you can't make it until morning that will be fine. Please be careful."

"I will. I'll be there tonight. I'll text when I'm on my way."

Jenna forced herself to focus on the details of taking last minute vacation days from work, and delegating responsibilities. Deborah would have to make her presentation tomorrow. They went over it, but Deborah knew it, since she had helped prepare it. Jenna was out of the office by 7:40pm.

As she packed for the trip, she called her own mother in Austin to tell her about Scout's mother, Penny. They had all lived in the same apartment complex when the girls were growing up. Jenna's mom, Sally, had always worked evenings, so Penny was the one home after school; the one who did all the driving to and from activities. Penny was the mom who baked cookies and made elaborate indoor tents by moving furniture to accommodate blankets and sleeping bags. Penny sewed Halloween costumes when they were in grade school, and taught the girls how to shave their legs when they were in middle school. It was hard to imagine the ever-moving, effervescent Penny laying still and quiet in a hospital bed.

Jenna was packed and, on her way, before she thought to call Brad. She hit the button for her hands-free car phone.

"Are you in the car?" he asked after saying hello.

"Yes. I'm on my way to Monticello, Illinois. Scout's mom was in a bad car accident. I'm going to be with her."

"You're driving there tonight?"

"Yes. I'll get there late. I'll be careful."

"You said you had to work, that you had a big presentation tomorrow. You said you couldn't get away," he reminded her.

"I couldn't, but now I have to," she said.

"What you mean is that you didn't want to, but now you do."

"That's not fair, Brad! What I want is to go comfort my friend. She needs me. Penny's always been like a second mother to me."

"I'm sorry, Jenna. I really am, but it's a little hurtful to me that as much as I begged you to take off work to be with me, it only took a call from a friend in need and you drop everything at work to be with her."

"Brad, you know how important Scout is to me," she said.

"Exactly!" he replied.

"Brad, Penny might die! This is not a vacation."

"I'm sorry about Penny and Scout, Jenna," he said, "but I am also sorry about us."

"What are you talking about? I have to go to her. She needs me. I would have thought you'd understand!"

"I think I do," he sighed.

"What's that supposed to mean. Oh, never mind. I have to drive. I'll call you tomorrow."

"That's not necessary," he said before the line went dead.

Jenna drove in stunned silence. Deborah had called Brad perfect; well, obviously, that wasn't true! How could he be perfect and yet so insensitive? How could he not understand *her* need to be in Illinois tonight was so different from *his* need to have her at his side at his mother's house? She and Brad practically lived together, spending most evenings and weekends at her place or his. What difference did one additional day together make?

Dismissing Brad's pouting from her mind, she drove on thinking of all the good times growing up with Scout and Penny. She was anxious to comfort and be comforted by her best friend who was like a sister. They may not see each other often these days, but the bond of friendship was as strong as ever!

Around midnight, Jenna slowly drove down the quiet residential street and parked in Scout's driveway beside two other vehicles. Scout and Jack lived in a hundred-year-old brick two-story, that they spent the past two years renovating and decorating. There are Christmas lights on the front porch. The dancing glow of a fire in the fireplace and the multicolored lights from the Christmas tree shine through the large bowed living room window. The rest of the house was in darkness. As she reached the heavy oak front door it opened and she stepped into Jacks outspread arms. She found comfort as her friend's husband held her; the warmth from the fire and his embrace contrasted with the snowy cold at her back. Jack led her in and closed the door.

"Where's Scout?" Jenna asked, as she placed her overnight bag by the stairs and removed her winter coat.

"My mom gave her something to sleep," he said. "Her brother Carson will be here in the morning. My brother, Boone, is here. You remember Boone. You guys met at our wedding."

She remembered Boone, the handsome chick-magnet that all the girls were talking about at Scout and Jack's wedding. He had moved out west after high school and some of the girls referred to him as a cowboy. Others said he was in a band. It seemed he was a rebel of some sort and had shown up at the wedding with a drop-dead gorgeous blonde hanging on his arm most of the weekend. Other than sitting next to each other at the rehearsal dinner they had little conversation. She had been with her then-new boyfriend Brad.

Boone stood as Jenna entered the cozy living room lit only by the fireplace and the Christmas tree. He was cuter than she remembered and had a warm smile, probably due to the seriousness of the situation.

"Hi," he said, "can I get you some tea, or cocoa, or a glass of wine? I'm doing the wine." He held up his glass."

"Maybe a small glass of wine," she said. "It might help me sleep."

Jenna took the leather chair closest to the fire and curled her legs under her. Jack handed her a throw that she put over her legs and Boone walked to the counter and returned with a short glass of red wine.

"Did you get any dinner?" Jack asked. "There is already food from the neighbors in the kitchen."

"I'm not hungry," she said, accepting the wine from Boone with a sad smile. "How's Penny? It doesn't seem real to me."

"It isn't real to any of us," Jack said, sitting across the glass coffee table from her. "I am so glad you came."

"How could I not come?" Jenna replied. "Penny was like another mother to me, and Scout is my best friend. She would do the same for me."

"It was nice of Brad to let you come at Christmas," Jack said.

"It was not Brad's call," Jenna told him. "I had to be here. Tell me what happened and how Penny is doing."

The three stayed up for another hour. Jack told her about Penny and the accident involving an out-of-control car that came across the highway and hit her. Jenna told them stories about Penny from when she and Scout were kids. Boone mostly listened. The few comments he made had her smiling.

When Jenna went up to the guest room, she got ready for bed and thought about what she remembered about Boone from the wedding. He had had a date, and she had been busy as the maid-of-honor, so they had not spoken much. She did remember that Boone had been funny and entertaining as part of the wedding party. At the time he lived out west somewhere. She knew through Scout that Boone had since come back to Monticello, and was working for his dad or something. Jenna crawled into bed and pulled the heavy comforter up to her chin. The long drive and the glass of wine made falling asleep easy.

Chapter 2

The first time Jenna opened her eyes the sun was up and shining through the open blinds. She could smell coffee and bacon so she quickly showered and dressed to go find her friend.

The bright, gray and white kitchen was a contrast to the gloomy, gray Illinois winter sky visible through the window wall behind the table. Boone smiled as she entered.

"Hi," he said, "get yourself a cup of coffee." He nodded toward the end of the counter where a Keurig coffee machine sat near a rack of K-cups and mugs.

"Thanks," Jenna said, "Where is everyone?"

"Scout left early for the hospital, and Jack just left to pick up Scout's brother, Carson, at the airport. I'm making you a bacon and egg wrap before we head over to the hospital."

"Oh, that's not necessary," Jenna began.

"Yes, it is," Boone told her. "You'll need the protein. It will probably be a long day at the hospital." He cracked two eggs into a small bowl and proceeded to beat them with a fork.

"Really," Jenna cautioned, "I don't eat breakfast." She held up her coffee mug and smiled. "This is fine."

"No, it isn't," Boone said as he emptied a second bowl containing chopped onions, red peppers, and spinach into the hot pan on the stove.

"Please," Jenna protested, "I'm serious. I don't eat eggs in the morning."

Boone stopped and turned to face her. His expression was kind, but Jenna was beginning to bristle at his insistence. She did not appreciate orders from men; she'd had more than enough during her time with Drake. Breakfast might be a small issue, but she was not going to eat something just because she was being told to.

"Are you allergic to eggs?" he asked.

"Well, no, but I'm really not crazy about them and I'm fine with the coffee. In fact, I probably should have just waited to get coffee at the hospital. I'm sorry I slept in and I certainly didn't expect you to cook just for me."

Boone turned back to the job at hand and dumped the beaten eggs into the skillet with the softened vegetables. He then added salt and pepper and began to mix them together.

"No problem," Boone told her. "Breakfast is kind of my thing. You'll hardly notice the eggs. I chopped all this for everyone. You don't want to start your day eating hospital food."

"But I shouldn't have slept in," Jenna told him. "I really am anxious to get to the hospital and see Scout and Penny."

"We can leave in 5 minutes," Boone said as he sprinkled a little cheese into the pan and then removed the baker's apron he had been wearing. "I made everyone wraps to-go to eat in the car."

Jenna watched his efficiency in the kitchen. She had never known a man who cooked.

"I'm really not a breakfast person," Jenna repeated, as she walked over to the sink with her empty mug. "I think we should go."

Ignoring her comment, Boone continued to put the cooked eggs and vegetables into a flour wrap and fold it into a precut piece of parchment paper.

"Healthy fast-food," he smiled, holding up the finished breakfast for the car. "Make another coffee in one of those to-go cups while I go get our coats from the front closet. We'll take my truck. It's parked next to your car."

He rinsed the pan in the sink and left the room, leaving Jenna with an all too familiar feeling. She was not happy. She stood looking at the wrapped breakfast and the coffee maker and didn't move.

Boone walked back into the room wearing his coat and carrying hers. He raised his eyebrows as he handed her coat.

"Not a coffee drinker?" he asked as he grabbed his own large to-go cup and her wrap off the counter.

"Well," she began, but he was already opening the door that led to the side drive. Looking longingly at the second cup of coffee that she would have loved, she figured she'd get some once they reached the hospital. She was, after all, anxious to see Scout and hear how Penny was doing. Shoving her arms into her coat and grabbing her purse off the table, she hurried to catch up with him.

"Just pull the door behind you," he called. "It will lock on its own."

Jenna did as she was told, but suddenly slowed her pace. Feeling like she was taking back a little control, she sauntered to the car.

She's cute, Boone murmured as he sat behind the wheel and watched her saunter to the car; *a little hard to figure out, but cute.*

Jenna opened her car door and looked back at Boone. "I think I'll take my own car," she told him.

"That's fine," he said, "do you know where the new hospital is?"

"Well, no, but I'm sure I'm capable of finding it."

"Your call," he shrugged, "but we're both going to the same place."

Feeling a little ridiculous, Jenna closed her car door and got into the passenger seat of the truck. As he handed her the breakfast wrap that she would have left on the counter, she felt a little embarrassed, as she realized he was only trying to be nice.

"Listen," she began, "I don't mean to be difficult, but I'm really not an egg eater in the morning."

"Well, it's made and better than hospital food, but no one is going to force you to eat it."

Boone put the truck into gear and backed out of the drive.

Jenna realized she had come to Monticello to be an encourager, but instead her morning behavior bordered on rude. She unwrapped the egg to-go, and before taking a bite, asked, "Any word on Penny this morning?"

"Jack called the hospital before he went to bed and Scout called early this morning. They told her there was no change, but they also said that Penny's vital signs are good. Everyone is hoping she wakes up today. It will make Christmas a lot happier if she does."

They rode the rest of the way with limited small talk about the weather.

As Boone pulled into a hospital parking space, Jenna wadded up the paper that had contained the egg wrap she consumed. Neither of them mentioned that she had eaten the entire breakfast Boone had made, and her pride kept her from thanking him for feeding her against her will—although she did feel good as she exited the truck. Boone carried his to-go cup as they walked to the entrance. Jenna was thinking maybe she shouldn't have been so stubborn about not fixing the one he had suggested, ordered, her to make. Not wanting to overthink the situation, she returned her thoughts to the task at hand.

"Do you know her room number?" she asked Boone as the hospital doors opened for them.

"I was here yesterday. She's in 3029, third floor. The waiting room is near her room and it isn't bad for a hospital waiting room.

When our dad was sick, the sofas we spent days on were like sitting on a park bench. These are much better."

"We're not here for comfort," Jenna said as they stepped into the elevator.

"No, but at the end of the day you'll be glad they aren't like a park bench."

They were walking down a normally busy corridor when Jenna spotted Scout walking from a room three doors down on the left. Scout looked up and saw Jenna at the same time. Her sad face broke into a smile as she hurried to the only person she could call a sister.

"Jenna! You came!" she cried as she wrapped her arms around her friend and hung on. "What will we do if she doesn't wake up?"

"Scout," Jenna sighed, "I am so sorry. I got here as soon as I could. Is she any better?"

Scout let go and took Jenna's hand. They continued the path that Jenna and Boone had been walking.

"They're taking her down for another set of tests," Scout said. "I guess we'll know more when they're done."

The three walked forward as Penny was wheeled out of her room. Jenna and Scout walked to her. The orderly stopped a moment as Jenna took hold of the hand laying on the white sheet.

"Hey, Momma Penny," she whispered, "I need you to wake up and talk to me. It's almost Christmas," she continued as her voice cracked. "We all know how much you love Christmas and I have so much to tell you. Please, Momma Penny. I love you. Please wake up."

The orderly began to gently push the bed forward and Jenna leaned in to kiss Penny's cheek. She, Scout and Boone then walked into a room filled with sofas, end tables covered in magazines, with a flat screen TV on one wall.

"It's strange to see her so quiet," Jenna commented. "Penny is never quiet."

"She just has to wake up today! The doctors said it was quite possible, but they can't say anything for sure." Scout said as she tipped her to-go cup and found it empty.

Looking at Boone and Jenna as they removed their coats and put them on top of the one Scout had left on a chair, Scout said, "Boone, why didn't you tell Jenna to fix herself a to-go cup? Jack just called to say he and Carson were stopping at Starbucks and I told them to get me a refill. Do you want me to see if they have left there yet?"

"No," Boone said. "I'm fine. These are tall cups you left for us. Evidently Jenna isn't much of a coffee person."

"Wow!" Scout exclaimed, "When did that happen? Jenna used to outdrink all of us when it came to morning caffeine."

Before Jenna could answer, Scout gave her another big hug.

"I am so glad you came," she said. "I wasn't sure if you would be able to."

"Why would you think that?" Jenna asked her as they both sat on a seafoam green sofa.

"Well, you do have a life, a job, a boyfriend, and it is Christmas."

"My job is important, but I have time off coming and I can answer questions and handle office problems on the phone. Anyway, I love being here for Christmas; it's my favorite place to be!"

"What about Brad?"

"He's with his family. He'll be fine. There are a multitude of them. They won't even know I'm not there." She smiled.

"I'm sure that's not true, but it's nice of you to say it. I know I have Jack and Boone and their mom and dad, but I needed my sister."

"And I needed to be here," Jenna took Scout's hand and squeezed it. "I would not have been happy anywhere else."

Boone sipped his coffee. Jenna wished Jack was bringing her a Starbucks, but her pride wouldn't let her mention it. She'd wait a while and get a coffee here at the hospital.

The morning hours dragged by. Jack and Carson came in with their large coffees and one for Scout. Friends stopped by and left. People rotated going into Penny's room and talking to her. She didn't respond, but the nurses said she could probably hear them so they made sure someone was always talking to her. Carson said she'd probably wake up just to get people to shut up and let her sleep. He rarely left her side.

"Remember when we were little and she'd put us in bed with her and tell us we were all going to take a catnap?" he asked Scout. "Most of the time we would fall asleep for an hour or more, but after a 15-minute nap she would be revived and get up. Once in a while she'd fall asleep and we wouldn't, but then we'd get in trouble for waking her up."

"Well, it just wasn't natural to be awake and have her sleeping," Scout said. "Mom was always so active."

"I don't remember her taking naps," Jenna said.

"By the time we were friends she didn't," Scout said.

"She might have when you weren't looking," Carson said. "She could close her eyes for 10 minutes and be refreshed. I never learned to do that."

The morning progressed with stories about the old days. Boone listened quietly and drank his coffee. A few times his phone rang and he would leave the room to talk down the hall. Around 1pm, Jack announced he had to go work at the store for a while and suggested Scout, Jenna, Boone and Carson go by his mother's house for lunch. Beth had called to say she left stew in a crockpot. Scout and Carson didn't want to leave, so Jenna left the hospital with Boone.

Chapter 3

As they exited the parking garage onto the main street, Jenna made small talk by asking, "Were your phone calls this morning about work?"

Boone shrugged. "Nothing that important."

"Is your employer ok with your time off?" she asked.

"I'm kind of my own employer. How about you? Is your job missing you this week?"

"I'm in touch with my administrative assistant. We spoke this morning. She is handling a big presentation for me today, but I have every confidence that she'll do it well."

"You seem a bit concerned."

"Well, it is my first quarterly report since taking a new job. It would have been good for me to have presented it myself, but I did prepare it, so maybe it doesn't matter who reads it."

"You don't sound so sure."

Jenna smiled, "She'll do fine. I have vacation days, so they're working around my absence."

"Scout was worried about you coming after your recent promotion," he said as he turned into a tree-lined street with large, manicured lots and two-story brick homes.

"Deborah, my assistant, is very competent. She and I spoke early this morning and she'll text me throughout the day with updates."

"I'm guessing you're a numbers person," Boone said.

"Yes, I am. I'm sales manager and I keep a lot of numbers accessible at all times," she told him.

"In your head or in a file?" he asked.

"Both," she said, "but I remember numbers. It makes me good at my job."

"I'm sure it does," he commented as they pulled into a long driveway approaching a beautiful, brick home tastefully decorated for Christmas.

"Your parents' home is beautiful," Jenna said as they walked up to the covered front entrance.

"It is," Boone said. "My mother is a designer, so the interior is even more impressive. She has the ability to impress without losing a sense of welcoming comfort."

"Are you in advertising or something?" Jenna laughed, "That sounded straight out of Traditional Home magazine."

"Just fact. You'll see," he said, as he opened the door and stepped back for her to enter.

"Well, you're right," Jenna looked around, "It's just as you said."

She glanced from side to side as she followed him through to a large, modern, gourmet kitchen. There she put her purse on an antique side table.

"Where's your mother?" Jenna asked, appreciating the aromatic smells of the kitchen. On the counter was a covered plate of rolls with a post-it note that read, *"These will be better microwaved. There is honey butter in the bee-hive jar."*

"She and Dad are working the shop. This is their busiest time of year. Scout usually works there and Penny helps out if they need her, so they are even more busy being short-handed. That's why Jack went over. He also helps evenings and weekends this time of year."

"Why aren't you helping at the shop?" Jenna asked.

"Me?" he smiled.

"You can run a cash register, can't you?" she asked.

Boone smiled and shrugged. "Why didn't you go with Jack?" he responded.

"They didn't ask me," Jenna said.

"They didn't ask me either," Boone said and pointed toward a door, "Get us something to drink from the garage over there. I'll have a root beer."

"What do I look like?" Jenna asked, "your servant?"

"Okay," Boone replied, "then just sit at the counter and as soon as I warm the rolls, ladle the soup and set the table, I'll get our drinks."

Jenna sighed and walked to the garage where she found a large refrigerator filled with drinks. She returned with two root beers.

"Are you always so bossy?" she asked.

"Probably. Are you always so touchy?"

"I am not touchy!"

"Really?" he stopped setting the table to look at her. "My guess is you have a controlling ex, or maybe you just don't like men?"

Wondering if he had heard about Drake, she replied, "I don't dislike men."

Boone shrugged again as Jenna twisted the cap off her root beer and sat in front of one of the plates Boone had set at the granite kitchen counter.

"What ever happened to that blonde who couldn't keep her hands off you at Jack and Scout's wedding?"

"Oh," Jack turned with a smile, "you remember that, do you?"

"Vaguely," Jenna shrugged.

"What happened to that milk-toast you were with that weekend? He didn't look the controlling type, but then people can fool you."

"His name is Brad," Jenna said.

"Brad," Boone repeated, "He looked like a lost puppy waiting for an atta-boy pat on the head."

"Brad is nothing like that!" she snapped, "and for your information, we're still together."

"Congratulations. Did he ever grow up and put his big-boy pants on?"

Surprised and a little annoyed that she shared his opinion, she felt the need to defend Brad. "He's a gifted teacher."

"I'm sure he is," Boone said as he set a steaming bowl of great-smelling stew on each plate. He took the plate with four rolls from the micro and put it near the honey butter he had placed on the counter. Opening his own root beer, he sat across from Jenna and tipped his bottle in the air. "Here's to Penny's recovery," he said.

"Yes," Jenna said, lifting her own bottle and touching his, "to Penny!"

For a minute they both concentrated on eating.

"So, tell me when you returned to Monticello," Jenna began. "Scout told me once you were the rebel in the family; that you left and were not looking back."

"Yeah. Jack was the one to stay and keep everyone happy. He's a born pleaser; not that that's a bad thing. He followed Mom and Dad's footsteps and went to U of I, and then came back here. He had a couple office jobs, but after he met Scout, he got his Real Estate license and began helping with the business. He's a natural at all of that business and numbers stuff. As Mom and Dad get older, they depend on him more and more. I'm sure he'll own the store at some point; plus, he's good at real estate. He'll probably also have his own real estate business one day."

"That's not your thing?"

"No. I guess you could say I'm more of a free spirit."

"Do you live here with your parents?" Jenna asked.

Boone smiled. "I have a trailer on the outskirts of town. It's on land that belonged to my grandfather. It's kind of perfect for me."

"You don't help out with the store?'

"I do a little wood working. I also practice with a local band," he admitted, "but we don't get many gigs around here. I think mostly we like to practice."

Jenna looked at her empty bowl. "This lunch was amazing," she said.

"Mom's a great cook," he smiled as he stood taking both of their bowls to the sink. "You don't want Dad helping in the kitchen. Even on the grill, Jack and I are better than he is."

"Well, thank your Mom for me when you see her."

"I'm sure you'll have a chance to thank her yourself," he said as he rinsed the dishes and loaded them in the dishwasher. "We should get back to the hospital. Maybe I'll fill a thermos and take some back to Scout and Carson."

"That's thoughtful," Jenna said.

"I'm a thoughtful kind of guy," he smiled.

Boone and Jenna were fastening their seatbelts when Boone's cell rang. He answered it, "Hey, Dad."

After listening he replied, "Jenna and I are just leaving the house. We'll stop by and pick it up."

He listened again and replied, "We haven't heard anything. I'm going to drop Jenna at the hospital. If there's been any change, I'll let you know."

Ending the cell call, Boone backed out of the drive and said to Jenna, "We have to stop by the store. A delivery I've been waiting for came in. Then I'll take you to the hospital and see how Penny is doing."

"I guess no news is good news," Jenna said.

"Good news would be that she was awake," Boone said.

"You're right," Jenna replied as they headed toward town.

As he approached the area called the Square, Jenna sighed and smiled. "It has been a long time since I've been back," she said. "Even the wedding weekend I didn't really get into town."

"That's right, I forgot you grew up here too," Boone glanced her direction. "I'm surprised I don't remember you from when we were young."

"I knew who you were," she commented, "but there was no reason you should remember me."

"And why is that," Boone asked. "I'll bet you were a cute kid."

"That's just it. I was just a kid when you were in high school."

"Hey!" Boone feigned indignation. "How old do you think I am?"

"I know how old you are and six years is a big deal when you're young. You were one of the jocks I saw when I got to go to the big kids' games."

When Boone rolled his eyes, she laughed, "Boone, when you got your driver's license, I was ten; I probably weighed 50 pounds. Why would you ever notice me? If you had it would have been creepy."

"Okay. You're right," he said. "Tell me about high school."

"Not much to tell. I spent most of my time from 8 to 18 with Scout. We lived in the Westside Apartments and Penny always said we were joined at the hip. We couldn't have been closer if we had been twins."

"I forget sometimes that you and Scout grew up in the apartments."

"Another reason you would not have remembered us," she said. We weren't townies and we weren't the country kids. We were the apartment kids and that made us not quite as acceptable as the other two groups."

"That's not true."

"Of course, it is! Think back to growing up here. There was the country crowd that wore jeans and boots and had horses and their own language. Then there were the town kids who walked to and from school and hung out around the square. Then there was the group of apartment kids who got on a bus after school. Most of us had single mothers or moms that had to work because dad had a minimum wage job. We didn't know all that at the time; but we knew we were a tier below everyone else. There was no activity bus, so even if you wanted to stay after school, you had no way to get home. Therefore, we became our own social group. The problem was most of the kids our age were boys and by the time we got to high school many of them were making bad choices. Penny kept a close watch on Scout and me. We spent most of our time just the two of us, but Penny made it as fun as possible. I spent more time with her growing up than I did my own mom who often worked two jobs."

When Jenna finished talking, they were pulling into the parking lot behind Arch Design, the store Beth and Joe Archibald owned. Jenna wrapped her collar tighter as they walked across the lot to the back door for which Boone had a key. They walked through a crowded store room with a tiny bath and into a brightly lit and busy, fashionable showroom. Jenna looked with approval at the furniture and accent merchandise she saw. As they entered, Jack, who was working behind the glass counter, handed a large gift-style bag to a customer and wished her a Merry Christmas. He looked up and waved to them as the next one in line put her purchase on the counter. Boone's dad, Joe, was explaining the virtues of the fabric on an upholstered chair, and his mother, Beth, was laughing with two women helping themselves to the free hot cider on a cloth-draped serving table. A small girl was excitedly showing her mother a reindeer with a lit red nose. The room smelled like apple cider and cinnamon; a happy, warm retreat from the cold outdoors.

"This is a great shop," Jenna said.

"And a busy one this time of year," Boone commented.

Joe looked up and smiled at them. Boone signaled that they were leaving out the back and they turned to go.

"Shouldn't we thank your mom for lunch?" Jenna asked.

"Their priority now is the customer. We'll see them later."

They walked back to the storeroom where Boone inspected a couple boxes by the back door. He lifted the heavier one and asked Jenna to get the door. After depositing it in the back of his truck, they got in and drove around the square. Jenna commented on how little had changed.

"Some of the shops are different," she said, "but many are the same. There's a tattoo salon on the town square?" she noted with surprise.

"I'm sure that was not an easy permit to acquire," Boone added.

"And look! Tony's Pizza and Bennie's Pub! They're still here!"

"Tony had a stroke last year, so young Tony pretty much runs the place now, even though I heard his dad is there a lot—mostly entertaining the customers."

Jenna smiled. "Everyone always loved Tony Senior. Bennie can't still be running his pub though. He must be nearly 80 by now."

"Bennie retired to Florida right after Tony had his stroke," Boone told her. "I think he decided to find a warm place where he could fish year-round. The new owner wisely chose to keep the name Bennie's Pub."

As they pulled into the parking lot at the hospital, Jenna and Boone's cell phones rang at almost the same time. They looked at the screens and saw Scout and Jack's faces. Looking at one another, they hesitantly answered.

"She's awake!" they both heard and broke into big smiles.

"We're in the parking lot," Jenna announced, "We'll be right up!"

Chapter 4

For someone who had slept for two days, Penny looked tired but happy propped up in her hospital bed as though hosting the get-together in her room. Carson and Scout were beaming.

"Jenna," Penny reached her hand up as Jenna hurried to her side.

"Boy am I glad to see those baby blues open again," Jenna leaned in to kiss Penny's cheek, being careful of the IV line. "How do you feel?"

"Like a celebrity and I didn't do anything," Penny said.

"What you did was scare us half to death," Carson told her. "Promise to never do that again."

"I'm sorry baby," she smiled adoringly at her youngest. "I only ran to the store for butter. It didn't seem like a life changing event at the time."

"Well it nearly was," he told her, "next time you want butter—have it delivered!"

Everyone laughed and Penny saw Boone hanging back near the door.

"There's my Bum," she smiled at Boone. "Come give me a hug. What are you standing back there for as though you were a visitor?"

Boone walked to the bed and as Jenna let go of Penny's hand to step back, Boone leaned down and kissed Penny's cheek.

"When I get out of here," she asked him, "will you make me some of your famous pancakes?"

"You know I will," he smiled and stepped back, "but I have to leave you now. The lights for the wagon came in. I need to get them up before Sunday."

"Well, you go. I realize I gave everyone a scare, but I feel fine now."

When he gave her a skeptical look, she added, "Okay, maybe a little bruised and, believe it or not, a little tired, but all-in-all I'm fine." She looked around the room and smiled. "I love you all and I'm sorry for the scare."

"We all love you, too, Mom," Scout said with tears threatening again.

"Hey," Penny said to Scout, "aren't we supposed to be helping at the store? Take Jenna and get out of here. I've got Carson to watch me sleep if anyone feels the need to hang around. Plus, he may have secrets to tell me that he doesn't tell everyone."

It was an old joke between Carson and his mother. He blushed a little as he smiled at her. "Can I adjust your bed or your pillow?" he asked as he stepped closer to her bed.

"If you lower my bed and talk to me, I think I may take a little cat nap."

"Listening to Carson talk could always put me to sleep, too," Scout teased.

"Never you mind," Penny said to her, "go be responsible."

"The story of my life," Scout said as she leaned in to kiss her mother goodbye, "it's good to have you back."

"Tell Beth I'm sorry," Penny said, and then smiled at Jenna, "but I'm sending a good replacement."

Boone, Scout and Jenna said their goodbyes and left the room. They walked the halls of the hospital each with his or her own thoughts.

"Well, that's a big relief," Boone finally said.

"I don't know what I would have done if she hadn't come back to us," Scout teared up again.

Jenna put her arm around her friend, "But she did," she remined her with a smile, "And she's back to telling us what to do and doting on Carson—just like the old days."

"For once I don't mind her being bossy, but you're right—some things never change," Scout said. "Can you stay a few days, Jenna? It's so good to have you here, and Beth could really use the help at the store if you're willing. Wait till you see how cute it is. She has great merchandise."

"We stopped for a second on our way back from lunch," Jenna told her, "and yes I can stay a few days. In fact, if you'll have me, I think I'd like to stay for Christmas. It feels like home here. I've missed that feeling."

Scout hugged her friend as they reached the door to the parking lot. "I love you, Jenna. This is your home and always will be."

"Go sell Christmas stuff and have a good time," Boone said as he headed toward his truck, "I'm so happy about Penny, Scout."

"Thanks Bum," Scout smiled, "You know she loves you too."

They all waved as Scout and Penny reached Penny's little lime green Mustang.

"OMG! Is this really your car?" Jenna exclaimed.

"Yep," Scout smiled. "Jack found it for me for my last birthday. I don't think it was even that expensive. I mean, who else would want a car this color?"

"It is so cool," Jenna gushed as she got inside. "I still remember your award-winning short story in Mrs. Hurley's English class about Slimy, the green Mustang."

Scout just smiled, patted the dashboard, and started the car.

"You didn't?" Jenna laughed, "You call this car Slimy?"

"What else would I call it?" Scout said as she hit the accelerator and headed for town.

"Beth has hot cider this time of year, but I'd rather have a coffee," Scout said, "There's a drive-through on our way if you want one."

"Oh, please! You know me and coffee."

"Yeah, what was that thing this morning with Bum about you not wanting any?"

"Just a misunderstanding," Jenna said, "Why do you and Penny call him Bum?"

"Oh, it goes back a long way," Scout said, "We were all out for dinner one night when Jack and I first started dating. An old high school teacher—Mr. Cartwright—remember him?"

Jenna nodded, "Kind of a jerk, if I remember correctly."

"Yeah, that's the one. Anyway, he walked out of the restaurant with some high school girl and Joe said, 'and he called our son a bum!'"

"Really?"

"For all we know his dinner with a student was perfectly reasonable, but then Boone's dad told the story of how the teacher had called Boone out in front of the class and called him a bum who would never amount to anything. When Joe heard about it, he confronted the teacher at a football game and they almost came to blows. After that, Mom and I affectionately took to calling him Bum instead of Boone. It's kind of our little thing."

"He doesn't seem to mind," Jenna said.

"I think he gets a kick out of it. We've done it so long he may not even notice anymore. Anyway, Boone has always had plenty of confidence in being his own person. He knows he's not a bum and he knows we love him."

Scout pulled into the drive-up window. "What coffee do you want?" she asked.

Chapter 5

The afternoon at the shop went by quickly. The place was packed when they got there and they immediately put Scout on the second register, and had Jenna helping Jack and Scout by wrapping and bagging. After a while Scout was able to roam the floor helping customers and relieving Beth and Joe to have a break. It was a happy place as customers shopped, sipped cider and visited. When there was a lull around the dinner hour, Jack sent Beth and Joe out to get a bite to eat. Beth had cheese and crackers in the back room that the other three snacked on when time allowed.

Jenna was surprised to see it was 8:45 when Boone walked in the front door. Jack and Scout had left about an hour earlier when the crowd became a smattering of customers coming and going. There had not been a moment since Jenna arrived that the shop had been empty. A high school friend of Boone's and his wife and baby were in the shop when he entered. He chatted with the husband while the wife shopped and checked out. One customer behind her paid for a chair that Joe promised would be delivered Saturday and then there was quiet. At 9 pm, Beth walked to the back of the store and turned off the Christmas music and then she, Joe and Jenna walked to the recently sold chair and the coordinating sofa and dropped into them. Boone smiled and walked over and pulled up a nearby stool to sit on.

"Good day?" he asked.

"Very good day," Joe answered.

"But we couldn't have done it without Scout and Jenna showing up," Beth told him. "We were drowning in customers when they walked in. I was afraid people would leave instead of waiting the long line."

"Well, if you have to be drowning, I guess customers is a good thing to be flooded with," Boone smiled. He turned to Jenna. "Wishing you were back in that plush office chair being a boss?" he asked.

"I had a ball," she beamed, "Everyone was so upbeat and they love the merchandise. Corporate sales aren't near this much fun. I even met a girl who lived across the hall from Mom and I when I was a kid. She now has three kids of her own!"

"Did you get those lights up by yourself?" Joe asked.

"Yeah," Boone told him. "It would have been easier with help if they had come last month like they were supposed to, but they are up and I should have plenty of time tomorrow to get everything ready."

"We're closing at 5 tomorrow, so we'll have tomorrow evening and Sunday morning to help with the finishing touches."

"How is the merchandise going here?" Boone asked.

"We'll pull what we have left from the back room, but it is getting low," Beth told him. "Oh, and Mrs. Hart asked about tea towels and I remembered that I bought some last spring that didn't get pulled out for the holidays. I guess it will be nice to have fresh stock this weekend, but I don't want them left over till next year."

"Where are they?" Joe asked.

"There should be two boxes I forgot about on the top shelf along the side wall on the left. They will be from Paddy, the Peddler; a blue label with yellow print."

Joe started to get up and Boone stopped him. "I'll get them down and put out whatever else needs to come out front. If Jenna wants to stay and help arrange things, I'll drop her off at Scout's later. That way you and Mom can go on home and rest up for tomorrow."

Beth leaned her head back on the sofa cushion. "That would be nice," she said, "anything on the "A" shelf that fits on the floor can come out front. I think those two Paddy boxes are the only Christmas I have left. They are small, light boxes on the top shelf on the left."

"Got it," Boone smiled at his Mother. "Take her home, Dad, before she falls asleep."

"I'm not that tired," Beth said as she sat up and looked at Jenna, "Would it be okay if Boone drives you back to Scout's? We live the other direction."

Jenna looked at Boone and replied, "That will be fine."

"Good," Beth said as she stood to leave, "top shelf on the left."

"I got it, Mom," Boone said, "two little, light boxes with blue and yellow labels."

As Joe stood, Beth leaned down to give Jenna a hug. "Thanks, Sweetie," she said. "We couldn't have done it without you. Tell Penny we'll be by after these next few days are over."

Boone and Jenna stood as his parents left through the back door. Boone walked to the front door and locked it, hitting a switch that lowered the lights in the showroom.

"Sure you don't mind helping?" he asked, "It shouldn't take much time to set out the new merchandise."

His cell phone rang. He answered, smiled and said, "No problem."

"My parents are really tired when they forget to put the cash in the safe," Boone said.

He walked to the register, opened it, and put all the cash and checks into a black bag that he took from under the counter. Once in the back room, he opened a trapdoor in the floor, knelt down, turned the combination, opened the door and put the bag of cash into the safe. He then closed the safe door, dropped the piece of flooring and put the rubber floor mat back in place.

"That's handy," Jenna said, "do most small shops have a set-up like that?"

"I don't know," Boone said. "Dad was commenting last summer that he hated carrying a bag of money out of the shop at night, so I made a safe place for him to put it until he can go to the bank during the day."

"You made that?" Jenna was incredulous.

"Not that hard," Boone said, "dig a hole, drop a safe."

"It looks a little harder than that to me," Jenna said.

"Maybe not a Sales Manager kind of job," Boone said. "Now let's get this stuff out on the floor and we can go."

As they began moving merchandise to the showroom, Jenna realized that Boone knew exactly what he was doing and what needed to come out to the floor.

"I thought you said your family didn't ask you to help at the store?" Jenna asked as he walked out with a box of candles.

"I said they didn't ask me to help today," he said, putting the candles on the counter next to the candle holders he had already placed there. "Put these in places where they look natural."

"Excuse me?"

"Oh, that's right," he said, "Jenna, would you *please* put these around the room for my mom."

"What's that supposed to mean?" she asked.

"It means anywhere that looks like it needs something put a pair of candlesticks."

"I could figure that out. What I meant was what's with the attitude?"

"I just remembered you're touchy about being told what to do, so I asked," Boone told her, as he walked back into the storeroom.

Jenna started to argue, but decided to just put the candlesticks around the room.

Boone came out with another box of stuff and placed it on the counter.

"Are the candles supposed to go in the candlesticks?" she asked

"The loose ones can. The ones that are still wrapped go over on that baker's rack where the other candles are. The items in this last box can go where ever you think they look nice. I'll go find those two Christmas boxes Mom was talking about."

"They're on the top shelf . . ." Jenna started and stopped when she looked up and saw his expression.

"Now who's being bossy?" he asked, and disappeared into the back room.

Jenna was artfully displaying items around the room when she heard a loud crash and moan. She dashed to the back room to find Boone on the floor with his hand on his head and blood oozing through his fingers. She quickly grabbed the nearest towel and put it over his hand.

"Not that one!" he snapped.

"What?"

"You just grabbed one of the Christmas towels."

"I know. You're bleeding. What happened?"

"I decided to use the stool instead of dragging out the ladder. When I pulled on the Paddy box of tea towels, the other, not so light box came with it. As I tried to grab it, the stool tipped and the corner of the box hit me in the head."

Boone started to get up.

"Sit still. You're bleeding," she pushed on his shoulder.

"You already said that."

"But you're bleeding a lot!"

"Head wounds do that," he said, "Stop being so bossy and let me get up. What's in that other box, anyway? It weighs a ton."

"It's not that big," Jenna and picked it up. "Oh, it is pretty heavy. Oooohh. Look at these cute snowmen."

"What are they made of?" Boone demanded, smearing the blood across his forehead.

Jenna looked at the box.

"Onyx," she said, "Is this what hit you in the head?"

Boone merely looked at her.

"You should probably go in the bathroom and wash off. Then we can see how bad you were hurt."

"Would you please put the 11 remaining tea towels and the snowmen out in the showroom. And don't feel bad if my mom rearranges them tomorrow."

Jenna did as she was asked and returned to the bathroom. Boone had done the best job he could but the bleeding had not stopped.

"Maybe we should go by the hospital," she said, "You might need a stitch in that."

"I'm not going spend the night in the emergency room," Boone said.

"Oh," Jenna thought for a moment. "do you have an old hat in your truck?"

"Probably, why?" he asked.

"I was just thinking if you put some paper towels on the hole in your head and then put an old cap over it, we could go by and say goodnight to Penny and let one of her nurses bandage it for you." Jenna smiled, as though proud of her idea.

Boone thought about it for a moment and decided it had merit. Grabbing a handful of paper towels, he reached in his pocket and handed her a ring of keys.

"Lock the back door when we leave," he said as he turned out the bathroom light then hit a switch that put the rest of the place in darkness.

They walked toward the small emergency light at the back door. Boone opened the door for her and after they both exited, he pointed to the key that would lock it. Jenna did as she was told and followed Boone to the truck.

"You're driving," he said.

She started to protest, but then closed her mouth and got in the drivers' side. Boone got in the passenger side and used his free hand to pull his seat belt across his chest. Jenna fastened his and then her own, and started the truck.

"Thanks," he said, as she pulled away from the shop.

Jenna parked the car near the secondary entrance to the hospital. The lot was fairly empty at that time of night.

"There's an old hat behind the seat," he told her.

Jenna found it and help put it over the paper towels he had his hand on. There was already more blood oozing through. They slipped in and immediately turned to the left to the elevators up to Penny's room. Exiting on the third floor, they had barely taken a dozen steps when a nurse said, "Well if it isn't Boone Archibald! You disappeared after high school. What are you doing back in Monticello?"

"Hi Cindy," Boone smiled.

Before he could say more, a trickle of blood ran from his cap.

"Boone, what happened? Where are you going?" she asked.

"We were going to see Penny Newton," he said.

"He dropped a box on his head," Jenna said at the same time.

"Let's take a look," nurse Cindy said, and led Boone over to a chair to sit down.

Since Penny was asleep, Boone and Jenna left fifteen minutes later with a butterfly bandage and a gauze pad over his cleaned wound.

"That was a good call to skip the emergency room," Boone said as he opened his hand for the truck keys.

"I can drive if you want," Jenna said.

"No, I'm good," he answered.

As they pulled out of the parking lot, he asked, "Are you hungry?"

"Not so much," Jenna said. "It's been a long day."

"How about a drive-through subway sandwich and a glass of wine?"

"Your Subway serves wine?" she asked.

"Well, the sandwich is up ahead on the right and the glass of wine is at my place where we can relax and eat the sandwich."

"Wouldn't we disturb your parents?"

"Not unless they're sleeping in my trailer," he said.

"Oh, that's right," Jenna said.

"Are you nervous about going back to my trailer with me," Boone asked, mildly surprised.

"No, of course not," she replied.

"I can take you back to Scout and Jack's if you'd rather," he said.

Realizing she was not ready to fall asleep, she answered, "A glass of wine at your trailer would be fine."

Recognizing she said "fine" and not "nice", Boone drove to his place without saying anything more.

After seeing his parents' lovely home, and knowing Jack and Scout's place was small, but beautiful in the coveted historic part of town, Jenna was curious that Boone was taking her to his trailer on the old property that his grandfather had left. He didn't seem apologetic nor embarrassed that a trailer was his current dwelling. Chastising herself for being a snob, Jenna sat back in the quiet of the truck. Maybe he had stopped talking because he was second-guessing his idea to take her there. Well, she would put his mind to ease right at the beginning. She wondered if the furniture had come with the trailer or if he had purchased new. His father had been in the furniture business, so he probably could get deals on things like sofas and recliners.

Boone turned off the street onto a gravel road that led them through dark fields. The headlights illuminated nothing but the path before them. They made two turns before the light struck a large building ahead. As the car approached the barn-like structure, motion-censored security lights began to flood the area. To the left of the building was a trailer, or rather a long, sleek motor home, landscaped and inviting. Boone pulled up in front of it and turned off the motor.

"Home, sweet, home," he announced.

Being embarrassed by her earlier thoughts, Jenna chose to say nothing.

They both got out of the truck as a yellow lab came bounding up to Boone.

"My guard dog," he laughed. "He always waits to make sure it's me before he makes himself known. I tell myself he'd bark if it was an intruder, but I'm not sure that's actually true."

"What's his name?" Jenna asked.

Upon hearing Jenna's voice, the big, yellow dog looked her direction.

"Yeller," Boone answered, petting the dog's head as the two of them walk toward the front door. Pulling a large chewy bone from his pocket, he gave it to Yeller who walked back toward the barn.

"Yeller?" Jenna asked, "You're kidding, right?"

"What else would you name a yellow dog?"

Boone put his key in the lock, opened the door, reached in to flip on the lights and then stepped back for Jenna to walk in ahead of him.

Classy was the first word that came to mind. The floors were wood, or maybe laminate, the small kitchen had can lighting, granite counters and stainless appliances, including a dishwasher she noticed.

The colors were muted Pottery Barn with just a splash of burnt orange on a throw pillow and two picture frames—one of the family taken at Jack's wedding, and the second of an old man by a barn that Jenna guessed to be the grandfather.

"Impressive without losing a sense of welcoming comfort," Jenna commented as she walked in and ran her hand along the smooth granite.

Boone laughed. "I let my parents give suggestions, but I wanted something simple. This seemed to work. Have a seat. I'll get us a paper plate for the sandwich and that glass of wine I promised you."

Boone hit a switch and George Strait sang softly on some hidden speakers.

"The music choice is all mine," he said as he uncorked the wine and aeriated it into a clear decanter.

Jenna leaned back into the soft cushions and relaxed.

"This is a nice place to come at the end of the day," she said.

"It has a tiny office, an adequate bedroom that fits a king-size bed, and a bath and a half. It's all I need. You'll have to come back in the daylight. I built a deck on the back. It's where Yeller and I spend our summer evenings."

Jenna's cell phone rang. She pulled it from her purse and looked at Brad's picture on the screen. Funny, she thought, she hadn't thought of Brad all day.

"I should probably take this," she said.

Boone nodded.

"Hi," she said, walking across the room and looking out the window into the darkness.

"How's Penny," Brad asked.

"Oh, she woke up. It seems she is going to be fine," Jenna said.

"That's great," he said, "then when will you be heading this way?"

"I'm going to stay here for Christmas," Jenna said.

"But you said Penny is fine," Brad challenged, "Why do you need to stay there? I miss you. My family will be so disappointed. I'll be disappointed."

Boone's cell phone rang and he answered it, "Hey."

"I'm sorry Brad," Jenna said into the phone.

"Yeah, I'm fine," Boone said when Jack asked about his head, "But, how did you hear about it already?"

"Who is that you're with?" Brad asked Jenna.

"Oh, that's Jack's brother," she answered.

Boone laughed, "That's right. I forgot you took Cindy to freshman homecoming."

"Then you're not with Jack and Scout?" Brad asked.

"No, they left early," Jenna looked at Boone who was watching her. "Listen, I've got to go."

"Jenna," Brad said, "we've been together for two years. You know how I feel about you. What's going on? Why are you really staying there for Christmas?"

"We'll talk tomorrow. It just feels like home here. I want to stay for Christmas."

"How can it feel like home? Your apartment isn't there! Your job isn't there! You don't even have family there!"

"We'll talk tomorrow," Jenna said and heard the phone disconnect at the other end.

Jenna shrugged and put her phone back into her purse.

"Problems?" Boone asked.

"I guess it would depend on who you ask," she answered.

"If I ask you?"

Jenna merely smiled and asked, "Is one of those wine glasses for me?"

"Unless you want them both," he said.

"One will be fine," she answered. "Tell me about your time out west."

Boone recognized the shift in conversation for what it was and decided to entertain her with stories of his wild and crazy days.

Jenna was grateful and laughingly got lost in what she figured were exaggerated tales of his western exploits. She ate the entire sandwich she hadn't thought she wanted and the bottle provided them each with two generous glasses of wine. The alcohol didn't seem to be affecting Boone, but Jenna felt herself getting sleepy.

Boone noticed and said, "Let me get you back to Scout's."

"I shouldn't have come here," she told him.

"Why not?" he asked.

"Now you have to drink and drive," she said.

"Two glasses don't affect me like they do you, but you're welcome to stay if you think I shouldn't drive."

When Jenna looked about to react, Boone laughed, "Your virtue would remain intact, but your reputation might suffer. I can drive. I promise."

He put his hand down to pull her to her feet.

"Come on," he smiled. "I told Jack you'd be home by 11. He said they'd leave the side door unlocked for you."

Ten minutes later they pulled into Scout and Jack's drive. Boone walked Jenna to the side door and opened it for her. As she started to walk in, he put his hand on her arm. She turned and looked up at him, and he said, "I'm glad you're staying for Christmas. I'm glad this still feels a little like home to you."

Jenna smiled. "Goodnight, Boone."

"Goodnight, Jenna."

Jenna walked inside and locked the door. Boone drove home to once again be greeted by Yeller.

Chapter 6

Saturday morning was sunny and cold. Jenna woke to the smell of coffee and talking. She put on her robe and padded down to the kitchen. Scout was alone and talking on her cell.

"I know, Mom," she said, "but what's one more day? You won't be able to help with the Christmas Faire anyway."

Scout waved Jenna into the room and pointed toward the coffee pot.

"Listen, Jenna just came in. We're going have a little coffee and girl talk. We hardly spoke to one another yesterday at the store it was so busy."

After listening and smiling she said, "I will Mom. I'll get all the scoop on Bum's injury."

After listening again, she said, "I will. I'll find out what Jenna thinks of Bum and what's going on with Brad. Okay, I'll tell her again, but she knows you love her." Scout smiled at Jenna. "Rest Mom. I know but try. I know. Carson should be there soon. I'll talk to you later."

Scout set her phone on the table and picked up her coffee.

"Penny says 'hi'."

"I got that," Jenna smiled as she sat. "And she wants all the scoop."

"On everything. She's going nuts having to stay in bed and in the hospital."

"Doesn't she have a headache or anything?"

"I'm sure she does, but she wouldn't admit to it. Carson's going to spend the day with her. He'll probably be the one with the headache by the end of the day."

Jenna laughed. "She hates the fact that stuff is going on without her."

"Especially the Christmas Faire. She and Bum have worked so hard on it this year!"

"What's the Christmas Faire?" Jenna asked as she took a sip of her coffee.

Surprised, Scout said, "Okay, now I want to know the scoop."

"What's that supposed to mean?"

"Beth said she left you and Boone alone at the shop, and Jack said you two were out at his place at the barn last night."

"Yeah, so?"

"What were you two doing?"

"Nothing. We were taking merchandise out of the storeroom, getting Boone's head patched at the hospital, and eating a sandwich at his trailer, which is very cool, by the way."

"It is very cool, but if you spent the evening right next to the barn, didn't the subject of the Christmas Faire come up at least once?"

"If it had, would I be asking what it was?"

"Okay, we'll get back to what you talked about later," Scout said. "The Christmas after Jack and I got married, Maude Gator, remember Maude?"

"Yes. In fact, her daughter, Camellia, came into the shop yesterday. She has three children."

"I know," Scout said, "she married a doctor. They live a few blocks from here."

"Wow!"

"Anyway," said Scout, "Maude was trying to put together a program for the kids out at the Westside Apartments. It seems some guy named Walter Thompson, and I don't know who he was or where he came from, set up a perpetual fund when he died to fund a Christmas party with gifts for all the kids living in the apartments."

"That's amazing," Scout said.

"Well, Maude isn't a youngster and Cammie had her hands full with three children under five, so she approached Joe to help her because she heard he was retiring that year. Joe said he'd look into helping and talked to Jack and me. Of course, I loved the idea and since Boone always came home for Christmas, we drug him into it too. That first year we planned games and food for the families and got a toy for every kid. Boone provided music and helped with the games. Maude and her friends set up all the food, and Beth and Joe dressed up as Mr. and Mrs. Claus and handed out the gifts."

"You did all this at the barn?" Jenna asked.

"No. The first year we did it at the apartment complex under that carport like thing in the back, but it was cold. Boone came up with the idea of cleaning up their Grandpa's old barn and having it inside. That was a great idea, because the second year was colder and wet. Plus, the barn was bigger than the carport. The following summer Boone moved back to Monticello and spent as much time as he could working on the barn. He bought the trailer and moved to the barn so he would have more time to work on it. I think he also likes the idea of being out there by himself."

"It was so dark last night I couldn't really see the barn."

"Well, there's not much to see on the outside anyway, but the problem we had last year was that some of the kids couldn't come because they didn't have a way to get out to the barn. We tried to get in touch with every mother and carpool, but we still missed a few kids who were really disappointed."

"I can see how that could happen."

"So, this year Boone came up with the idea of creating a Christmas wagon that will pick up families and deliver them back home when the day is over. We sent out flyers and got many volunteers to be chaperones and work the game area. We have prizes donated and a free raffle for either a computer or one year of free house cleaning for the mom whose name is drawn."

"Really?"

"At first, we just were going to offer a computer, but then realized that meant someone might have to pay for internet service they couldn't afford, so on the back of the ticket there is a place to mark which you would rather have. It was a last-minute thing so the kids don't even know about it. No mom will get in trouble for not getting her child a computer."

"You guys thought of everything."

"We tried. I still can't believe Boone didn't tell you anything. It's become his baby."

"It didn't come up," Jenna said.

"So, what did you guys talk about?"

"Just stuff. Brad called shortly after we got to Boone's trailer."

"How are things with Brad?" Scout asked, as she held up her coffee mug and motioned toward the pot.

"Yes please," Jenna said and handed her empty mug to Scout who filled both and walked back to the table.

"How are things with Brad?" Jenna repeated Scout's question. "It's hard to say. I told him I was staying here for Christmas."

"How did he take that news?"

"Not well, as I guess you would expect. He's a nice guy, Scout," Jenna said.

"But?"

"I don't know."

"How long have you two been together?"

"Two years."

"I thought so," Scout said, "I can see why he would be disappointed you chose to stay here instead of spending Christmas with him and his family."

"I understand his feelings more than I understand my own," Jenna confided.

"Well, guys can complicate your life. I remember the dating years. So, tell me about your promotion. Is it nice to be one of the top guns in the company?"

Jenna snorted a laugh. "I'm hardly a top gun, but my new job has changed everything at work, that's for sure."

"In a good way?" Scout asked.

"In some ways, yes," Jenna told her. "I have more control of the sales area and am able to input some good ideas that are making a positive difference."

"That sounds good. You've always been an innovator."

Jenna laughed. "And you have always been my biggest encourager, but the job has damaged my girlfriend relationships. I used to get together after work with the girls in the office, including Deborah, who is now my assistant. We would talk about our lives, which included complaining about work and management. Now I'm management. I went out with them a couple times after the promotion, even though my peers advised against it. It felt uncomfortable. I started making an excuse for why I couldn't go and the girls stopped asking me. They either are happy to not have me there or they think I'm a snob for not going. Either way, I miss them; they used to be the majority of my social life."

"Do you like the job? Are there peers you can connect with?" Scout asked.

"I'm the only female in what feels like a good-ole-boys club. They have a working dinner every Thursday night at a nice restaurant. I went twice. It isn't what I would call a business dinner. The only thing I felt was job related was that they all work for the company and they expense the dinner. They talked sports and politics and made either stupid or sexist jokes; the latter they would apologize for as they laughed. I didn't fit and I felt like they too were relieved when I stopped going."

"So, what do you do besides work?"

"I hang out with Brad."

"Because you love him or because he is there?" Scout asked.

"When you put it that way, I feel so shallow. It's been two years and I care about Brad. I do. The problem is I know he cares about me more than I care about him, and I don't know what to do about that. I know I have hurt him by choosing to stay here for Christmas, but, Scout, I feel so empty these days, but here I feel like . . . I don't know," Jenna sighed.

"Your emotional tank is being filled?"

"Yeah, maybe that's a good way to put it, but what does that say about me and Brad. I stayed awake last night wondering if I've just been using him so I'm not alone. What kind of a person does that make me?"

"It makes you normal. I've met Brad. He is a nice guy and I'm sure you're being too hard on yourself. You know the two of you have had good times together."

"We have, but I see how you and Jack are. Is your marriage as great as you two make it seem?"

Scout beamed and answered. "The first year was an A+. It seemed like everything was fun and exciting. My mom said we were connected at the hip – kind of like you and I were as kids--only grown-up better."

"Because marriage includes sex," Jenna teased.

"Yeah, that does add a special touch," Scout smiled. "The second year has been a bit more challenging, though, as we have had to learn what to do when we were stressed or angry or just when we just made wrong assumptions about one another. What we are discovering is that loving someone means figuring out all the tough stuff together. I think we are learning that life is a bunch of highs and lows, so we try not to make too much of the more difficult times. We kiddingly say we'll be really good at it by our 25th anniversary."

"Maybe I should try harder with Brad," Jenna said.

"I'm not an expert, but I think if you have to try then it's not really love," Scout said. "When I realized I couldn't imagine not having Jack in my life, I knew I was a goner."

"Maybe I'm not cut out for that kind of love, Scout. I thought I loved Drake and by the divorce I wanted nothing to do with him. I thought Brad was safe, but if I'm being honest, I think he's a bit boring. I'm not sure if the problem is Brad or if it's me."

"I don't think either you or Brad are the problem. Maybe you just don't fit. Drake . . . Drake was another story. No one knew what you saw in him."

"Really? You never told me that," Jenna said.

"By the time I met him, you told me you were in love," Scout told her. "What was I supposed to do? You're my best friend, so I supported your decision."

"What did you see in Drake that I didn't?" Jenna asked.

"He was handsome and could be very charming, but he always loved Drake more than he loved you. I was young at the time, too, but I worried about you. If you were just meeting him today, I'd tell you that."

"So, I'm a sucker for cute and charming?"

"Hey! Who isn't? Brad, Jack, Boone—they're all cute and charming! We just get older and wiser. I think you're looking for more these days. I'm sure there will be someone who you can't imagine life without. You have too much to offer some lucky guy, but it has to be the right guy."

"Boone thinks I'm too emotionally touchy," Jenna told her.

"Why did he say that?"

"I told him he was bossy," Jenna said.

"He is bossy," Scout agreed.

"That's what he said."

Scout laughed. "See you did find things to talk about." She looked at the clock over the oven. "Let's get dressed. We need to be at the shop in an hour."

Chapter 7

The shop was busy from the moment the front door opened. Jenna was glad she was there. Penny was being released from the hospital, so Scout left around 2:30 to help Carson get her settled at home. As the day wore on, she realized how much she was enjoying the people and the festive mood of the shoppers. She wondered if every shop felt this way so close to Christmas or if it was the atmosphere of Arch Design. Everyone was welcomed as though they were a friend, and the customers appeared thrilled with their options for last-minute gifts. Jenna, it turned out, had a talent for gift-wrapping beautifully in record time. It didn't feel like work; she was having fun.

One thing that surprised Jenna was how often Boone's name came up in conversation. She supposed it was because his parents owned the shop, but everyone was excited about the Christmas Faire, and Boone, it seemed, was a large part of that function. Some people were just excited to take their children, but most were excited to minister to the Westside Apartment kids, of which Jenna used to be one. It was a warm feeling to see the town people trying to enhance the Christmas experience for what she suddenly thought of as "her people." She was also surprised to hear how much customers were anticipating hearing Boone's band. As the day wore on, she realized she was too.

Around 4pm, a striking woman with her hair pulled severely back into a long, platinum ponytail walked through the door. She wore tall pink boots in soft leather, cream-color leggings and turtleneck, and a fabulous pink, shaggy, faux-fur jacket. Her nails were perfectly manicured on gold-ringed fingers. She had more gold dangling from her earlobes. Her confident stride got the attention of every eye in the shop. She walked up to the counter and announced she was looking for Boone Archibald.

Joe reached out to shake her hand.

"Merry Christmas," he said, "I'm Boone's father. May I help you?"

"Oh, Mr. Archibald, it is so nice to meet you!" she said, "My name is Amber Golden. I'm sure Boone has mentioned my name. I'm his agent and I have wonderful news for him. Can you tell me where I can find him?"

"Well, he's pretty busy today," Joe said, "Did you come all the way from Texas?"

"No, I'm based out of Nashville, although I did spend a lot of time in Texas when Boone was there. That's a very talented son you have, Mr. Archibald," she cooed.

"Please, call me Joe," he said, "Let me get you a cup of my wife's famous cider. She's the lady in red, and this guy at the register is my other son Jack. This is our friend Jenna."

Amber acknowledged them both with, "Nice to meet you."

"Hi," Jack said.

"Merry Christmas," Jenna added.

Jenna and Jack continued to handle the two registers, one of which Joe had abandoned to host their guest. Amber seemed to expect the attention. Joe walked her to the cider table and poured her a cup of cider, handing it to her with a napkin and a besotted smile. "Here ya go, Miss Golden," he said.

Amber put her hand on Joe's arm, and with a practiced smile of her own said, "I would like to be Amber to you, Joe. I'm sure Boone will be anxious to see me. It's been oh so long since we've been together."

Jack turned to Jenna with raised eyebrows and a smirk. Jenna wasn't sure how to read his expression, so she just stuffed a little more tissue in the gift bag, and then smiled as she handed it to the customer with a "Merry Christmas."

Jenna was a little surprised at the amount of attention Joe was giving Amber. She glanced over to witness the same expression on Beth's face. At that moment, Joe looked up from Beth to the registers and excused himself.

"Please have a look around, Ms. Golden," he said, "I'm afraid I have to get back to work. I'll call Boone and see when he will be able to meet with you and where."

"It's Amber, Joe," she smiled, "remember?"

Joe walked to the back room where Jenna assumed he called Boone. He came back out to give Amber written directions to the Barn.

"I do have a GPS, Joe," she smiled, again with her pink-nailed hand on his arm.

"Well, I'm afraid a GPS might not get you all the way out to where Boone is today," he grinned, "it's kind of out in the boonies, especially for a lady like yourself."

"Oh, Joe, Boone and I have been out in the boonies together before, but I'll let him tell you those stories," her voice dropped to a conspiratorial low.

Another look from Beth prompted Joe to clear his throat and excuse himself to get back to the register.

"You have a lovely establishment here," Amber called to Beth with a smile and a sweeping wave of her arm as she strode toward the front door.

There was almost a collective sigh as the front door closed, as though every eye and ear had been tuned to the pink Amber Golden's presence.

"She was sweet," Joe commented as he returned to register 2 so Jenna could again concentrate on wrapping.

Jack coughed to cover a laugh, and said, "Merry Christmas, Mrs. Landon. How is your daughter doing?" to the next customer in line.

Life in the shop continued as before, but Jenna continued to consider Amber Golden and when she did, sweet was not the adjective that came to mind.

The sign on the front door read 'Closing at 5PM,' but they did not lock the doors until 5:35 when the last customer left. By then, Beth had cleaned up the cider table and was rearranging merchandise to cover the areas that looked bare. She also had made a table for the few Christmas items that were left and pulled out a Sale sign that she placed on that table. The shop would be closed now until Wednesday morning, the day after Christmas.

Jack locked the door behind the final customer as Joe pulled the day's proceeds from the two registers, put them in the black bag, and carried them to the back room. Jenna and Jack joined his mother on the brocade sofa as Joe returned from the safe.

"I tried to watch the sales as we rang them up today," Jack said. "I think we ended the holiday season well. It will be interesting when we total it all."

"I'm pretty sure we had a record year again. Can I send your check to you, Jenna? I'll do all the numbers later in the week. I'll fax you an employee statement to sign if that's okay."

"Oh, Joe. I was just here to help. I'm not an employee."

"Of course, you are," Jack said. "Scout gets paid when she works."

"But I had fun," Jenna smiled.

"Work doesn't have to be a chore," Joe said. "We all enjoy working here, and we would have been in trouble if you hadn't helped. So, like it or not, you're an employee."

"Besides," Beth added, "you gave up Christmas with your boyfriend to be here. We really appreciate it, Jenna. Thank you."

"It really has been my pleasure," she replied, "and this is where I wanted to be. The people in this town are so nice."

"And what about that Amber Golden?" Joe spoke up.

"What about her?" Beth asked.

"She was pretty nice," Joe smiled.

"I'm more curious about her 'big opportunity' for Boone." Jack said, "I wonder if it's as big as she makes it sound and what decisions Boone will make after hearing it."

"Do you think he'll leave again?" Beth asked.

"Amber seemed pretty impressed with the news she had for him.," Joe said.

"I think Amber was pretty impressed with Amber," Jack said, "Scout will be really disappointed she missed her."

"You think she'll stick around for tomorrow?" Joe asked, "She did come a long way to see him. I mean, she could have called him with the offer."

"My guess is we'll see that pink jacket again," Beth said.

Joe's cell phone buzzed. He read the text and announced, "Boone said everyone is done at the barn for the evening. He'll see us tomorrow."

"Let's go out for dinner," Beth said. "Jack, do you think Scout will join us?"

"I'll text her and see if she'll leave Penny."

The evening turned out to be relaxing and pleasant. Jack joined them even though Scout chose to stay home with Penny and Carson. Jenna thought she might feel uncomfortable, but it was just the opposite. She was treated like a special family member. They asked about her mom and her job. They included her in their discussions which ranged from family to future plans for the shop to what to expect at the Christmas Faire and then to the sudden appearance of Amber Golden and what that would mean for Boone.

"I think it must be an awfully big deal for her to drive all the way here from Nashville at Christmas," Joe said.

"Jenna drove here from Nashville. It's not *that* far," Beth said.

"Maybe she has no one in Nashville and wanted to see Boone," Joe said.

"You don't think she'll stay for the holiday, do you?" Beth said, and then with raised eyebrows, "Do you think she's staying at the trailer?"

"Mom, Boone's a big boy," Jack reminded her.

"But she's not his type," Beth said, "He's seemed so happy since he's been back here. He went out with Paula's niece when she was in town. Now, that was a nice girl—cute and wholesome."

Jack laughed. "And boring. Mom, Boone went out with her because you put him in a position where he had to be rude to not go."

"I did no such thing!" Beth declared.

"I'm afraid you did," Joe added. "She was a nice girl, but they didn't stay in touch after that one date."

"Maybe she didn't like Boone," Jack laughed.

"Of course, she liked Boone!" Beth said, "What's not to like?"

"Spoken like a mother," Joe said. "I think we can trust Boone to make his own decisions about his life. I'm sure he'll carefully consider whatever she offers."

"A girl like that—there's no telling what she's offering!" Beth said.

"Now, Beth," Joe said, resting his hand on top of hers on the table. She moved her hand.

No one responded.

"We have a long day tomorrow," Jack said, "Why don't Jenna and I get back to the house. You two need to rest up for your big appearance as Santa and Mrs. Claus. Wait till you see them, Jenna. They are amazing and the kids love them!"

"We love doing it," Beth said as they stood to leave, "the kids are all so sweet and so excited."

"Well, I've heard so much about the Christmas Faire, I can't wait to experience it," Jenna said.

"Just like at the shop," Jack told her, "I'm sure you'll be put to work."

Jenna smiled.

"And you'll get to hear Boone sing," Beth added as they left the restaurant.

"Yes, I'll get to hear Boone sing," Jenna commented.

They said their goodbyes and headed toward their respective cars.

Chapter 8

Jenna had not known what to expect, but the Christmas Faire was an amazing day that began for her when she, Scout and Jack arrived at the barn around 9am. There were people everywhere putting up signs, hauling in food and coolers, and calling out orders to one another. The inside of the barn was even more remarkable. There were large plywood panels that had been painted like theater sets to resemble snow scenes. There were others with traditional Christmas themes. On the right as you entered stood a large creche big enough for a live nativity, which Jenna was told it would be by the time the children began arriving. From somewhere in the distance she heard a donkey bray.

"This is incredible," she said, trying to take it all in.

"Glad you like it," said a familiar voice behind her.

She turned to see the proud face of Boone. He wore tight jeans, western boots, and a very cool denim jacket.

"Great job!" Scout said, giving her brother-in-law a high-five. "I helped with some of this, but seeing it all together is amazing. Is there anything left to do?"

"There are still a lot of details to take care of. We will be serving dinner, but it is catered and the local retirement community is bussing a group at 4 pm to serve the food."

"I saw food coming in now," Jack said.

"Some of that is for the workers today. Maude is handling all the food and the organization of helpers. A lot of my contribution is already done," said Boone.

"Your manger turned out beautiful," Scout said, as she walked over to tough the smoothly carved wood. "Did you make those rustic chairs?"

"Yeah," Boone replied, "it was a last-minute idea. It's probably not very authentic, but they are comfortable since Mary and Joseph will be on display for several hours. The shepherds will be busy protecting the animals and kids from one another."

"Animals?" Jenna asked.

"Just a donkey and a couple lambs for the kids to pet. After all, it is in a barn."

Jenna said, "Why don't you show us around. Is there anything for us to do?"

"I actually saved a project for the four of us. It involves being up in the loft and I figured the liability was less if family fell from up there."

Jenna looked at the height of the loft and back at Boone. "I'm not family," she said.

"Are you thinking of suing us?" he asked.

"Not until now," she said.

"Don't worry," Jack said, "We won't let you fall." He turned to Boone, "What needs done up in the loft?"

"I have lights all up in the rafters that look incredible after dark," he said. "Maude and a group of ladies made these angels that they wanted to move in the sky. At first, I was afraid it would look like ghosts, but when I say them I got motivated to figure out a system. It took a while but once I had an idea of how to make it work, I decided we could have snowflakes moving in the rafters in other places. I need the four of us to hook the system up."

"Who helped you hook up the angels?" Jack asked.

"Dad, but he's been a little busy lately and I think the four of us can get it done in an hour or so. Come on," Boone said, putting a brotherly arm around Jenna's shoulders, "Let me show you the rest of the Christmas Faire."

"We got lucky with the weather this year," Scout said as they moved further into the barn.

"We have been watching the forecasts and have moved most of the relays out back. That gave us more space to set up tables for dinner and room for Santa."

Behind the first row of hinged plywood was a craft area. There were three different craft areas with tables and supplies being organized for the kids to make Christmas gifts.

Behind the next set of boards was a large painting of Rudolph with a hole where his nose would be. Boone explained there was a red flood light that will shine on the hole and prizes for any kid that can throw the bean bag through the hole.

"They made it hard enough that we won't go broke giving away prizes, but the prizes are nice enough it should entertain the most competitive for a while.

"This is where we will serve dinner," he continued as they got to an area where people were decorating tables and setting up a refreshment area. "And that raised platform over there is the throne for Santa and Mrs. Claus to hand out gifts."

"This is incredible," Jenna said again.

"Outside these back doors are the relay games. There are small prizes that are age appropriate as are the various relays. Again, that's not my area of expertise, but the people in charge think of everything."

Jenna looked to another platform and guessed what it was for. "That's where your band will play?" she asked.

"Yeah, you get to hear the Mules play," Boone smiled.

"The Mules?" Jack said, "that's the best you could come up with?"

"We're musicians, not marketers," he said. "Yule time—Mule time. I don't know, by the end of an evening it kind of sounded good."

"Were you drinking that particular evening?" Jack wanted to know.

"We're singing in a barn. What can I tell you?"

"Hey, by the way," Jack said as they retreated to the front of the barn, "we met the very pink Amber Golden yesterday. What was that all about?"

"She said she met my family," Boone said.

"Dad was smitten," Jack told him.

Boone laughed.

"I didn't get to meet her, but I heard about her," Scout said.

"I'm sure," Boone replied, "The barn wasn't really her thing and yesterday was pretty much grunt work, so I was tired and dirty when she showed up. She waited in the trailer till I showered and we had dinner in town."

"Was her offer something to consider?" Jack asked.

"Amber's offers are always worth consideration," Boone said.

"That's what Dad said," Jack replied.

Boone laughed again.

"Since you're all dressed for work, let's head up to the loft. Everything we need is already up there," was all he said.

The time in the loft turned out to be longer than Boone had anticipated. The concept he had developed was simple but the logistics of setting it up took all four of them. Boone's plan had been that he and Jack would do the hanging in the rafters as the girls balanced on tall stools he had provided to lift the snowflakes. To show them what he meant he sent Jack up into the first rafter and showed Jenna how to balance on the stool and lift the wired snowflake to where Jack could reach it. The wires were shorter than it turned out were really needed, so Jenna had to reach far over her head with the snowflake. Her first try ended with her tipping the stool and Boone catching her as she landed in the hay, attempting to save the snowflake from harm.

"Are you alright?" Jack called down from above, as Scout ran over in peals of laughter.

"Nice save, Boone," she said, as she reached down to help Jenna up as she lay face to face on top of Boone.

"I wish I had a video of that move. A stunt man couldn't have done it better!" Scout said, as Boone picked himself up out of the hay.

Boone and Jenna looked at one another and then began brushing hay from their clothes and hair. It was obvious they needed to rethink their operation.

"Don't you have a ladder around here?" Jack asked.

"I do," Boone said, "but it's too big. That's why I was going to use the stools."

As it turned out, each snowflake was a three-person job. Either Jack or Boone in the rafter, one of the girls on a stool and the other guy balancing the girl on the stool. They talked about doing it with a guy on the stool, but the stools weren't made for the guys' weight, and the girls were insulted that they were being excluded. The project succeeded, but it took longer when only one snowflake at a time could be attached. The project also meant that a good portion of the time Boone had one hand on Jenna's hip and the other on her leg balancing her on the tall stool. Jack insisted on being in the rafter most of the time, and Scout offered to go up and down with coffee or water. Boone was a bit suspicious about their motives, but, then again, he couldn't complain about his part of the job.

"This should be our last one," Scout finally said.

"How're you doing?" Boone asked Jenna as she prepared to climb onto the stool for the last time.

"My arms are getting a little tired holding these things up," she said, indicating the last snowflake.

"Mine, too," he smiled looking to her rear end.

"Hey!" Jenna gave him a mock scowl.

"I haven't heard any complaints," Scout accused.

"That's because I'm a gentleman," Boone explained.

"A gentleman with a big smile all morning," Scout said.

"I'm just a happy guy; what can I say?" he replied.

"Could you guys quit fooling around down there," Jack called. "All my blood has pooled in my head I've been upside down so long."

"You're the one that wanted that job," Boone reminded him.

"Only because you seemed to be enjoying your job so much. That's what brothers do for one another; but I think I smell pizza, so let's get this over with."

As they hung the last snowflake, Jenna was more aware than ever of Boone's hands on her back side and thigh. What had previously seemed utilitarian, suddenly seemed more intimate. Instead of letting him help her down as before, she jumped form the stool into the hay, and heard Boone softly chuckle as the stool went one way and she again landed sprawled in the hay. Feeling herself blush, she jumped up, brushed herself off, and was the first one down the ladder to the barn floor.

Just as the last of the three stepped off the ladder, the sound of jingle bells could be heard coming through the front door. Santa and Mrs. Claus smiled and waved as they walked back to where the smell of pizza filled the air. The four from the loft followed.

"They look wonderful," Jenna told Scout.

"I know," Jack beamed, "I am so proud of them every year."

"I would hardly recognize them," Jenna said, "the white wigs and beard, the wire glasses, and the vintage, velvet suits. I want to be a kid again and sit on Santa's lap!"

"I'm sure he'd let you if you're serious," Boone said. "You can take home a souvenir photo if you want."

"Not like this," she said looking down at her dusty clothes. "Can we go home and change?"

"Of course! Let's grab a couple pieces of pizza and go," Scout said. "The wagon leaves to start picking up kids in a half hour."

"Oh," said Jenna as she grabbed Scout's hand, "won't the kids feel special?"

"Maude has buckets of wrapped candy for those on the wagon. As it goes through town they get to throw candy to any kids they see. She had to get a permit from the city for both the wagon and the candy throwing. Boon, don't forget you have to take along a shovel and bucket."

"For what?" Jenna asked.

Boone beamed. "It's a surprise this year. We actually have horses instead of the wagon to pick the kids up."

"Boone built the wagon sides and seats and strung lights like a canopy, so it will be lit to take them home at dusk," Jack told them.

"I means cutting the day a little shorter, but I think the kids will get a big kick out of it," Boone said.

"The wagons have to leave by dusk," Jack said, "Boone's band has agreed to play into the evening for all the volunteer families or those who have cars. I heard talk of the evening party being a BYO."

"Let's get pizza and go get changed," Jenna said.

"Well if the wagon is horse drawn, it will take a while to get back. We have time to look good!" Scout said.

The girls got their pizza and took off. The guys sat with some friends for a break. Fifteen minutes later the wagon was heading to town.

Chapter 9

Jenna and Scout walked to Scout's car.

"I am so glad they are having a sunny day for the Faire," Jenna said as they reached the car.

"Me, too," Scout said as she got into the car and started the engine.

"I'm excited for tonight," Jenna said.

"I can see why," Scout said, "with all the chemistry going on between you and Boone."

"There was no chemistry," Jenna declared. "If he enjoyed having his hand on my butt, that was his issue. It was not chemistry."

"Okay, if that's what you want to think."

"No, that's how it is! There is no chemistry. I have a boyfriend and you should have seen Miss In-the-Pink! That girl had chemistry!"

Scout laughed. "You sound jealous. A girl can't have chemistry by herself!"

"You didn't see her. She had chemistry with everyone in the shop."

"She's Boone's agent!"

"She implied she was more."

"Jack didn't say anything about that," Scout said.

"You ask Beth. She'll tell you. She was actually flirting with Boone's father!"

"First of all, a lot of women flirt with Boone's father. He's kind of a flirt himself, yet he's wholesomely harmless. I think women sense that so he is fun to flirt with," Scout answered.

"Does Beth get upset with him?" Jenna asked.

"No. She knows he's harmless, too."

"Well, she didn't like Amber being all touchy/feely with Joe. I'm telling you, that girl has chemistry."

"That's interesting about Beth. I've never seen her react to Joe's kidding with other women. You didn't see Amber and Boone together. It's possible they're just friends."

"I thought she'd be here today," Jenna said. "Maybe you're right. Maybe she did just come to deliver a contract or something."

Scout smiled. "So, would it bother you if Boone liked her?"

"Of course not!" Jenna retorted, "After all, I have Brad."

"Who you aren't seeing for Christmas; who you have hardly spoken to or even mentioned since you got here."

"It's only been a couple days," Jenna reminded her.

Scout smiled. "So, what should we wear tonight?"

"I didn't bring a lot of outfits, but something warm," Jenna replied.

"Warm and sexy would be good," Scout said.

"It's a children's program!" Jenna reminded her. "Aren't we going to be playing kids games and stuff?"

"No, I've got clout with the people in charge. You and I are going to be Santa's helpers. We'll be there to call names, help hand out gifts, and take pictures. It will be fun, and then after the kids leave, we're going stay around and listen to the band. We can be groupies. Jack packed some wine."

When Jenna rolled her eyes, Scout continued, "Okay, you can just do warm, but I'm thinking I want to look good tonight. Who knows? Maybe I'll get to meet Miss Pinky if she's still in town."

When Jenna squinted her eyes, Scout laughed. "That's what I thought! I have some stuff you can borrow. Trust me; we're going to look good!"

The girls got back to the barn dressed for the event. Scout was wearing a red sweater with a short black and red plaid skirt, black tights, and tall black boots. Jenna was wearing a black turtleneck that she thought was a little tight, but Scout assured her it wasn't. She had tailored black pants with short black boots and a wide red belt. She topped off the outfit with this expensive red, white, and black scarf she had splurged on to take to Brad's for Christmas. They had taken time on their makeup and hair, and had guaranteed one another the results were perfect. They had fun taking selfies to make sure. It reminded both of them of the many times they had done the same when they were young.

The wagon was just pulling in from its second pickup of the day. There was Christmas music coming from the barn and excited kids piling off the wagon. Jenna was surprised to see so many adults getting off with the kids; mostly moms of the younger ones she suspected. She realized the families were invited.

They walked into the barn; Scout speaking to many and introducing Jenna to a few. There was actually an older woman that

Jenna remembered from when she and her mom had lived there. Sweet Mrs. Coolidge looked older, but her hair style and clothes were the same.

"Why Jenna, dear, you haven't changed a bit," she remarked. Remembering her awkward teenage years, Jenna chose to take the remark as a compliment.

"Neither have you, Mrs. Coolidge" she replied.

They wove through the crowd of children and adults, laughing, talking and snacking on hot or cold drinks and pretzels. The craft tables filled up quickly. The more energetic children were ushered out back where the relays with prizes had already started. The line for the Rudolph toss was growing as competition for the serious prizes escalated.

"What do Santa and Mrs. Claus do now?" Jenna asked.

"I think they are over at Boone's trailer, staying warm and waiting for their grand entrance. I saw Mr. Jeffries horse trailer off to the side. Jack and Boone are probably helping with the horses."

"I hate it that your mom is missing this," Jenna said.

"Me too, but she is loving having Carson to herself for a couple days. I promised I'd take a bunch of pictures, so maybe I should get started before the gift giving starts and we're busy."

"Maybe," said Jenna, "I'll go out where it's a little quieter and call my mom. I missed a call from her when we were getting dressed."

"Why don't you go over to the trailer. You can keep Mom and Dad company. Plus, you don't really know many people. I don't know most of them either, but I am the Picture Lady. I want to get as many as I can while the light is still good."

Jenna walked over to the trailer talking to her mother on the phone. She told her how well Penny was doing, and about how so many people had worked hard to make Christmas special for the Westside Apartment kids. She said she would send her mother some of Scout's pictures. When her mother asked about Brad, Jenna told her it was a complicated situation and she wasn't sure what would happen once she got back home. Her mother said she was sorry. Jenna said she was too. After ending the call, she knocked on the trailer door. Santa answered with a ho-ho-ho!

Jenna was being entertained with stories of the kids on the wagon when Boone walked in the door.

"Time to change into my entertainment gear," he said, "Scout will be calling soon to let us know it is time for all of us to be at the barn."

Joe and Beth decided to use the bathrooms. As they left the room, Boone got a text. He responded and then walked to his bedroom. Jenna carried the small plates and cups they had used to the little kitchen.

It wasn't long before Boone returned to join the others in the living room. He had changed into a western-style red shirt with multiple colors on the yoke and cuffs. He was wearing tight jeans, fancy boots, and carrying a white cowboy hat. Scout called to say it was time. As they opened the door for the four of them to go to the barn, they were met by Amber's furry, pink jacket over an outfit equally as dramatic as the day before—long silver sweater, black, white and silver leggings, and white boots.

"Hello, darling!" she said as she stepped forward to kiss Boone.

"I believe you met my parents," he said, stepping back from her embrace, "Mr. and Mrs. Claus."

"Oh My, Joe," she gushed, "you two look amazing! I love it! Yesterday a designer shop—today a barn decorated for Christmas! This is small-town America at its best!"

"We try," Beth said with an attitude that only Amber seemed not to notice, "but we have to keep moving. Our small-town people are waiting for us."

Beth led Joe past Boone and Amber, with Jenna bringing up the rear.

"Janet, wasn't it?" Amber addressed her.

"Jenna," she responded.

Amber smiled, "You look cute, too."

Boone looked back at Jenna. "Dad and I are the luckiest men in the house tonight," he said.

"You mean in the barn," Jenna said as pulled the front door of the trailer shut. "Does it lock on its own?" she asked.

The three followed Mr. and Mrs. Claus to the barn in silence, Amber mostly watching the ground so as not to soil her white boots.

As they entered the beautifully lit barn, Scout rushed up to them with her phone in her hand.

"They're hear," she said into the phone. Then to the group entering, she said, "Boone you're up first. Go. We'll see that Amber is seated."

Amber started to speak when the band playing Christmas carols stopped and one of Boone's band buddies spoke into the mic.

"Wait!" he shouted, "I think we may have a guest joining us."

Scout started shaking the leather strap of large jingle bells in her other hand and the kids on the other side of the plywood wall began to cheer.

Boone ran around the screen, pulled off his hat and in a dramatic fashion bowed and ran to the stage.

The adults cheered and the kids booed. He hopped onto the stage and walked to the mic as his buddy backed up smiling.

"I thought you were waiting for me," he yelled into the mic and the kids all yelled back "Boo" and "No!"

"What!" he yelled incredulously, "Well, who were you waiting for?"

"Santa," they yelled.

"Who?" Boone yelled back at them.

"SANTA!" they repeated louder.

"Oh," Boone took off his hat and in a grand gesture, bowed toward the end of the screened wall. "Here they come, now!"

As the jingle bells continued to ring, Santa Claus and Mrs. Claus appeared and walked to their seats amid thundering applause and shouting. The kids were barely able to contain themselves as they jumped up and down and pounded on the tables.

Jack walked over and took Amber's elbow. Scout and Jenna followed pulling a large wagon with four huge red bags loaded with gifts. The children continued to cheer as the band played 'Here Comes Santa Claus.'"

Jack took Amber to a seat where he had filled a paper plate with food and a drink in a paper cup. Since the roar in the room outdid even the music, he motioned and she sat.

Boone raised his hands as the music softened. All eyes turned back to him when he spoke.

"We are so glad Santa and Mrs. Claus are here. They spent the afternoon unloading presents from their magic sleigh."

The kids went wild again. Boone let them for a minute, and then quieted them down by raising both hands and speaking into the mic.

Jenna could tell this was not the first time he had played to a crowd. He was not only commanding, but he seemed in his element; he was thoroughly enjoying himself.

"Santa has drafted two beautiful helpers," he smiled and gestured toward Scout and Jenna, who bowed for the crowd. "They have only one job today and that is to make sure that all the presents in those big bags get handed out to all of you."

Again, the barn erupted in cheers.

"Because there are so many of you, we have a plan. Jenna will pull a gift from the bag and call out a name. When your name is called, you get to walk up to Santa. You can either sit on his lap, or stand on the red X so Scout can take your picture. Then Santa will ask you to tell him something you are grateful for, and Mrs. Claus will hand you your Christmas present. Our only request is for you to not open your present until you get home."

There was a collective "aaawww" from the group.

"I know it will be hard, but haven't you already had a great day?"

More applause.

"That's what I thought. I think we should all give a big round of applause for the many people who made this Christmas Faire possible. If you did anything to help with today will you please stand."

People all over the room stood and received a big round of cheers.

"Now," Boone said, "before we start passing out your gifts, we have two gifts we would like to give to two moms. The first gift from Mrs. Claus goes to Maude Gator, without whom this day would not be possible. I happen to know that she is already working on next year's Faire. Maude, please come up and receive a gift from Mrs. Claus."

Everyone applauded as a red-faced Maude hurried up to receive an envelope with a thank you card and a gift card inside. She posed for her picture with Mrs. Claus and Santa.

"Now," Boone said, "we have one more gift to give. Each Mom when she entered the barn today was asked to sign a card that was put into this magic Christmas box. Boone looked back and smiled at Amber. We have a special out-of-town guest with us today, Ms. Amber Golden from Nashville, Tennessee. I am going to ask her to come up and draw a card out of the magic box. We then have a special gift for the Mom whose name is drawn."

Although surprised by the request, Amber stood and sashayed to the stage, waving to the crowd as though she were the main attraction. Boone reached out his hand to assist her upon the stage, and she beamed and waved as she leaned into the mic.

"This is such a surprise," she announced, "I am honored to present a gift to a special mom. We all know how special moms are, right kids?"

The children and adults all responded to Amber just as she expected them to with smiles and applause. Jenna walked across the room with the magic box, took the two steps up to the stage and held it high for Amber to pull a name from it. Amber put her hands to her face and then shrugged her shoulders and made her eyes twinkle as though it were the event of the evening. Everyone applauded again. With a dramatic wave of her hand, she reached into the box and removed a card. She silently read the card and then looked at the crowd with the dramatic pause of an awards show presenter. Finally, she read the name in a flourish as though it was exactly who she was hoping it would be.

"Liza Brown!"

Everyone applauded and looked around as a young, brown-skinned girl handed her baby to an older woman sitting next to her and walked to the front of the room. Boone again reached down to assist her up onto the stage. Jenna took the appropriate envelope off the small table behind her and handed it to Liza.

Boone put his hand on Liza's shoulder and with a big smile said, "We are going to make one exception tonight. Liza we would like you to open your gift and tell all these waiting people what it is."

Liza opened the envelope and removed a card. Inside the card was taped a gift certificate for 12 cleanings of her apartment in the coming year. Liza, gasped as she realized what it said. Boone adjusted the mic lower so she could speak into it.

"Oh, my," she smiled. "I have a toddler and a baby. My poor mother watches them while I work and we all live in my little apartment. This says that for the next year, I will have a Merry Maid come to my place and clean it once a month. I can't believe it. Mama," she said, looking to the back of the room, "won't that be wonderful? Thank you everyone!"

Boone told her to go by Santa to get her picture taken, and helped her off the stage. He then turned to do the same for Amber.

Picking up his guitar, he said, "The band and I would like to play softly for you as Santa and Mrs. Claus have the honor of presenting each child here with a gift. The first bags are for the younger children."

A big sigh of disapproval came from the floor.

"Now I happen to know that the boys and girls of Monticello are loving and kind at heart," he said, "so as you older ones think of what you will tell Santa you are thankful for, the younger ones will get their presents so they can be on the first wagon to go home and get a good night's sleep."

The band started up and softly played 'Jolly Ole Saint Nicholas' as Jenna called out a child's name and the gift giving began.

When Jenna signaled Boone that the last of the young children's gifts had been presented, Boone announced that the pictures taken would be available to download from a website by the end of the week. Jack stood at the back of the room. He and his good friend Jeff would accompany the tractor-pulled wagon as the first group was taken home. By the time the wagon returned, the second group was waiting. Because they had to wait to open their presents, getting them to leave was not a problem. Many of the presents had ripped wrapping due to their curious and impatient recipients. The volunteers were busy cleaning up. Some would head home. Others would stay for more music. Boone noticed many friends and neighbors arriving. Word must have spread that his band was playing tonight. As the people were leaving the barn, the band took a break.

Chapter 10

Boone walked off the stage and greeted people who had recently arrived. Scout and Jenna folded the big red bags, and Beth took them with her and Joe as they went back to Boone's trailer to remove their Santa gear and wigs. They returned a while later in normal street clothes and also greeted people. Jenna and Scout walked over to Cammie.

"You two appeared to be having fun," Cammie said.

"It reminded me of when we were kids," Scout said. "Remember all the times we did make-believe?"

"I got in on some of those times," Cammie smiled. "How's your mom doing, Scout?" she asked.

"So much better. She's home and fought to be here tonight, but we left her with Carson."

"My goodness, I haven't thought of Carson in years," Cammie said. "I'll tell you as a mother, it's hard not to spoil the baby in the family."

"I'm sure it is," Scout said, "but I guess in many ways Penny spoiled all of us."

Their conversation was interrupted by a big, booming voice from across the room.

"Jenna Mcguire!"

As Jenna turned to see who was addressing her, she was rushed and then caught up in a big bear hug that ended with a big, loud kiss on the mouth.

Startled, she pulled her head back as she realized her feet were dangling off the ground. Her surprise turned into a big smile.

"Donny Melton," she laughed, "could you put me back on the ground."

"Jenna-bear," he said, "I've been trying to sweep you off your feet since you were ten years old."

"No, Donny, you've been lifting me off the ground since I was ten years old. Do you still live around here?"

"I'm in town to see my folks for Christmas and they said I had to bring them tonight to hear Boone's band."

"I didn't realize you and Boone were friends in school," Scout said.

"We weren't. We met up in Texas a few years ago and were surprised we were both from Monticello. I was there when his song first hit the top country music charts."

"What song?" Jenna asked.

"Don't Lie, by the Squires," he announced. "You didn't know our own Boone wrote that song?" he asked at her look of surprise.

"I didn't know he was a songwriter," Jenna said.

"Oh yeah! It made number 39 using the Squires arrangement. Personally, I always liked Boone's arrangement of the song better."

"So do I," Amber said from behind Donny.

"Holy crap!" Donny cried, when he turned. "Golden, what are you doing here?"

Hugging Donny's arm, she gave him a conspiratorial look as she said, "I wanted to hand-deliver Boone's new contract to him. He's opening for Barry Barns' first tour starting in March."

"No kidding! I like Barry's new song—saw him do it on the CMA Awards this year." Donny looked around the room and saw Boone leaning over a little old lady who was talking into his ear. "Good for Boone," he said, "he deserves a chance. Does he know who will be traveling with him?"

"He was caught off guard with the holidays and all. I just told him last night, so I'm sure he hasn't had a chance to form a definite band."

Donny smiled. "It's good to see you Amber. Did you set up Barry's tour?"

"Of course," she said.

"So, you'll be touring with them? Well, I hope to see you soon," he said. "Think I'll go congratulate my buddy. Nice to see you again, Jenna!"

When he looked as though he was going to pick her up again, she stepped back and he laughed his big laugh and gave her a high five. Hitting Scout's high-five, he strode across the barn toward Boone.

"So, you all grew up together?" Amber asked.

"Sort of," Jenna said, and then made the introduction, "This is our friend Cammie. The three of us grew up in the apartments all these kids today live in. Many of them live with single moms, just like I did."

"That is so sweet," Amber said. "This place is like stepping back in time. It's hard for me to picture Boone and Donny coming from here, though."

"Where did you grow up?" Cammie asked.

"I was an army brat," Amber said, "We lived everywhere. My parents retired in Arizona. I don't get to see them often, but they are still together and happy, so I'm happy for them. Do you still live in the apartments, Cammie?"

"No, I live down the street from Scout and Jack," she said.

"Cammie's husband in a cardiologist," Scout said.

Before Amber could reply, Boone walked up, and Amber took his arm, and kissed his cheek. "This has been delightful," she said, "You could always work a crowd."

"It's not too hard when the average age is twelve, and in reality, Santa was the main attraction." He looked back toward the stage, "The guys are going back, so I need to join them. I see Jack approaching with a bottle of wine and glasses. Find a seat; I'm leaving you in good hands."

"Darlin', you'll be entertaining much bigger crowds than this next year," Amber said, squeezing his arm as he pulled away.

"Why don't we sit up front," Jack said, handing the glasses to Scout. He pointed toward the stage as his parents headed that way also. Cammie said goodbye and went to join her family. Others were getting seats and pulling cold drinks or hot chocolate from coolers. There were still a few waters and soft drinks on the back table.

Jack, Scout, Jenna and Amber reached a round table just as Joe and Beth did. Jack's friend, Jeff, walked over and asked if he could join them. Amber seated herself between Jeff and Joe, and flashed her appealing smile from one to the other. The men looked pleased, Beth did not.

Suddenly, an electric guitar chord was played and Boone's clear, rich voice sang the words to "Don't Lie" with the tempo and the country rendition that Boone originally wrote it to be played in. Jenna sat spellbound as Boone moved with his guitar and sang the words.

Tell me what's true
Don't lie
I can't be with you
If you lie

Don't lie
Don't lie

I can handle the truth
Don't lie

I saw you with him today
You said it meant nothing
Don't lie
You lay in my arms at night
Your lips are so warm
But they lie

Don't lie
Don't lie
I can handle the truth
Don't lie

You know how to talk about love
How I wish that your words
Weren't a lie
I thought life with you was real
Now I know what I thought
Was a lie

Don't lie
Don't lie
I can handle the truth
Don't lie

Don't lie
Don't lie
When you look in my eyes
Don't lie

Don't lie
Don't lie
I can handle the truth
Don't lie

The song ended with applause. Jenna couldn't believe how much better it was the way Boone sang it than the way the Squires had recorded it.

The band went right into the cover of another song and each one Jenna thought better than the one before.

"He is really good," she leaned over and said to Scout.

"I know. Jack and I go hear him whenever the band plays."

"Do they play often?" Jenna asked.

"Not enough," Beth said.

"Not nearly enough," Amber added, "and as much as the people of Monticello love him, it is not fair to the rest of the country to be denied his music."

"Has he written other songs?" Jenna asked.

"Yes, but none of them have hit the charts like 'Don't lie.'" Jack said.

"That's why I want him out there singing on tour this year. By the end of next year, maybe he'll be preforming an original song on the CMA's." Amber smiled. "I will be with him promoting him as much as I promote Barry. The only difference is Barry is a name people recognize. At this point, Boone's isn't, but that's about to change."

"When is his first show?" Joe asked.

"Austin, Texas, The second Saturday in March. That's not a lot of time to get it all together, but I've been planning for this day even though Boone hasn't. He was becoming much too comfortable here. I needed to get him on the road. It's going to be an amazing ride!"

The people at the table turned their attention back to Boone on stage. Each in his or her own way wondered how this ride was going to change the Boone they knew.

Chapter 11

Christmas Eve morning dawned bright and clear. The air was crisp and cold making the snow on the ground crunch underfoot. Penny still didn't have her normal energy back, but she oversaw the holiday plans in her usual take-charge manner. She had "chores" for Scout, Jack and Carson in order to get the house and the food ready for Tuesday dinner. Her sister Betty and friend Margaret were coming for Christmas dinner and Penny wanted everything perfect. It had been six years since her sister had come for Christmas. Scout, Jack and Jenna were at Penny's by 8:30 looking for their second cup of coffee. Penny and Carson had fresh coffee cake coming from the oven.

"This is how I remember Penny," Jenna said. "As a kid I wondered if she ever slept. She was busy when we went to bed and busy when we got up."

"That's why it was so hard to see her in that coma," Scout said, "Mom is the original Energizer Bunny!"

The back door opened and Boone walked in.

"You were recruited, too?" Jenna asked.

"I wouldn't feel like family if I'd been left out?" Boone said.

"Your family doesn't need you guys today?" Carson wanted to know.

"I think today they're happy to be alone. The six weeks leading up to Christmas are getting harder for them as they get older. They love it, but they wear out a little faster."

"Oh, Bum," Penny entered the room and gave him a hug, "I am so glad you are here. They wouldn't let me go to your concert last night."

"You've heard me before. It's more important for you to get better than go out in the night air."

"She acts like we tied her down," Carson said. "She was asleep by 9:15."

"Well, I'm not asleep now and I have a project for you, Bum."

"What can I do?" he asked.

"You can take Jenna with you and make a run to Hampton Farms. I ordered a fresh turkey and an order of homemade sausage from them. Then I need you two to go by the Vineyard Nursery. They're not open today, but they promised to leave a box of fresh garlands by the back door for me. I paid for them online."

Boone looked at Jenna and smiled, "We can do that. Is there anything else we should pick up while we're out?"

"No. Other than that, you're free to enjoy your day," she said. "Carson, will you pull the cooler out of the garage and put an icepack in the bottom. That should keep the turkey and sausage in the back of Boone's truck for the day."

After loading the cooler in the back of the truck, Boone and Jenna were on their way. They had been on the highway for a few minutes when Boone said, "Thank God for Penny!"

"And why is that?" Jenna asked.

"I have wanted time alone with you for two days and here we finally are."

"I've been here," she said.

"But I've been busy," he replied.

"With Miss Pink Fur," Jenna said, sorry as soon as the words left her mouth.

"Oh, not you too," he moaned.

"What does that mean?"

"I already got an earful from my mother this morning. I don't want to talk about her."

"That's fine. Neither do I," Jenna said.

They rode for a few minutes in silence.

"Why did no one tell me you were a country singer/song writer?"

"I don't know."

"Well, it's kind of a big deal it seems," she stated.

Boone merely shrugged.

"You're going on a national tour," she said.

"Just as an opening act," he told her.

"Who has an original song in the top 40."

"Sung by someone else. You didn't even know I had written it."

"It appears that's about to change. By the way, I liked your arrangement last night much better than the one on the radio."

Boone smiled, "Thanks. Me, too."

"You must be so excited about this opportunity. Amber says it's a big deal!"

"I'm not sure its what I want any more," Boone told her. "I have enjoyed my time back home. Maybe this is who I am now."

"You're thinking of not going on tour?"

Boone shrugged. They rode is silence again for a while.

"You know," Jenna said, "I worked my butt off to get the promotion I received this past fall. It wasn't the only problem with my short marriage, but it was one of them. Being one of the big wigs, as my mother calls it, was my focus. I knew I was as smart and as motivated as those at the top and I was going to prove to myself and to others that it was true."

"And you did it," he said.

"And I did it," she repeated.

"So, your point is?"

"I'm not sure I like it at the top."

"Maybe you haven't been there long enough to know," he suggested.

"And maybe you need to go on tour to find out if that is what you really want," she said.

"Wow," he sighed.

"What?"

"I've been mulling this thing around in my brain for two days, and you just simplified the entire situation."

"Really?"

"I was going to go, anyway, but I wasn't sure why—only that it seemed I should. You're right. I have to go and give it a chance. I think that's what Amber has been trying to tell me, but it made sense when you said it."

"Are you saying Amber and I are the same?" she asked.

Boone laughed, "Not at all!"

He reached over and squeezed her hand.

"Well, that's a relief," Jenna said, and Boone laughed again.

It was a 40-minute drive out to Hampton Farms where the turkey and sausage were waiting for them. The nursery with the garland was twenty minutes in another direction. Boone and Jenna talked in the car, comfortably getting to know one another with softly-playing Christmas music in the background.

"Is there anything else you want to do while we're out?" Boone asked her.

"I did not know that Carson was going to be here," Jenna said. "I would like to get him a Christmas gift, but I haven't thought of what that might be. Any suggestions?"

"I know a great place that is a little out of the way, but you might find something there. It is a working farm with a Farmers Market, but the owner has a great eye for unique gifts. I have purchased a few items for my parents there and they have all been hits."

"Do you mind going there?" she asked.

"Anything to get a little more time with you is okay with me," he smiled.

Jenna returned his smile, but she questioned the warm feeling those words gave her. Was she was enjoying her time with Boone a little more than she should?

"Will it be hard to be away from your boyfriend for Christmas?" he asked.

"He's not really my boyfriend," Jenna surprised herself so she added. "I mean we have been dating for a while, but we also have no permanent commitment to one another. I mean we have been exclusive, but . . . it's a difficult situation to explain," she ended feebly. To change the subject, she asked, "Were you and Amber an item in the past?"

"Not really," he said. "She's been my agent and we have spent a lot of time together, but, as you put it, there was no commitment."

The Farmers Market Shop was jam-packed with happy people filled with Christmas spirit. It seemed the owners, who had a small vineyard, were serving small samples of their own wine. Jenna figured it added to the cheer of the place. Everyone seemed to know everyone else and many of them were happy to see Boone.

"Hey Buddy!" an older guy sporting a full beard and wearing a warm flannel shirt and bib-overalls wrapped his arm around Boone's neck. "I hear you're about to hit the big time!"

"Where did you hear that?" Boone laughed and returned the hug.

"The music grapevine is far-reaching," he said, "I even heard the always effervescent Amber was in town."

"That she was," Boone replied.

"She'll get her pussycat paws back in your life if you let her," the older guy warned. Nodding to Jenna, he said, "This one looks more your style to me."

"Uncle Pete," Boone stepped back to make the introduction, "this is Scout's friend, Jenna Atherton. She's here for the holiday. Jenna, this is Pete Urban, a friend of the family since before I was born."

"It's very nice to meet you, Jenna. I'll bet Penny had something to do with the two of you being out alone today," he laughed a booming laugh.

"I'm not complaining," Boone assured him.

"I hear Penny is doing better. That sure was a scare!" Pete said.

"She was up early making coffee cake and giving orders," Jenna told him.

"I knew she wouldn't be quiet for long. It takes more than a bump on the head to keep her down! What are you guys in here for? They just brought out the Christmas wine for sampling," Pete said.

"It's a little early for us," Boone told him, "We're just here for a couple last minute gifts."

"Join the crowd," Pete said, and then turned as someone walked in the front door and greeted Pete with a voice as big as his.

Boone and Jenna began to walk the store. There were wooden shelves and tables with everything from homemade jams and salsas, to pickled vegetables and a few things Jenna didn't recognize. Mixed in were tables and racks with unique items that Jenna perused to find something for Carson. When she wandered over to Boone, he was looking at a belt buckle.

"That's cool," she said.

"Yeah," he replied, "Amber commented that the one I wore last night was too worn and plain for the tour. The problem is I'm not naturally the splash and sparkle guy she would like me to be. I know I'll have to dress it up for the stage, but it feels like a costume to me, more than a style. I'm sure I'll get used to it."

"Hey," she said, picking up an oval belt buckle with a cursive "C" on it, "What about this for Carson? It kind of has a Carson look about it."

"I think that's a good choice," he said, as another older guy entered and spotting Boone, called his name.

Boone left her to go hug another guy in flannel. Jenna took the "C' buckle and also the one Boone had admired and walked to the register. The buckles were wrapped in brown tissue and put in a Farmer's Market bag. She walked to meet Boone who was enjoying the company of two men. As she approached, two twenty-something girls came through the front door. Upon spotting Boone, they both lit up and slid into flirt mode. Jenna recognized one from the night before concert.

"Hey, Boone," she cooed, "When you get famous, can we get back-stage tickets to a concert? We're two of your biggest fans."

"Thanks," he said, then he reached out and put an arm around Jenna's shoulders, "have you met my friend, Jenna?"

"Hi," they both said, somewhat deflated.

"It's nice to meet you," Jenna said.

Uncle Pete and his friend laughed. Pete winked at Jenna as she and Boone headed toward the door.

"Don't become a stranger," Uncle Pete called as they left.

"Never," Boone replied.

As they got in the car Jenna's phone rang. It was Scout.

"Hey," Scout said, "where are you guys?"

"We're just leaving Farmer's Market," Jenna told her.

"Well, we're heading home. Have Boone drop you off at our place. I have a few gifts to wrap still and then get ready for tonight."

"Do you have extra wrapping paper?"

"I have gobs of it."

"Okay," Jenna replied, "I'll see you in a little while."

"Buckle your seat belt," Boone said to her.

"Are you being bossy again?" Jenna asked.

"No," he said, "just law-abiding."

"In that case," she said, and buckled her belt. "Scout asked that you drop me off at her place. Is that out of the way?"

"No problem, now that you're buckled in," he smiled.

"I am actually an easy person to get along with," Jenna said.

"I never said otherwise," Boone glanced her way as he answered.

Jenna continued to watch out the front window, "I just don't like being told what to do."

"That's pretty obvious."

Jenna's phone rang again. She assumed Scout wanted to add something to the previous call and started to answer it when she saw Brad's face on her screen. Boone saw it also and raised an eyebrow. Jenna let the phone continue to ring.

"Aren't you going to answer it?" he asked.

"I'll call him back when I get to Scout's," she answered.

"It is Christmas Eve. I'm sure he misses you," Boone said.

"Yeah," was all Jenna replied.

"Are you sorry you stayed?" he asked.

"I don't want to talk about Brad if it's alright with you."

"I was actually talking about you, but we can switch to the weather if you'd like. I heard me might have a light snowfall tonight – you know, a white Christmas."

"That's what I was dreaming of," she replied.

"Good one," he smiled.

Boone turned on the radio and they listened to Christmas music the rest of the way to Scout's. As they pulled into the driveway, a florist truck pulled in behind them. The driver got out of the truck with a long box and walked up to Jenna as she exited the car.

"Jenna Atherton?" he asked.

"Yes."

"These are for you. Merry Christmas." He handed her the box and returned to his car.

Not knowing how to act, she looked back into the car and said, "I'll see you tonight."

"See you tonight," he said.

Jenna closed the car door and walked to the front door as Boone backed out of the drive. Scout met her at the door.

"You got flowers?" she exclaimed.

"It seems so," Jenna replied.

"From who?" Scout asked.

Jenna rolled her eyes and walked past her friend.

"Well it could be your mother or your office," Scout said.

Jenna put the box on the table and opened the attached envelope. The note read, *Wish you were here as we planned. I'm writing this through my tears. I love you. Brad.*
Jenna opened the box to find a dozen long stemmed red and white roses. She put her face into the blooms and took a deep breath.

"They're beautiful," Scout replied. She then walked over to the buffet and picked up a small package. As she handed it to Jenna she said, "This came in the mail this morning. It was addressed to me with a note to not give it to you until the family opened their presents. I decided to let you make that choice."

"Thanks," Jenna said, "I should go upstairs and call him. He called while I was in the car and I let it go to voice mail, but he didn't leave a message."

"I'm wrapping gifts in the sunroom when you're finished. We don't have to be at the Archibald's until 5."

"Okay," Jenna looked at the flowers and hesitated.

"I'll put them in water for you," Scout said.

"They are beautiful," Jenna commented, "It was sweet of him."

She walked to the foyer and up the stairs.

Scout carried the flowers into the kitchen where Jack was slicing cheese.

"Wow," he said, "Looks like I've been out-classed."

"She didn't seem that excited about them," Scout told him.

"Well, the guy is certainly trying. I wonder what the jewelry box he sent contains?"

"I gave it to her, so we'll probably know soon."

"I thought the note said to wait until everyone was together," Jack said.

"Depending on what's in the box and how she really feels about him, I thought that might be uncomfortable for her," Scout said.

"I thought he was her boyfriend," Jack said.

"I thought so too, but there's something amiss with their relationship."

"Amiss?" he smiled.

"I'm not sure what else to call it," Scout said, "Jenna and I need another girl-to-girl talk. It's a busy couple of days, but we'll find some time."

"Drop a hint to Penny. She'll get Jenna talking."

"Not a bad idea," Scout lightly punched his arm. "You're smarter than people give you credit for."

"What people?"

Scout smiled and gave Jack a quick kiss as she passed him.

"I have to get these gorgeous roses in water," she said and walked to the pantry to retrieve a tall vase.

Upstairs, Jenna sat on the edge of the bed with the small box in her hands. She decided to open the beautifully gift-wrapped box before calling Brad back. With a sigh, she untied the silver ribbon and unwrapped the gold and silver foil paper to find a gift box from an expensive jeweler in Nashville. Opening the box, Jenna found a lovely gold bracelet chain with a gold heart bordered in gold braid. She turned the heart over and was pleased to find it was not engraved. Taking it from the box, she wrapped it around her wrist. It was elegantly simple; exactly what she would expect from Brad. She scooted back to the middle of the bed and dialed her cell phone. Brad answered after only one ring.

"Happy, happy Christmas, Baby," he sang. She could hear the smile in his voice.

"Merry Christmas," she smiled back at him. "I just received the roses. They are beautiful, Brad. Thank you."

"Not as beautiful as my girl," he said, "I miss you so much, Jenna. It's not the same without you here."

"Be sure and tell all of your family hi and Merry Christmas for me," she said. "I'll miss Aunt Mary's Christmas pudding. Make sure you tell her I said that."

"Oh, Jenna," Brad sighed, "Why are you there? I'm trying to understand, but I don't."

"Brad," she said, "it's only for one holiday. It's hard to explain, but it is a little like coming home for me. I grew up here and these are the people I grew up with. I didn't realize I had missed it until I got back here. I guess it is a little like the way you feel going home for Christmas. It's not like I need to be here every holiday from now on, but I only have my Mom and she has her own life in Texas. I don't really have family."

"You have me," he said.

"I know and I am grateful to have you the other 360 days of the year, but this one year I needed to be here. Penny is improving and Scout is so happy to have me here, and I have somehow felt fulfilled being here—like this year it is the right place for me to be. I have been helping at the family shop with Penny out of commission. I may not be saying it very well, but I hope you can understand."

"I hear what you're saying, but I just miss you so," Brad said, "I wanted this to be a special Christmas for us, but I guess we'll have many more to be together. I can be a brave soldier."

Brad always used that phrase "brave soldier" like it was an endearment, but it always made Jenna feel like a mother dealing with her young son. Shaking off her negative response, she scooted to the edge of the bed and stood. As she did, Scout poked her head around the partially open door.

"Listen," Jenna said into the phone, "Scout just came in looking for me. I'm supposed to be downstairs helping her wrap Christmas presents. I'll have to give you yours when I get back in town."

"When will that be?" he asked.

"I'll leave here Wednesday morning. I have to be back at work on Thursday."

"I'll be waiting for you. I love you, Jenna-boo," Brad said.

"Me too you," Jenna responded, "and thanks again for the beautiful flowers. I'm sure Penny will love displaying them tomorrow for everyone to see. Goodbye, Brad."

Jenna stood staring at her friend after she ended the call. Neither spoke for a few seconds.

"I'm hope I didn't cut your call short," Scout said, "I came up to see if you wanted hot cocoa or a glass of wine."

"Wine," Jenna said, without hesitation.

"Let's go wrap gifts," Scout said.

Jenna grabbed the vintage Farmer's Market bag off the dresser and agreed, "Let's go."

"Still glad you're here?" Scout asked as they descended the stairs.

"Absolutely!"

Chapter 12

For their evening at the Archibald's, both Jenna and Scout wore little black dresses. Scout's had a full skirt, fitted waist, and thin straps. She wore a red choker, red drop earrings, and red heels. Jenna's dress was a simple, black sheath with a v-neckline. She wore a silver antique heart on a flat silver chain, with small silver earrings, and silver cuffs at each wrist. Her feet were in sling-back black heels. Scout's hair was loose waves; Jenna's pulled back and up.

The mood at the Archibald's was already upbeat and busy when they arrived. Joe's sister, Dorothy, and all of her family were also present. Her husband, Carl, was on the sofa with their son, Alec, who was helping him with his new iPhone. Alec and Kelly's teenage daughters, Brooke and Anna, were playing a duet on the piano. Their younger daughter, Maddie, was chasing her little cousins, Nicky, Joey and Bailey, who belonged to Dorothy and Carl's daughter Ally and her husband Jay. Jay, Joe and Boone were in the morning room watching football on TV. The women were in the kitchen talking and finishing preparing food.

As Jack, Scout and Jenna entered, Jack was attacked by Nicky and Joey who each grabbed a leg.

"Whoa," Jack called as he balanced two platters over their heads. "Let a guy in the room before you attack. You want a tray of yucky stuff to spill on your heads?"

"Ewww," they hollered and ran the other way.

Beth appeared from the kitchen and rescued one of the platters.

"Just throw the coats on the bed of the first bedroom," she said, as she welcomed them and then headed back to the kitchen.

Scout and Jenna put down the large shopping bags they carried, and removed their coats as Joe and Boone appeared from watching TV.

"Need any help?" Joe asked.

"There's just a couple more bags in the car, but Jack can get them," Scout said, kissing her father-in-law, as Jack handed her the remaining platter, and headed back out the front door.

"Merry Christmas," Boone smiled. "You ladies look beautiful."

"Merry Christmas, Bum," Scout said and kissed her brother-in-law. "Looking pretty sharp yourself!"

Boone and Jenna smiled at each other. "Merry Christmas," they each said.

Boone took her and Scout's coats and walked to the first bedroom to deposit them. As he returned to the foyer, Jenna and Scout were headed toward the kitchen and Jack was struggling through the door with his arms loaded. Carson and Penny were right behind him. Boone helped them all in and unloaded arms and again took coats to the bedroom.

"Penny!" Dorothy called in a loud voice, and the rest of the adults in the room crowded into the foyer to embrace the recent patient.

When the greetings and Merry Christmas wishes were exhausted, the group spread back into the living room, kitchen and adjoining meeting room. Joe dispersed drinks, and food began appearing everywhere. Introductions were made and happy conversation rang from every corner of every room.

Jenna felt like she had been part of this group her whole life. Brooke and Anna wanted to know what it was like living in Nashville. The younger children and adults acted like she had always been a part of the family. Carson made himself at home in the kitchen, and Penny was forced to confine herself to a stool at the counter so as not to overdo. With so many people to talk to she seemed perfectly content.

As Jenna observed the big happy family atmosphere, there was one thing of which she did take note. There were a lot of orders shouted from person to person that no one seemed to even take notice of.

"Joe, see if anyone wants another drink!" and he did.

"Boone, go get that Christmas platter from the hutch in the dining room!" and he did.

"Anna, take little Bailey to the bathroom!" and she did.

"Boys, leave Uncle Alec alone for a while!" and they did.

"Scout, put this back in the garage and bring in another container!" and she did.

"Carl, answer my phone; my hands are full!" and he did.

Boone walked over and asked if Jenna needed anything. When she smiled and said she was fine, he sat next to her on the sofa with his arm behind her resting on the sofa back.

"Enjoying your day?" he asked.

"Yes," she said, "your family has taken me in as one of their own."

"They're good at that, but they also like you," he replied.

"It must be fun to be part of a big family," Jenna said. "It was always just Mom and me."

"Jack and I always had cousins around growing up, plus my parents included so many others as family that we were never sure if the people we called Auntie and Uncle were even related to us."

Jenna smiled.

"You also had Scout and Penny and Carson, didn't you?" Boone inquired.

"Yes, but their family was little, too. Scout and I talked as kids about what it would be like to have lots of siblings or cousins. Neither of us really had fathers we knew."

"Jack and I were fortunate. We had lots of people to boss us around."

Jenna laughed, "I have noticed there are an awful lot of bossy people in this family, but no one seems to care. They just do what they're told."

The doorbell rang, and Beth stuck her head around the doorway to the kitchen and spotted her son sitting next to Jenna.

"Boone, answer the door," she yelled over the confusion of running boys.

"See what I mean?" Jenna laughed, as Boone stood to see who had arrived.

"Auntie Sherie!" Boone smiled and stepped aside as a smiling, round lady carrying a box entered and turned her cold cheek to receive an expected kiss from Boone.

Jack appeared from nowhere and also kissed the rosy, cheek of the smiling woman at the door. "The day wouldn't be complete without Christmas fudge from the Fudge Lady! Did you make some peanut butter?"

"Jacky Boy, would I forget that's your favorite? I made a new one this year with just a touch of Bourbon in it that I think you'll like also."

"You've never made one I didn't," Jack told her. "Come in and greet the family."

Sherrie walked further into the room and Boone introduced her to Jenna who was looking over the back of the sofa. Jenna stood, but before she could respond, it seemed everyone in the house came to kiss the cheek of the Fudge Lady. Boone walked over to Jenna and casually draped his arm around her shoulder. Jenna was surprised, but Boone seemed not to even notice the natural act.

"The Fudge Lady?" Jenna whispered.

"She lives down the street and has been making and delivering fudge to the neighborhood for as long as I can remember. For many years it was her and her husband, but after he died, she continued the tradition. Her fudge may be the best you have ever tasted, and she loves giving it as much as she loves making it, maybe more at this stage. I can't imagine how much fudge she makes a year."

"Come in and join us for a while," Beth said.

"She says that every Christmas Eve," Boone told Jenna.

"Oh, Sweetie, I couldn't possibly. I have fudge to deliver, but I sure appreciate the invitation. I'll come by for tea in January."

"And," Boone said, "she says that every Christmas Eve."

Jenna smiled.

Sherrie left and the family went back to their respective activities. Around 6 pm dinner was served, although Jenna could not figure out how anyone was hungry after all the food that had been consumed already, but she tasted as much as she could and it was all delicious.

Jenna helped clean up the kitchen, a project that took little time with so many willing hands. Then the group headed toward the living room with the big tree for gift giving to the children.

Boone again sat by Jenna on the sofa. "I've been thinking about your observation that everyone here is bossy," he said.

"Oh, I didn't mean to be rude," she quickly said.

"I didn't take offense," he replied, "but if you spent your childhood around Penny, didn't you get a lot of orders?"

Jenna laughed, "I supposed I did, but that was different."

"Why?" Boone asked.

"Well, for one we were kids, and because that's just how Penny is."

"You know what I think?" he asked.

"What?"

"I think you didn't mind her bossiness because you knew she loved you, and you loved her."

Jenna thought a moment. "You're probably right," she said.

"So, what happened that made you so touchy?"

"I'm not touchy!"

Boone merely raised an eyebrow, as Joe took the floor and began the gift-giving tradition. He reminded everyone that the reason for giving gifts at Christmas is because it is the time of year we celebrate the birth of Jesus, God's greatest gift of all time.

"What's our Christmas verse?" he asked the children.

In unison, everyone quoted John 3:16, "For God so loved the world that he gave his only son, that whosoever believes on him shall not perish, but have everlasting life."

"Who does God love?" he asked.

"The whole world," the kids replied, as the parents smiled.

"And what did he do?" Joe asked.

"He gave his son," they also replied, showing Jenna this was indeed a Christmas Eve tradition.

"So, what should we all do for others?"

"Give gifts."

"Love."

"Help people." The children all called out answers.

"Do to others what they do to you!" Joey happily shouted, and the adults laughed.

"I think what you mean, Joey," Grandpa Joe revised, "is treating others the way you **want** them to treat you, not always the way they **do** treat you."

Joey smiled, "Can we open our gifts now?" he asked.

Joe shrugged to the adults and said, "Every year I try." Turning to the children he said, "Yes, now we will have the drawing to see who gets to pass out the gifts."

Beth produced a red bowl decorated with poinsettias and held it over Joe's head. He reached in and drew out a piece of paper. With fanfare he read the name Maddie, and everyone applauded. As though a great honor had been bestowed on her, Maddie smiled and stood to begin taking gifts from under the tree and reading the names on the tags.

When the children's gifts were all opened and the wrapping paper had been cleared away, Brooke walked to the piano and Anna left the room. Boone also stood and walked to the piano where he retrieved his guitar. Anna returned with a guitar and a banjo.

"Whoa!" Uncle Boone exclaimed, "when did this happen?"

A beaming Anna announced she bought the banjo with her own money and had been practicing to surprise him for Christmas.

"Let's hear it," Boone smiled.

"We want you to join in," Brooke said.

"Okay. Lead us," he said.

A rousing rendition of Jingle Bells began with piano, banjo, and Boone on his guitar. The family sang along, and one song led into another.

After several sing-along numbers, Anna said, "Brooke and I have been practicing a song we'd like you to sing with us, Uncle Boone."

"That's not fair," he teased, "I didn't get to practice."

"Improvise," Brooke told him.

Boone looked to Jenna and winked.

Anna switched to her guitar, and with beautiful harmony, she and Brooke began Dolly Parton's Hard Candy Christmas. After a while, Boone joined in with soft harmony. When it ended, Boone began Silent Night, and again the three of them harmonized as the rest of the family softly joined in. The only lights were those from the tree and candles on the mantle, besides the lamp near the piano. It was sweet and meaningful and uniting. Everyone in the room was somehow bound by the words and the harmonies, and Jenna felt like she belonged in a way she may have never felt before. She couldn't image being anywhere else.

When the music ended, it seemed everyone was ready to leave. Bailey was asleep on her dad's lap. Penny looked happy, but tired. Everyone had another busy day tomorrow. As people rounded up their empty cups and glasses, coats and children, and said goodbye, it appeared Boone was driving Jenna back to Scout's. No one questioned why she wasn't riding with Scout and Jack, and Jenna realized she was glad she and Boone would have time alone. A fleeting thought of Brad crossed her mind, but she quickly put it aside to consider later. She thanked Beth and Joe, and told the others she was glad to meet them. Boone held her coat for her. He called goodbye and held the door so she could precede him. It was a moonless night, with a spattering of snowflakes as they walked to his truck. He assisted her in and walked around to the driver's side. Jenna wondered if he had a plan, but decided not to ask. It was somehow a little exciting to not know.

"So," he asked after a few minutes of driving in silence, "what did you think of your first Archibald Christmas Eve?"

"It was warm and lovely and fun," she said. "Your niece has a beautiful voice."

"Brooke?" he asked.

"Well, actually, both of them have nice voices."

"They do, but Brooke's is amazing. Anna has more diversity in her musical ability. She loves all kinds of music and can play several instruments. She has a great ear. Brooke only plays the piano, but she excels at it, and her voice is so pure. I don't know that I've ever heard her off pitch, even as a little girl. She plans on majoring in music. I'm not sure what she'll do with it when she graduates, but I'm sure she has dreams. She's the quieter of the two."

"I can see that," Jenna said, "and then there is Maddie."

Boone laughed. "And then there's Maddie. She's a pistol! She borders on being a brat at times, but how could she not be? She's so darn cute with her assumption that she is the center of the family universe."

"She kind of is," Jenna said.

"She absolutely is," Boone replied, "and the funny thing is none of the others seem to mind."

"Maybe because she is so much younger," Jenna said.

"She's not younger than the boys, but they put up with her the same as the others do. I don't get it, but she works it!" he laughed. "I just hope she outgrows the center-of-attention attitude."

"Ally and Jay seem to be good parents," Jenna said.

"Yeah, they're the best. I'll probably be a terrible parent someday," Boone said.

"Why would you say that?"

"I'm not a laid-back guy like your Brad, but I think I might have a hard time being tough on my own kids."

Ignoring the fact that Boone brought up the subject of Brad more than she did, Jenna replied, "I disagree. You were raised with rules and respect, and I believe you would see to it that your children were the same. Maddie may be a bit spoiled, but she is not a whiney, needy child. She is happy and respectful."

"She can be pretty willful," Boone said.

"And your cousins know that and will help her channel her passion as she grows up. Look what a good job they have done with the older girls."

"The other girls were easier, more compliant," Boone said.

"More compliant is not always the best," Jenna said.

With a raised eyebrow, Boone looked at her and asked, "Is this coming from the girl who hates bossy?"

Jenna pretended an attitude and said, "Even you pointed out that all bossy isn't the same!"

"I did, didn't I?" Boone smiled. Changing the subject, he said, "Do you mind if we go out to the barn? I have something for you at the trailer."

"Is it a cup of hot cocoa? Your mother said you make the best hot cocoa in the county."

Boone laughed. "She only said that because for some reason she hates making hot cocoa, so she patronizes me so I'll make it for her."

"Your cousin agreed with her," Jenna said.

"Well, I guess I'll have to make some and let you be the judge," Boone told her.

"I'm not going to be bias just because I like you," she said.

"You like me?" He cocked that eyebrow again as he smiled at her.

"You're not bad for a bossy guy," she said.

"Good enough," he said, as he turned into the lane leading to the barn and the trailer.

When they stepped into the trailer, Boone turned on a small lamp and then lit up a 3' Christmas tree with only four ornaments and white lights.

"You have a tree!" she announced.

"What? Do you think I'm a Scrooge?"

"No, but you're a bachelor living in a trailer, and it wasn't here yesterday." Walking to the tree she said, "However, if you're going to have a tree, you should put ornaments on it."

"I did," Boone stated.

"Four," she said.

"That's all I have."

"You could get one in every city you tour this year. Then you'll have a collection for next year's tree."

"Good idea. Maybe I will," he said as he turned on some soft instrumental Christmas music.

"Now would you rather have a glass of wine or hot cocoa?" he asked.

"I've had a glass of wine already today, but I've never had the best hot cocoa in the state."

"County," he corrected, "best in the county."
"So far," she teased."

Chapter 13

Jenna sat at a stool at the granite counter while Boone pulled out a pan and ingredients for his hot cocoa.

"How are you feeling about your upcoming tour?" she asked him

"Everything," he responded. "It was my dream for many years to get this opportunity. I love to play for people and a big stage seemed like the utopia I was striving for. Then when the Squires recorded *Don't Lie*, I was surprised at the amount of the pride and fulfillment I received just hearing my song. One day I was checking out at an auto parts store and the clerk was humming *Don't Lie*. He didn't know who I was and I didn't need to tell him. Well, to be honest I almost blurted out 'I wrote that!'"

"I would have," laughed Jenna.

Boone smiled. "I didn't because at that moment I realized it was about the song more than about the performance. Does that make any sense?"

"I think so."

Boone added a splash of brandy to the chocolate syrup he had concocted while they were talking. He slowly poured it into the milk warming on the stovetop.

"I don't struggle over songwriting," he explained. "I get an idea in my head and sit down and put it on paper. It's like once the inspiration comes, I'm only a vessel to put the notes and words together. They are already in my head and are straining to be released."

"That's because it's a gift, a talent you possess," Jenna said.

"Okay," Boone stopped stirring and looked at her, "but because it was easy it felt more like a hobby or a pastime until *Don't Lie* hit the charts. Then the idea of a career as a songwriter took shape. I came home and started creating a life here. I began doing woodworking, my other passion, because orders for small pieces came in through my mom's contacts. I didn't solicit business, it just came. Then I got involved in this Christmas Faire, and I kept writing songs, and I bought the building on the square, and life just seemed to be falling into place for me."

"Wait a minute," Jenna stopped him, "you bought a building on the square?"

"Yeah, the block with Arch Design on one end and Bennie's Pub on the other."

"You own Bennie's Pub?" Jenna asked.

"No. I own the building. I rent the space to the people who own the businesses. Mostly I collect checks and let them do their thing."

"How did you end up buying a block of buildings?"

"It's actually all one long building," he explained, as he went back to stirring the hot cocoa. "It was one of those foreclosure messes about the time I came back. I was getting my first royalty checks from the song, and my parents approached me with the idea. Someone needed to buy the building to save the existing businesses. So, I did. It just sort of happened."

Boone poured the warm cocoa into two mugs, and retrieved a store-bought whipped cream from the refrigerator. He loaded the top of each mug and carried them to the sofa in the living area. Jenna followed him and sat. Boone placed the mugs on the coffee table and walked across the room to a small package under the tree. He crossed back to where Jenna sat and sat beside her. He put the gift bag on the coffee table and picked up his mug. Jenna picked up hers.

"Merry Christmas," he said, holding his mug up to gently touch hers.

"Merry Christmas," she responded, and took a sip. "Hmmm, this is really good!"

"Thanks," he said, and took a sip of his own.

"No, I mean it is really, really good!"

"Glad you like it. Next time I'll make fresh whipped cream. Tonight, I had other things on my mind."

"Really" she smiled, "like what?"

"Well," he stated and picked up the small bag. "it is Christmas Eve and I'm enjoying a cup of cocoa with a beautiful woman; a woman who I find interesting and adorable, so I got her a Christmas present. I'm afraid I'm more of a shopper than a wrapper."

"I'd say more of a country singer than a Rapper," she smiled.

"Good one," he said, and handed her the gift bag.

Jenna opened the bag and pulled out a small plaque that read

I'm not Bossy,

I just know

what you

should

be doing!

Jenna laughed. "Tell me what you were thinking when you bought this," she said.

"Well, I have been thinking about the fact that you claim to not like bossy people, so . . ."

"Wait," she interrupted, "I never said that!"

"Okay. You don't like bossiness, but at your job, you are the boss, so you must have to tell people what to do. When I saw the plaque, it just kind of reminded me of you."

Jenna looked at the plaque and then back at Boone. "I'm not sure what I think of this, but I can't help but love it—in a strange sort of way."

She looked at the plaque again and announced, "I'm going to hang it in my office. The more I read it the more I like it. Maybe bossy isn't always so bad after all!"

Boone laughed and leaned back into the sofa cushions. "It depends on which side of bossiness you find yourself?"

"I guess it does," she smiled. "Thank you. This is a perfect gift and will always be a reminder of this Christmas in Monticello."

Taking her purse off the end table, she retrieves a small box expertly wrapped. With a smile she handed it to him.

"You are a serious wrapper," he said.

"That's wrapper, with a 'w'," she stated.

Smiling he sat up straighter and carefully removed the bow and paper. Inside was a box that he opened to find the shiny belt buckle he had been looking at yesterday.

"Wow! You got me the buckle for the tour!"

Before Jenna realized what was happening, he leaned forward, put his hand behind her head and pulled it forward to kiss her. It was a quick kiss, but it seemed to affect both of them more than expected. He drew back and stayed close, looking into her eyes. After a few seconds, he removed his hand and leaned back.

"Thank you," his voice was a bit hoarse. "I will wear this at every concert and think of you. It will remind me that I have to sample my dream and find out if it is still my dream or if my dream has changed."

Jenna smiled. "The nice thing about dreams is that they give us hope," she said. "Sometimes we push forward and pursue the old dream, but then sometimes we trade it in for a new one. Either way, they give us hope."

"I like that," he repeated, "Either way, they give us hope. Sounds like it might become a new song. I'll call it Jenna's song."

"Don't you dare," she laughed, "just call it *Dreams.*"

Boone and Jenna stayed on the sofa comfortably telling each other about their lives and their dreams.

"Do you know anything about Walter Thompson?" she asked him at one point.

"Not a thing other than the fact that his foundation started the Christmas Faire. Why he had a heart for the Westside Apartments no one seems to know. The foundation was not discovered until after he died," Boone told her. "You lived there. You never heard his name?"

"Never. Even the name Thompson doesn't ring any bells. I wonder if it will always be a mystery."

"You're the one with a theory on dreams—maybe it's connected to a dream of his," Boone speculated.

"You have the heart of a romantic," Jenna smiled.

"I'm not sure that's true, but if it is, let's keep it a secret."

"Why," she laughed.

"I'd rather be known as a cowboy than a romantic," he said.

"You can't be both?" she asked.

"Well if I can, let's still keep it our secret."

"I think I like having a secret with you," Jenna said.

"So, in all fairness, you should now share a secret with me," Boone told her.

"I don't have secrets," she said, "I'm really an open book."

Boone laughed, "You think so, do you?"

Surprised, Jenna asked, "You think I'm secretive?"

"Let's just say I think there are a lot of layers below the surface."

That sounded better to Jenna. "Maybe," she admitted.

Jenna felt like she could sit on that sofa in the soft light of the sad little Christmas tree and talk forever. Around midnight a yawn slipped out and Boone looked at his watch.

"I should get you back to Jack's," he said, "but I hate to see this evening end."

"Me, too," Jenna smiled.

Boone stood and held a hand out to her. She let him pull her to her feet and they stood facing one another for a minute, trying to read what was not being said.

Boone broke the silence by saying, "Let me get your coat."

As they walked to the truck, it was still snowing. Boone deposited her in the passenger seat and walked around to the other side. After he started the engine, he took a scraper from behind the seat to clear the windows of the snow that had accumulated since they parked earlier. Jenna watched him with a feeling she could not completely identify. She had known him such a short time, and their time together had been so limited, yet they had exchanged Christmas gifts and shared secret thoughts and dreams in a way she didn't remember doing with either Drake or Brad. She smiled. She was glad she had one more day before she headed back to Nashville and he started following a long-held dream. Boone opened the driver's door and brushed snow off his coat and pants before climbing into the seat.

"Boone?"

"Hmmm?" he lazily replied.

"May I ask you a question? You don't have to answer if you don't want to."

"I'll probably answer it. What do you want to know?" he asked.

"Did you and Amber live together when you were both in Texas?"

He looked at her with one raised eyebrow.

"I'm sorry," she quickly said, "That's none of my business."

"I think I like that you asked," he said. "If you were going back to work every day with Drake, I would wonder about it."

"That's different. Drake and I were married," she said.

"Well, Amber and I were not married and we did not live together, but I'm glad you thought about it," he smiled.

She smiled back at him, and then asked, "Why did you mention Drake and not Brad?"

Boone laughed. "I don't know Drake and you married him, so I suppose there was something attractive to you about him. I've met Brad. I'm sure he's is a nice guy, because you've been dating him for two years, but he's not what you're looking for."

Jenna bristled a bit, "How would you know that?" she asked.

"Because you're here," he replied.

Boone put the truck into reverse and backed around so he could drive forward away from the barn and trailer.

"Didn't you say your first concert is in Austin, Texas?" Jenna asked him.

"That's what Amber said," Boone replied as he turned the truck toward the road.

"My mother lives in Austin," Jenna said. "I could visit her and be at your first concert if you'd like; that is if you don't mind. I mean, my mom and I; we could get tickets online or something."

Boone reached over and put his hand over hers. "There is nothing I would like better. I'll send you tickets."

Without thinking, Jenna turned her hand over and linked her fingers with his. She didn't know what this relationship was, but tonight it felt good and it felt right. She would think through the questions later.

"What does tomorrow look like for you?" she asked.

"I'll spend the morning with my parents. Uncle Pete usually shows up for brunch. Penny has invited us for dinner around 4. I guess we'll get a little more time together before you leave."

"When will you be leaving?" she asked.

"I'm not sure. After tomorrow I'll have to find out what all is involved in this new path my life is taking."

When they got to Scout and Jack's house it was still snowing. Boone stopped in the drive and without turning off the engine, he walked around to Jenna's side of the truck.
He took her hand again, and they walked to the front door.

"A White Christmas," she stated.

When they got to the front porch where the light had been left on by the door, they turned to one another. Boone took her other hand in his and said, "Merry Christmas, Jenna."

"Merry Christmas, Boone," she said and then ever so slightly leaned toward him. Without letting go of her hands, he leaned in and kissed her. Their second kiss was as stirring as the first and lasted a bit longer.

Jenna sighed and released his hands. She opened the front door, but before going in she looked into his eyes and said, "Thank you for a beautiful memory."

"The pleasure was mine," he said, and watched her disappear into the house.

Jenna watched through the window as he walked back to his truck. When he had left the driveway, she locked the front door and quietly slipped up to her room to dream about a sweet kiss and a singing cowboy.

Chapter 14

Jenna woke Christmas morning to the smell of coffee and the soft sound of voices downstairs. Would she always be the last one awake, she wondered? Quickly adorning robe and slippers, she brushed her hair and teeth, and hurried downstairs.

Jack was mixing something in a bowl, while Scout sat at the kitchen counter with a cup of coffee and a look of happy contentment.

"Merry Christmas," Jack smiled.

"Merry Christmas," Jenna returned.

"Hey, Sleepyhead," Scout teased.

"I know," Jenna replied. "Where's the coffee?"

"Over here," Jack nodded toward the pot in the corner.

Jenna looked out the window as she crossed the kitchen to pour herself a cup.

"It is really snowing hard out there," she said.

"Yep," Jack commented, "It's really accumulating."

Jenna moved to the counter island and took a stool next to Scout.

"What smells so good?" she asked.

"It's Scout's Christmas coffee cake," Jack said.

"And what are you creating?" Jenna wanted to know.

"It has become tradition for me to make Christmas Pecans to take to Penny's."

"Sounds good. Is she coming over this morning?" Jenna asked.

"She usually does, but she is staying home with Carson this morning. Her sister and friend are supposed to arrive around 10. We'll head that way around noon or so."

"So, this is a lazy morning?" Jenna asked.

"Our favorite kind," Scout said, pulling her robe tighter around her. "Let's take our coffee in by the tree. I'll turn the fire on and we can visit while Jack finishes up in here."

Jenna and Scout walked into the living room where Jenna got comfortable on the sofa while Scout hit the switch for the fire. "It's not as nice as Archibald's big wood-burning fireplace, but it's a lot easier," she said.

"I think it's lovely," Jenna told her. "I'm so happy for you, Scout. Boone and I were talking about dreams last night. You're living yours, aren't you?"

"I guess I am," Scout smiled. "I love my life and my husband. We've decided we'd like to have a baby on the way by next Christmas."

As Scout sat down, Jenna leaned forward and hugged her friend. "That is exciting news! I'm going be an auntie!"

Scout laughed. "Well, not for a while. Baby Archibald is only in the planning stages at this point."

"Never the less, I'm happy for you."

"So," Scout said, "it was pretty late when I heard you come in last night. What kind of dreams were you and Boone talking about? Is there anything going on between the two of you?"

"Oh, Scout," Jenna sipped her coffee, "I wish I knew. He kissed me. Well, I kissed him. I mean, we kissed!"

"Okay," Scout said. "Tell me what you're feeling."

"I don't know. I'm feeling everything—happy, confused, worried. I think mostly I feel like smiling. It sounds foolish, but all I want to do is smile."

"That doesn't sound foolish. It sounds lovely. I like Bum. I can't think of anything nicer than the two of you being friends."

"Friends," Jenna repeated quietly.

"Okay," Scout added, "friends that kiss."

"Scout, what am I doing?"

"You tell me," Scout replied.

"I don't know. This is just so crazy. I have only known Boone a few days and we have not spent that much time alone together. And what about Brad?"

'What about Brad?"

"Well, he's a nice guy, and we've been dating two years, and he loves me."

"Do you love him?"

"I care deeply about him. He is good to me and our lives match. Boone is about to go on a world tour as a country star! How does that enter into a relationship?"

Scout laughed at her friend's drama. "Jenna, I think you have two separate dilemmas here. You expressed doubts about Brad before you had hardly spoken to Boone. You didn't seem all that concerned that you were not spending Christmas with him when you knew that was what he wanted."

"I'm a bad person!" Jenna whined.

"No," Scout corrected her, "you're a woman who has come to realize that the relationship she is in is not a forever kind of relationship. You and Brad have had a good connection, but you know your feelings have been fading lately. You've questioned if it was time to step away."

"I think I have tried not to question it, because there is really nothing wrong with Brad. I worry that there is something wrong with me that I don't love him like I should."

"I'm not even going to comment on how many ways that statement doesn't make sense," Scout told her.

"Really?"

"Really! There is nothing wrong with a good relationship that has run its time. To continue it when you know its not what you ultimately want would be the wrong thing. At least that's how it looks to me."

"But how can I have a relationship with Boone when he is traveling all over the place performing? You should have seen these two young girls at the Farmer's Market when they saw him. They went starry-eyed—and at this point he performs in Monticello! He's going to be on a big stage with lights and big amps and real country stars!"

Scout reached over and touched her friend's hand. "First of all, Boone is not going on a world tour. He'll be mostly in the south, I think Jack said Texas to the Carolinas. And what do starry-eyed girls have to do with anything? He'll still be Boone, and you really haven't had time to build anything with him. You had an afternoon and an evening together and a kiss," Scout said.

"You're right," Jenna said, "I'm probably making too much out of a simple kiss—well, two kisses."

"A simple kiss or a very good kiss?" Scout teased.

"Okay, a very good kiss," Jenna smiled.

"Who's kissing whom?" Jack asked as he walked in carrying his coffee cup.

"Your brother and my sister," Scout told him.

"Ah, I'm not surprised," Jack said as he set his coffee on the end table and asked, "can I get either of you a second cup? It's time to take the coffee cake out of the oven."

Scout stood. "I'll get us another coffee and take care of the coffee cake. You talk to Jenna."

Scout took her and Jenna's cups and left the room.

"Why are you not surprised?" Jenna asked Jack.

"I know my brother," he said.

"What does that mean?"

"It means—I don't know—it means I could tell he was interested in you. Why wouldn't he be? You're attractive, sexy, smart, funny. What's not to like?"

"So, he kisses girls he thinks are interesting?" she asked.

"Well, he doesn't kiss girls he isn't interested in, at least as far as I know," Jack responded.

Jenna looked at the fire and frowned.

As Scout returned with a tray carrying three small plates and two cups, Jack cleared magazines off the coffee table so she could set it down. Scout looked at Jenna and then at Jack.

"What did you tell her?" Scout asked him.

"What?" Jack defended, "I said she was sexy and smart. Why wouldn't Boone want to kiss her?"

Scout handed each of them a plate of coffee cake and sat back down with hers.

"He's adorable and the love of my life, Jenna, but don't turn to Jack for romantic advice."

"Hey," he objected, "I'm romantic!"

"You are very romantic," she assured him, "it's the advice part you're not that good at."

Jack took a big bite and with his mouth full, said to Jenna, "She's probably right, but I am very romantic. In fact, I have a romantic Christmas present for you. Can we exchange gifts now that Jenna is up?"

Jenna smiled, still a little unsure about Jack's remark concerning Boone, as Scout stood and removed two small gifts from under the tree.

Jack ripped into his and pulled out a box with a picture of a tool in it. He looked questioningly at Scout.

"The real one is in the trunk of my car. Boone put it there last week and it is too heavy for me to lift and wrap. Now you won't have to drive to the barn and use his all the time."

"Wow, Babe! Thanks," he said and stood to kiss her. Then he walked to the tree and picked up a small box and handed it to her. "This is from me to you."

Scout opened the box and let out a squeal. "Yes!" she said, and turned to Jenna to explain. "It is a gift certificate to this great spa in Champagne! I'll use it the week before we go on vacation." Standing to kiss Jack, she added, "Thanks! You are romantic!"

Jenna opened her gift from Scout and found a beautiful pair of earrings that she loved. She was just about to thank Scout when the doorbell rang.

Scout looked at the clock on the wall and commented, "It's only 10am. Who would be stopping by on Christmas morning? We're not dressed, Jack; would you see who it is?"

"Thank you, Scout," Jenna said, "you knew I would like these. They are so much like the ones I've admired of yours. I love . . ." Before she could finish her sentence, her eyes showed her surprise as a familiar voice at the front door said, "Merry Christmas. I'm Brad Scott."

"Did you know he was coming?" Scout whispered.

"Of course not! What is he doing here?"

"I guess he missed you even more than you realized," Scout said.

They both looked toward the doorway as Jack ushered Brad into the family room.

"It's warm and cozy in here," he smiled. "Merry Christmas, Jenna."

"Brad! What are you doing? It's snowing and it's Christmas morning! What time did you leave Lexington?"

Brad walked across the room to the back of the sofa and put his hand on Jenna's shoulder. "Merry Christmas," he repeated. When she didn't move, he leaned down and kissed her cheek. "I missed you and I couldn't sleep last night knowing today was Christmas, so I just got up and started driving."

When no one spoke, he said, "I guess you're surprised to see me. Don't I even get a kiss hello?"

"Brad!" she said as she stood and turned toward him with the sofa between them. "You just don't get up in the middle of the night on Christmas and start driving in a blizzard!"

"The weather got worse as I came west," he said, sounding like a little boy who was in trouble. "It wasn't so bad when I left. I missed you, Jenna. I thought you'd be happy to see me."

"Oh, Brad," Jenna sighed. Then turning toward Jack she said, "Would you get Brad some coffee while Scout and I get dressed?"

As the girls headed toward the stairs, Jack said, "Let me take your coat. We have hot coffee and fresh coffee cake in the kitchen. How long did that drive take you?"

When they got upstairs, both girls walked into Jenna's room and closed the door.

"What's wrong with him?" Jenna shouted in a whisper.

"He's in love?" Scout suggested.

"Oh, please!" Jenna said.

"Jenna," Scout said, "I know this is not what you wanted for today, but it was kind of sweet."

Jenna rolled her eyes. "Who invited him? You don't just show up on someone's doorstep on Christmas morning! He's crazy."

"Jenna, if you were in love with him, you would have thrown your arms around him, delighted to see him."

"If I was in love with him wouldn't I have reacted a little differently to his pleas that I spend Christmas with his family, and then the flowers and the bracelet? What is he thinking driving three states without a word to me?"

"My guess is he may be wondering the same thing about now. What are you going to do?"

"Oh," Jenna dropped to the bed. "I don't want him here. I don't want to have Christmas dinner with Brad and Boone! And I was hoping to have time with Boone before our lives took off in different directions. What am I going to do?"

Instead of answering, Scout sat next to Jenna and put her hand on her arm.

"What should I do?" Jenna repeated.

Scout thought for a few minutes.

"I think the best thing to do is to head back to Nashville with Brad."

"What?" she shouted.

"Well, think about it," Scout said. "You said you don't want to spend the day with Brad in Boone's presence, nor can you very well spend the day with Boone if Brad is here. You have been dating Brad for two years and it is not his fault entirely that surprising you on Christmas Day backfired."

"Seriously?"

"Jenna, up until this trip he thought you and he were an item. You told him you were coming here because of Mom. He had no way of knowing you would not be happy he had left his family and driven through the night just to be with you."

Jenna sighed. "I hate it when you make sense. But it was still a stupid thing to do!"

"Some girls might call it romantic," Scout said. "You can't blame him because you have changed your mind about him. Remember, he doesn't know that."

"What about Boone?" Jenna whined.

"He's trying to figure out all this change in his life, too," Scout reminded her. "I'm sure he'll be surprised and disappointed that you aren't at Penny's today, but I'll tell him what happened. You can call him later and tell him whatever you decide. Don't expect too much from him just yet. If you two really have a good connection, the beginning of something special, let it naturally grow into something more. After all, he's my brother-in-law. You'll stay connected to him at some level through the years. Let it happen as its meant to."

Defeated, Jenna sighed, "Fine. I'll leave with Brad."

"You don't have to. You both can stay if you want."

Giving Scout a dirty look, she shooed her out of the room. "I have to get dressed and packed."

Scout gave her friend a hug. "I'm sorry."

"Me, too, but maybe it is my fault. I've known for a while I needed to break this off with Brad. Being a coward led me into this mess."

"Don't call my sister a coward!" Scout said, walking toward the door. "See you downstairs."

Jenna walked into the kitchen later to find Jack, Scout and Brad talking as though they were old friends. Jack was cooking something on the stove again.

"I was just explaining to Brad," said Scout, "that you and I had discussed you leaving for home today, since the snow is supposed to stop by noon, but start up again heavier tonight and tomorrow. I would feel much better about you driving alone with Brad following you in his car."

Brad stood and walked to Jenna smiling. "I should have texted you that I was coming, but it is so good to be with you again." He put his arms around her and drew her close. She let herself be kissed, then remembering Scouts words, she relaxed in his familiar arms. She needed to be fair to him. He was doing what he thought would make her happy. He was being Brad.

"Sit, you two," Jack said. "I'm making scrambled egg wraps for you before you head out into the cold. The protein and coffee will help you stay awake in case the roads are bad and the trip takes longer than usual. Scout, get me a root beer from the garage."

Jenna remembered Boone making the same breakfast and giving the same order the first morning she was here. She wanted so badly to talk to him before she left, but it looked like that was not going to happen. As she watched Scout carry in a cold bottle of root beer, she wondered why that request had put her off only four short days ago.

Brad pulled out a stool for Jenna and she sat. He sat next to her and reached for her hand. He seemed to be trying to judge her mood. She weakly smiled back.

"I guess this snow has changed Christmas for you," Brad said. "Spending Christmas Day in the car doesn't seem like much fun, does it?"

"The forecast makes it seem like tomorrow would be worse," Jack said, "Plus there should be less traffic on the road today."

Still holding Jenna's hand, Brad asked, "Did you open my gift yet?"

"I did," Jenna smiled. "The bracelet is beautiful and so are the flowers. Thank you."

"I'll tell you a secret about the bracelet one day," he said. "I can tell you are sad about leaving, but one day we will look back on this crazy holiday and laugh. Well, except the part about Penny's accident, but Jack was telling me she is recovering well."

"Yes, she is," Jenna said, as Jack passed out four plates with wraps filled with eggs, bacon, cheese and more. Scout had added fruit to each plate, and she put the rest of the coffee cake on the counter where she and Jack joined Brad and Jenna.

"Merry Christmas," Jack raised his root beer and the others raised their coffee.

For the next forty-five minutes, they ate and talked. Brad asked about Jack and Scout's life, and they asked about his. Jenna listened, commenting only when necessary. She kept thinking about all she wished she could say to Boone. She watched Brad, so naturally conversing with her friends, and wondered why she didn't feel more for him. He was sweet and steady and he always seemed to be thinking of her. Boone, on the other had was a bit of a mystery. Was that part of what attracted her to him? Was she no different than the starry-eyed groupies? She had a long drive today to try and sort it all out.

It was almost noon before the two cars pulled out of Scout and Jack's drive.

"I like him," Jack said, as he closed the front door to the cold wind.

"He's a nice guy. I can see why Jenna has dated him for so long," Scout added.

"Poor guy," Jack laughed, "he was definitely expecting a different response upon his arrival. What do you think? Do you think Jenna's going to dump him?"

"I'm not sure she even knows."

"Poor guy," Jack repeated, "Let's clean up and get ready to go to your mom's. One thing is for sure. This is a Christmas we will all remember!"

Chapter 15

Valentine's Day

Feeling lonely, Jenna picked up the phone and dialed her best friend. Scout answered on the first ring.

"Hello."

"Hi," Jenna said, "I hoped to catch you before you guys went out for the evening."

"I'm glad you called. We're not going out," Scout said.

"What happened?" Jenna asked.

"Jack and his dad spent the day working on some big project at the barn. He came home filthy about a half hour ago and went up to take a shower. I went up a few minutes ago to get ready and he is passed out on our bed. I didn't have the heart to bother him. We can go out to dinner another night."

"It's only a holiday for greeting cards and candy sales," Jenna said. "I'm planning a chick movie on the sofa with a bowl of ice cream."

"I thought you and Brad had plans for tonight," Scout said.

"We did, but he called me at work today to say that something came up and we'd have to cancel."

"Something came up? What does that mean? It's not as though his job has customers or business trips," Scout said.

"I suspect what came up was a better offer. What else could it be?"

"I thought you guys were good," Scout said.

"Oh, Scout," Jenna sighed, "I guess we're okay, but things haven't been good since Christmas. We've gone out several times and we talk on the phone occasionally, but its not like it was before. Maybe it wasn't all that good before either."

"I'm sorry, Jenna," Scout said. "You sounded like you were going to break things off with him when you were here at Christmas."

"I know, but I didn't," she replied, "When I got back to Nashville, I kept thinking of Boone."

"That's why you didn't break up with Brad?"

"No," Jenna sighed, "I had just about worked myself up to a decision. I was going to call it quits with Brad and call Boone. Then this article came out in Nashville Country Music Magazine. It was about him touring with Barry Barns. There were a bunch of pictures of him with his arms around all these girls, and one of he and Amber looking very cozy together. He had a big smile on his face in every shot, and I got scared."

"Of what?"

"Of making a fool of myself; of falling in love and getting hurt. A little voice in my head said, 'What are you thinking? You are not in the same league with these people. Stick with Brad; he loves you and he is safe.' I convinced myself that my attraction to Boone was merely an infatuation, and Brad is a nice guy. I could do worse. He treats me well."

"I have to say as your best friend, Jenna, the little voice in your head is not your friend."

"Maybe my little voice is the voice of reason," Jenna told her.

"Maybe your little voice is plain ole fear. You said Brad was safe. You can never be in a real relationship without risk, Jenna. Plus, there is nothing romantic about saying I'm with someone because they are safe. That's a good reason to move into a neighborhood, not a reason to be in a relationship with a man."

"I know," Jenna said, "we haven't seem that much of each other since Christmas, and he dumped me tonight, so I probably have already lost him as a boyfriend, anyway. I just don't know if thinking of Boone the way I have been is very smart."

"Speaking of Boone, Jack received 4 tickets yesterday to his Austin concert next month. Are you still thinking of going?"

"Four tickets?" Jenna asked.

"Well, the note said they were for us and his parents, but that he could get two more if you and your mom were coming."

"Oh."

"The thing is his parents have decided to wait and see a closer event. He'll be in Nashville this summer, so I already have tickets for you and your mom if you want to join us."

"Do you think I should go?" Jenna asked. "Do you think it's a good idea?"

"I thought you wanted to go. You said it would also be nice to go see your mom. I've never been to Austin. It will be fun. Yes, I think you should go!"

"It might be weird. Boone and I never talked after Christmas."

"Well, he's the one that mentioned you and your mom, so he must still be thinking of you."

"Probably more like Jack's sister-in-law," Jenna said.

"Jenna, what do you expect? You left and didn't call him. You've been dating Brad. He's been really busy according to Jack. He had to assemble a new band and work on music for the concerts. Amber has him doing promotional spots. He's about to release a new single they have been recording. I think the fact that he thought of tickets for you and your mom means he'd like to see you. For all he knows, he was just a way for you to spend time in Monticello until Brad came for you."

"You know that's not true!" Jenna said.

"I know what you were feeling, but he doesn't know for sure. You never called to explain anything to him."

"I didn't know what to say. I didn't know how he felt. I didn't even know for sure how I felt considering our totally opposite lifestyles."

"So, go with us to Austin. You can see your mom and we'll all go to the concert together. What do you say?"

"You're right," Jenna said after a moment of hesitation, "I at least owe it to myself to find out what I feel when I see him again. Maybe he's nothing to me but your brother-in-law and a good guy."

"Well, you'll never know for sure if you stay in Nashville, with or without Brad," Scout told her.

"Okay," Jenna said, "I'll call mom and make plane reservations. Are you staying for the weekend?"

"I think so. I'll talk to Jack about it and let you know. I mean, why fly there for one night?" Scout said, "So, what movie are you going to watch tonight?"

"I was thinking *Six Days and Seven Nights* with Harrison Ford," Jenna said.

"You can never go wrong with Harrison Ford, especially on Valentines Day," Scout said. "What about ice cream?"

"Oh, I'm all set in that arena," Jenna told her. "I've got a banana, mint chocolate chip and butter pecan ice cream, fudge sauce and whipped cream!"

"Wow! You stay prepared for these occasions! I'll have to settle for rocky road ice cream and chocolate sauce, but I'm good with that," she laughed.

"Have a good evening," Jenna said, "I'm glad I called. I'm getting excited about a trip to Austin."

"I'm glad you called, too," Scout told her, "and I think Austin will be fun. I'll let you know when our flights are scheduled. Have a good evening, Jenna."

"Bye, Scout. You too."

The next morning, Jenna was in her office when Deborah walked in all starry-eyed.

"A good Valentine's night?" Jenna asked.

"Does it show?" Deborah smiled.

"More than a little," Jenna said, "tell me."

Deborah sat in the chair in front of Jenna's desk. "Scotty and I have been talking on the phone a lot, and we had one movie date, but last night was perfect. He brought me flowers and candy, and he'd booked a private table at Kayne Prime."

"Wow! Classy!"

"I know. We talked and held hands across the table and the food and wine were out of this world. I have no idea what the dinner cost, but it was the most amazing date I have ever been on!"

"I'm happy for you," Jenna said.

"I'm happy for me, too," Deborah said as she stood to go back to her desk. "Do you need the Flynn papers finished today?"

"If you can get your head out of the clouds long enough, I'd like them by noon," Jenna smiled.

"I can do that and keep my head in the clouds. It's fun there," Deborah said as she left Jenna's office.

Jenna was happy for her friend. She thought about the fact that Brad had cancelled their date for Valentine's Day, and she really had been content with just Harrison Ford and a banana split. She wondered what Boone had done. Had he taken Amber out for a romantic dinner? Did Boone even do romantic dinners. Jenna wished she had not been such a chicken about calling him after Christmas. Scout said he had mentioned tickets for her and her mother, so he had at least thought about her. But there was a very long distance between sending a complimentary concert ticket and a romantic dinner.

Jenna shook her head back to reality. Boone was headed toward fame. She had an office job in Nashville. They lived in two different worlds. As she put her fingers on her keyboard, she thought about their two kisses and sighed. "Get a grip," she told herself, "it was only two kisses!" A relationship with Boone was probably as realistic as a relationship with Harrison Ford! Talk about having one's head in the clouds. Jenna turned her thoughts toward the sales figures on her computer.

Chapter 16

March in Austin, Texas

Jenna walked to the curb of the Austin-Bergstrom International Airport as her mother pulled up waving and smiling in her little red convertible. Jenna smiled back. The air was warm, the sun was shining, and it had been over a year since she had seen her mother. She had wrestled with her decision to come to Austin, but seeing her mother made her happy she had come.

"Jenna, Baby!" Sandy jumped out of her car and ran around the back to hug her only child. "It has been soooo long!" she said, "You look beautiful and so successful! I love your hair that way!"

Sandy took Jenna's suitcase and threw it into the little trunk. Jenna got into the passenger's seat as Sandy ran back around to the driver's side.

"I hope you don't mind the top down," Sandy said, as they pulled away from the curb. "The weather has been hot this week, and I just love the feel of the wind and the sun!"

Jenna knew her mother had always been a sun-worshipper. It was evidenced by her brown skin and spiky, sun-bleached hair. Sandy Davenport did not look or act her age. She was financially secure as a widow from her third husband; the only one with any redeeming qualities in Jenna's opinion. Sandy was trim and toned from spending five mornings a week at the gym. At 49, she had looked tired and frumpy; but, now at 69 she was the epitome of a happy energetic senior citizen. Craig, the last husband, had been good to her and for her. They had been a true second-chance love story, and Jenna knew her mom missed him since his instant death from a heart attack two years ago.

Jenna put her hair into a scrunchy, and enjoyed the ride as Sandy darted in and out of traffic, turning suddenly into the parking lot of a Mexican restaurant with outside seating.

As she parked the car and turned off the engine, she said, "I assume you are hungry since the airlines serve nothing but drinks anymore."

"This place looks lovely," Jenna said as they both exited the car.

"It's one of my favorites," Sandy told her.

Once they were seated, Sandy ordered them both strawberry margaritas, because she said they were to die for. Jenna leaned back in her seat and sighed.

"You look good," she told her mother.

"I am good," Sandy said. "Of course, I miss Craig every single day, but I have friends and I keep busy and I'm healthy. At my age, being healthy is the important part."

"You're going to be 70 this summer," Jenna said.

"Hush," Sandy said, looking around as though Jenna's words might have been heard.

Jenna laughed. "What I mean is that it's okay to look a little older at your age."

"Oh, yeah?" Sandy said, "Tell me that again when you're turning 70."

"Based on how you look and feel, you'll probably be planning my 70th birthday party someday," Jenna said.

"If I'm able, I will!"

"I'm sure you're right," Jenna replied.

"Now," Sandy said, as their drinks were delivered, "let's order and then you can tell me all about you."

They ordered taco salads, and then Sandy took a sip of her drink and leaned back in her seat to wait for Jenna to talk.

"Well," Jenna began, "my job is going very well. I am slowly gaining the respect of my peers. I suspected from the beginning that I was not their choice for the job, but I believe I have grown into it."

"It seems every time I talked to you this past year, you're at work," Sandy said. "You must like your job."

"I do. It's not as creative as I would like. There is more detail and paperwork than I originally thought, but I have made positive and productive changes. I think I have the respect of those I manage."

"I'm sure you do," Sandy said, "you're a good person, Jenna. I'm proud of you."

"Thanks, Mom," Jenna smiled. "I'm proud of you, too."

Sandy laughed and raised her margarita glass to Jenna as their salads were delivered.

"These look delicious," Jenna said.

"They are," Sandy told her, taking a bite and then returning to conversation. "What's going on with your love life? I have tried to determine your situation over the phone, but I must admit, I'm not sure what's what."

"That makes two of us," Jenna told her. "I think things are over between Brad and me."

"You don't know?"

"I think we're both cowards," Jenna laughed. "It just isn't working. It seems we like one another and we don't fight, so the death of our relationship has been a slow one.   We talk on the phone occasionally, but I was thinking on the plane that we haven't gone out once since Valentine's Day. It's like there's a mutual understanding that it's over, but no one wants to say the final words. I guess if either of us had someone else, that person would make the break.   Although, I suspect he had a date on Valentine's Day. He cancelled our date at the last minute."

"How did you feel about that?"

"I was okay. I called Scout, and then ate ice cream and watched an old Harrison Ford movie."

"Well, Harrison Ford is a good choice for Valentine's Day," Sandy said.

"That's what Scout told me," Jenna laughed.

"Speaking of Scout; Penny's doing well? She tells me she is, but I figure a second opinion is a good idea with her."

"She is doing well.   Scout said she's totally back to normal. Everyone is grateful."

"So, now we finally get to the topic of Scout's brother-in-law," Sandy said. "Have you spoken to him?"

"Boone?   No.   I'm a little nervous about just showing up tomorrow," Jenna said.

"Why should you be nervous? It's not like you're showing up at his house for dinner! You're going to his concert and he provided the tickets. Of course, he's expecting you to be there."

"I know, but we haven't spoken since Christmas."

"But you told me your time with him at Christmas was good," Sandy said.

"It seemed very good at the time, but I have second guessed every minute since then. I mean, there is a lot that I don't know about him. He's going to be a country music star for goodness sake! What could we possibly have in common?"

Sandy smiled at her successful daughter's insecurity. "Tell me what you do know about him. What attracted you to him? After all, you didn't even know he sang when you first met him."

"I forget that sometimes," Jenna said, "Boone is a good guy. He cares about his family. He is handsome and funny and focused and hard-working and talented and bossy."

"He sounds a lot like you except for the handsome part," Sandy said.

"He's nothing like me," Jenna countered, "He's strong and self-confident and did I mention bossy."

Sandy laughed. "Yes, you did. I'm anxious to meet him. If I remember correctly, you also mentioned he was a good kisser."

"I never told you that!"

"Was he?" Sandy raised an eyebrow with a twinkle in her eyes.

Jenna shrugged one shoulder. "Passable," she said.

"Ha! I knew it!" Sandy laughed.

Jenna returned her mom's smile. "Okay, he was good."

"Good?"

"Mom!"

Sandy waited.

"Okay. He was a very good kisser—but maybe that's because he's had so much practice. Maybe he kisses every girl he finds interesting!"

"Maybe, but my experience is that it doesn't matter how many girls he has kissed; a guy is either good at it or he isn't!"

Jenna laughed. "And I can't believe I'm having this conversation with my mother! Promise me if Boone and I ever become a couple, you will never, and I mean never, tell him we had this conversation."

"I'll try to remember," Sandy said, "but my mind is not what it once was."

"There is nothing wrong with your mind!" Jenna told her. "There might be something wrong with me for having this conversation with you."

"Now I'm insulted," teased Sandy.

"No, you aren't!" Jenna laughed. "You're loving every minute of making me uncomfortable."

"When do I get to meet Bum?"

"You've talked to Penny about this!" Jenna accused.

"Maybe a little," Sandy confessed.

"Oh, I'm doomed!" Jenna moaned.

"Not if we have anything to do with it!" Sandy assured her.

"Let's go see your condo," Jenna said, changing the subject. "I want to see the renovations you told me about."

"We have a nice pool. Maybe we can spend the afternoon outside so you can get a little color. You're kind of pale, you know."

Jenna shook her head. She loved her mother, but Sandy always spoke her mind. Jenna hoped she wouldn't embarrass her in front of Boone.

Jenna and Sandy spent Wednesday afternoon at her condo pool. Early Thursday morning, Sandy went to the gym. Jenna showered and finished the book she had started on the plane. She tried to keep her mind occupied so as not to stress about meeting Boone that night. Scout and Jack would be in around noon. They were staying downtown at the Westin and were going to meet Sandy and Jenna at Shady Grove at 6pm.

Shady Grove was a small venue Amber had booked for the evening before the big concert. Boone and his band were the main and only attraction for the night. They would be preforming on a small outdoor stage before wooden tables and plastic chairs. Scout said they would have time to connect with Boone on Friday. Saturday's concert was booked at the Stubb's Amphitheater, where Boone was the opening act for Barry Barns, country music's rising star. Jenna knew from Scout that Boone would be busy all day Saturday with promotional events in the morning and sound checks and stuff in the afternoon.

Jenna was hoping she and Boone might have some alone time. She wondered if Boone even wanted time alone with her. She should have called him after her unexpected departure Christmas Day. It might have been an awkward conversation at the time, but not calling made this situation more awkward. She wondered again if she should have come.

Sandy returned from the gym, showered quickly, and they got back in her convertible. Jenna was glad her mother insisted they go to the San Antonio Riverwalk for lunch. It was another beautiful day, a perfect distraction for her nerves about seeing Boone. It was over an hour's drive each way, which gave them time to talk. They were able to get an umbrellaed table along the water and commented on the people and activities they witnessed. After lunch they visited a few shops and Sandy bought her a pair of cowboy boots to wear to the concert that evening. They returned to the condo with just enough time to shower and change for their evening out. Scout had texted when they got to their room and they made plans to meet at the Shady Grove.

Jenna and Sandy exited their car that evening and were crossing toward the front of the restaurant as Jack and Scout pulled in driving the Jeep they had rented for the weekend. Scout jumped out as soon as Jack cut the engine.

"Sandy," Scout exclaimed, as she threw her arms around Jenna's mother, "you look wonderful! You remember Jack, don't you?" she asked as Jack approached.

"Of course," Sandy smiled, "How are you, Jack?"

"I'm well," he responded, "the weather is beautiful here. How could anyone be anything but great?"

"Gets pretty hot in the summer," Sandy told him, "but I still love it. I've become a Texan, through and through!"

"Well, let's get inside," Jack said, putting his arm out to usher the three women toward the door. "Boone said there would be a table waiting for us."

"This is just so exciting!" Scout said. "Jack talked to Boone a while ago. He said his brother seemed nervous about tonight."

The foursome went into the coolness of the restaurant. They walked through to the outdoor area where they saw Amber at a table concentrating on her phone. As they approached, she stood wearing open-toed pink boots, fringed denim shorts over tan, bare legs, and a tight vee-neck tee shirt that stopped just above her shorts, with the name *Boone* in large block letters down one side of the front. Jenna introduced her mother, and there were hugs and greetings all around. As Amber hugged Jack, Jenna noticed her pink shirt had a picture of Boone in a cowboy hat on the back with the words *I'm with Him.*

"How's my brother doing?" Jack asked her.

"You'd think he'd never done this before," Amber said, "I'm glad I got him this gig before the big stage tomorrow. But he'll be fine once the music starts. Boone's a natural entertainer."

"Is he here?" Scout asked.

"No," she replied, "He said he didn't want to get here until right before 8. They did a sound check earlier. Did you all have good flights?"

The four sat in plastic chairs at a wooden table under large pecan trees near the outdoor stage. They were early for the show, but not for dinner. The patrons were a combination of young people, senior citizens and families with children. Amber had suggested they get there early enough to sit near the stage.

As a young girl walked up to take their orders, Amber announced she'd be back by show time and left. After a short discussion on drinks, the girls ordered Ladybird Lemonades and Jack ordered a draft beer. They also ordered a plate of Nachos and an order of Queso, Salsa and chips.

"That was nice of Amber to get here early and save us this table," Sandy commented.

"She's his agent and very attentive to Boone wants and needs," Jack said.

Jenna wondered exactly what that meant, but decided not to ask.

It was a pleasant night in Austin. The temperature dropped a little as the sun set. Their drinks and appetizers were delivered to the table. Sandy and Scout interacted a lot. Sandy asked about Penny, and Scout asked Sandy about her life. They also reminisced about the years they all lived in the apartments.

"What do you do, Jack?" Sandy asked.

"Since I moved back to Monticello," Jack said, "I have helped my parents run the store and have a growing Real Estate business."

"Residential or commercial?" Sandy asked.

"Both," Jack answered, "but it's moving more and more into the commercial arena. Boone led me in that direction when he moved back and was looking to invest in our town. He bought the building in town where my parent's store is located. Mom loves the sales and personal interaction of the store, but I think Dad, who retired as a furniture rep, would like to be more retired. I think he misses the travel and diversity of his old life. Mom is more content with the sameness of her day to day life. I'm sure over the next couple years they'll work out an arrangement that works for both of them."

"Would you and Scout take over the store?" Sandy asked.

"Maybe, it depends on what life brings down the road. At this point I don't think anyone is looking ahead," he reached over and took Scout's hand. "Life is good for all of us. Boone is the only one looking outside of Monticello these days. It will be interesting to see where life takes him."

"Or if this is the life he really wants," Scout added.

"What's not to like about it?" Jack said. "Boone loves music and he is being given the opportunity to write and perform his own original songs. It comes naturally to him. When we played cowboys as kids, I was always the sheriff rounding up the bad guys. Boone liked trying to lasso the dog, playing his guitar, and singing cowboy songs he made up as he went." Jack laughed. "Someday he'll have to tell you about the one he wrote about our family."

"I've never heard one about your family," Scout said.

"It's ten-year-old boy humor; probably not nearly as hysterical as it seemed back then."

As the conversation continued, the group ordered another round of drinks and the girls ordered salad's for dinner. Jack got a club sandwich.

At 7:40, Boone and the band walked through the restaurant and up onto the wooden stage. Boone smiled down at their table, but was all business as he and the band tested sound with their instruments. Donny Melton looked at their table, pointed at Jenna and smiled. At exactly 8pm, Amber appeared from nowhere in tight shiny black pants, low black boots and her signature pink top – this one had long sleeves and a very low vee neckline, front and back. She was also sporting long silver earrings and a pink western-style hat that said AUSTIN on the band. As she stepped to the microphone, she received a round of applause and several catcalls. Jenna noticed the room had changed to a more adult crowd, although there were still some families present.

Amber leaned into the mic and yelled, "Good Evening, Austin!" The response was big and loud as she smiled and moved her body just enough to excite the crowd. Jenna suspected she could have yelled 'Fire!' and the response would have been the same. The guys in the band grinned as they waited for their cue.

"My name is Amber Golden."

Another round of cheers.

"Thank you," she smiled, "I wish to thank the Shady Grove for the invitation to perform here tonight. I can tell this is going to be a good crowd. Ya'll are cheering and you haven't met the main attraction for the evening. How many of you are lucky enough to have tickets for the Stubb's Amphitheater tomorrow night to see the amazing, up-and-coming country artist Barry Barns?"

A few people responded.

"Well, you are the lucky ones, but the rest of you get a taste of tomorrow tonight. On your humble stage tonight, the opening act for Barry Barns is going to perform. These handsome and sexy guys behind me . . ."

A response of cheers and whistles from the females in the crowd interrupted Amber. She gave them a minute to carry on.

"Ya'll have great eyesight and good taste," she encouraged. "Behind me is Country's new and talented group known as Southern Nights. Let me introduce you to them; they can't wait to meet ya'll."

Again, the yelling from the female patrons. There was a drum roll from the back of the stage and more cheers as one by one Amber introduced the members of Boone's band.

"And the cowboy who holds it all together, Ladies and Gents, the writer of the hit song *Don't Lie, the* one and only Boone!"

As the cheers exploded again, the band started to play and Boone, strumming his guitar, approached the mic with that slow, sexy smile. The boys in the band approached their mics also.

As the crowd cheered, Boone began to sing 'Tell me what's true, Don't lie,' looking directly at Jenna. As she felt the heat rise to her face, he turned his attention to the rest of the room. Jenna was mesmerized by the image of Boone; the guy who gave her the plaque hanging in her office, the guy whose kiss the last time she saw him was again in the forefront of her mind. She remembered him teasing her and making her laugh. She remembered his kindness to the people of Monticello and how they seemed to respect him and care for him in return.

Jenna looked around the room. Some people were talking to those they were with, but many were riveted on Boone and his band. They were enjoying what he had to give them, especially the young girls. Jenna watched what would be considered his groupies. Was she just another in that group? Was her attraction to him based on how sexy he looked in tight jeans, his smiling eyes and easy smile? Was she crazy to think he might be attracted to her? Was his singing that first song about lying sending her a message? If so, what message was he sending? Was he calling her a liar for her actions at Christmas, or was he asking her to be honest with him because he had feelings for her? Probably neither. Jenna tried to just enjoy the music and not think at all. Both Scout and Sandy had snapped pictures of Boone with their phones. She would be sure to get at least one of them. Oh, she hoped she wasn't just another girl caught up in the moment and music. After all, what girl doesn't love a singing cowboy?

When the concert was over, patrons were either leaving or partying. Many of the girls rushed the stage. The band handed over their guitars to the crew who showed up from somewhere to attend to the instruments and equipment. Amber was on stage for a few minutes giving directions to the crew. The guys from the band jumped off the stage to revel in the attention of the young girls. They accepted the flirting and signed autographs as they flirted back.

The waitress appeared to refill drinks. Jack ordered a beer for himself and one for Boone. It wasn't long before Boone pulled a chair up between Jack and Sandy. He tipped his hat back from his forehead and smiled.

"You must be Jenna's mother," he said, "I can see the family resemblance."

"Sandy Davenport," she said, holding out her hand to receive a firm, but gentle handshake. "I enjoyed your music. I never knew you wrote *Don't Lie.*"

"Most people don't," he responded.

"Have you written other songs?"

"Probably not any you would know, but I'm hoping to change that in the future."

"Great job, Buddy," Jack said, slapping his brother on the back.

"Loved it, Bum," Scout said.

"Me, too," echoed Jenna.

Boone smiled at Jenna. "Good to see you again," he said.

"I'm glad I came," she smiled back at him.

"So am I," he answered.

"Boone!" Two young girls approached the table. "Tonight is my bachelorette party," said the one with the long dark hair and beautiful dark eyes, "and the girls over there," she pointed to a table of maybe a dozen giggling girls. "they dared me, I'm Sarah, and this is my maid-of-honor Katy," Katy held out her hand to shake Boone's. "They dared me to get your autograph," Sarah giggled some more.

"I think I can accommodate," Boone said.

Sarah handed Boone a Sharpie and ran her finger over her heart. Lifting her chest toward Boone, she said, "Right here! I need you to write 'Boone' over my heart."

Boone's eyebrows raised and he took a deep breath. Taking the marker from the bride-to-be, he pulled the arm seam tight and signed his name on the left side of her shirt near her shoulder. The maid-of-honor looked disappointed, but the bride appeared to be thrilled with the autograph. Her friends back at the table were shouting, clapping, and taking pictures.

Katy turned to go back to their friends, but Sarah hesitated. She took the marker back from Boone and leaned down to kiss his cheek. "Thank you," she whispered, and followed Katy.

"Wow!" Jack said, "so that's what fame looks like!"

"I guess," Boone said. "Don't they serve beer in this place?"

"Here it comes now," Jack said, as the server approached with their two beers. Jack paid her, and he and Boone both took deep draws on their beers.

"I was thinking," Jack said, "if you have time to hang out tonight, there is a pool on the roof of our hotel that should have a beautiful view of the city at night. Why don't we finish these and go back there and hang out? You have a car here, don't you?"

"That works for me," Boone said. "Amber has my entire day tomorrow booked with stuff, and tomorrow night I have to go to this promotional thing after the concert and do interviews. I balked at the idea, but she said something about striking while the iron is hot."

"Well, it is a job," Scout said. "We knew you would have commitments. That's why we thought tonight might be our only time to visit."

Boone took another drink of his beer and looked around. Upon spotting Amber walking off the stage, he said, "Let me go tell Amber my plans."

"She can join us if she wants," Jack said, followed by "ouch!" as Scout pinched his thigh.

Boone smiled and excused himself from the table.

"What was that for?" Jack demanded.

"Why would we want Amber to join us?" Scout demanded.

"I was being polite."

"Well, don't be!"

"I think I'll skip the rooftop party, if you young folks don't mind," Sandy said.

Jenna didn't hear her mother's comment or Scout's reply. She was watching what looked to be an argument between Boone and

Amber. Amber was not happy, and after a few back and forth comments, she stamped her booted foot to make a point. Boone just grinned, leaned down and kissed her cheek, and walked back to the table. Amber went the opposite direction in a huff.

Boone was approached by a striking 40-something woman when he was a few feet from the table.

"My younger sister would like an autograph," she said, leaning toward Boone and putting her hand on his shoulder to steady herself. "Do you have a napkin or something?" she asked.

Boone reached over to the table and picked up a clean paper napkin.

"Hey, Jack," he asked, "got a pen?"

Scout reached in her purse and handed Boone a pen. Boone put the napkin across his palm and signed his name. As he handed it to her, she kissed a white business card, leaving the impression of her lips on it, and slipped it into the pocket of Boone's shirt.

"Thanks, Doll," she said as she winked and walked away, none too steady.

"Does this happen all the time?" Scout asked.

"No!" Boone said, "let's get out of here."

"Boone," Sandy asked, "if you don't mind seeing Jenna home later, I'd like to leave you young folks to do the late-night stuff. I have an early morning tomorrow, but if I take the car, Jenna will need a ride."

"I'd be glad to see that she gets home okay," Boone said. "I'm sorry we didn't get a chance to talk this evening."

"I hope we will have another chance in the future," Sandy said.

"I hope so as well," Boone said.

"Let's go while my brother's virtue is still intact," Jack said.

"Give me a break!" Boone barked.

"I'm trying to, Buddy! I'm trying to," Jack laughed.

The group got up and headed toward the parking lot without another interruption.

A half hour later, Jack used his room key to open the door to the pool deck of the Westin, as Scout and Jenna got four bottles of water from the vending machine. Boone held the door as the girls walked out.

"Wow," Boone said as they entered the dimly lit deck with blue lights shining through the water of the pool. Over the railing, the night lights of Austin were on display. "This is beautiful."

The girls passed out the water and the four of them walked to the railing to quietly look out over the sparkling lights of Austin, Texas.

Boone was the first to break the silence. "When I see a view like this, I am reminded that each of those lights represents a family or a person with hopes and dreams, problems and pain. It's humbling in a way to realize how small we are in comparison to the vastness of humanity."

"My brother, the philosopher," Jack said.

"Boone's right," Scout said. "Just think about how little we know about the world. Sociology wants to group people into categories, but each of those lights is a home or business with real people and real beating hearts that want deep down the same things everyone wants—to be loved and accepted; to have a life that has some sort of meaning."

"To have hope and dreams," Jenna added.

"That's the title of my new song that I'm debuting tomorrow night," Boone said.

"Hopes and Dreams?" Jenna asked.

"No, just *Dreams*," Boone answered. "It was going to be called *Jenna's Song*."

"Really?" Scout said, "Why did you change it?"

"She asked me to."

"Jenna?"

"He's kidding," Jenna said. "We were just talking one night at Christmas and he said he'd write a song and call it Jenna's Song."

"It was Christmas Eve," Boone said, "and you told me that everyone needs to have dreams, but that our dreams can change. I went back to the trailer and wrote the song. I was going to sing it for you on Christmas Day."

"Sing it for us now," Scout said.

"No, you'll hear it tomorrow with all the smoke and lights," Boone said.

"Do you like singing with all the smoke and lights?" Jack asked.

"Haven't done it yet," Boone shrugged. "Barry told me it's actually easier than a gig like tonight, because you don't really see the people. Even the sound is deafened by the ear pieces we use to hear our own music. I guess I'll find out."

"Are you nervous?" Jenna asked.

"I don't know how I couldn't be," he answered. "It's a big stage with big sound and lights and more people than I've every played for before. Barry said you kind of get into a zone and then the music comes naturally. I'm counting on him being right. I keep reminding myself that they all bought tickets to see Barry Barns, not Boone Archibald. That takes a little of the pressure off."

"Amber doesn't seem worried for you," Jack said.

"Amber has her own way of handling nerves. Unless you know her well, you'd never know she has a care in the world," Boone said. "She comes across as cool as a cucumber, but believe me there is a lot of passion under the surface. That combination of passion and control is what makes her a great agent. I'd be nowhere without her, although she can get under your skin."

"She didn't want you to come with us tonight," Jenna said.

"No, she was plenty pissed about it, but I know how to sweet talk her. I'll calm her down later tonight. She's probably soaking in a tub of bubbles, with a glass of Merlot, calling me every name in the book about now. By the time I see her, she'll have blown off steam."

Jack yawned and put his arm around Scout. "How about you and I head back to that big king-size bed. As long as we're paying for that room, we might as well make use of it."

"How can I resist such sweet talk," Scout replied. "You guys will need a key to get back in here, so don't leave the deck until you're ready to go."

"Do you mind if we stay up here a while?" Boone asked Jenna.

"No, but I will need a ride back to my mother's condo. I hope it isn't too far."

"I don't think I'll sleep much tonight anyway. I'm in no hurry to get back," Boone said.

"I'll call you in the morning," Scout said as she hugged Jenna.

"Will we see you at all tomorrow?" Jack asked Boone.

"Probably just on stage," Boone replied. "Amber has my attention from the time I wake up until past midnight. Wish me luck!"

"Good luck, Bro!" Jack said as he gave his brother a hug. "We're all proud of you!"

"Thanks, Man," Boone replied.

As the door quietly closed, Boone gestured toward two chaise lounge chairs.

"Warm enough?" he asked as she sat and put her legs out.

"I'm fine," she answered, "This side of the building is out of the wind."

Boone moved a chaise up against hers and stretched out.

"I miss the stars at the farm," he said, looking up at the black sky over the myriad of city lights.

"I guess all cities are that way," Jenna said.

"I guess you're probably right," he said. "How have you been?"

"Good," she replied, "I've been good."

"That's good," he responded. "Work is getting better? Are you feeling more comfortable in your job as a boss?"

Jenna smiled. "The plaque you gave me at Christmas hangs in my office." She was silent as she debated how much to say. "I think of you when I see it. I noticed you wore the buckle I gave you tonight."

"I told you I'd wear it for all my concerts."

"Yes, you did," she said. "Did you really write your new song Christmas Eve?"

"I did. I was so disappointed when I got to Penny's and you had left. Are you still dating Brad?"

"No. We still talk occasionally, but we've had dinner only a couple times since Christmas. I haven't seen him in a month. It wasn't the same after my trip to Monticello."

"Why not?" he asked.

"I don't know how to answer that question," she sighed.

Boone studied her face. She looked so miserable he smiled, and decided to change the subject for now.

"Are you still working so many hours?" he asked.

"I think it's the only way I know how to work," she replied.

"That doesn't really leave time for a social life," he observed.

"Or maybe it covers the fact that I don't have one?" she speculated.

"I didn't say that," Boone said.

"I know, but I ask myself that question sometimes." Jenna wondered again at how easy it was to talk to Boone about her true feelings. "Why do I do this with you?" she asked.

"Do what?"

"Share thoughts and feelings so freely. I do not easily open up to most people, but even though we have spent so little time together . . ." she didn't finish her sentence.

No one spoke for a minute.

"You really wrote a song about dreams?" she looked over at him and smiled.

"I really did."

'I never inspired a song before."

"Maybe you have."

"What do you mean," she asked.

"Well, you've had a husband and at least one long-term boyfriend. You are an inspiring person. You are intelligent and honest and open and . . . delightful. I'm sure you have inspired others before me; they just weren't songwriters professionally."

Jenna laughed. "You think they sang songs about me in the shower?"

Boone smiled. "Could be. Did any of your past loves write you poetry?"

"Danny Troutman," she confessed.

"There ya go!" he said.

"We were in the fourth grade," Jenna said, "Margo Smith stole the paper off my desk and read it to the whole class before the teacher came into the room. Danny never spoke to me again."

Boone laughed. "Poor Danny. I've been there, but you do remember Danny after all these years."

"Yes I do. I don't remember the poem, but I do remember Danny."

"Well, maybe you'll remember my song," Boone told her.

"Since you will be singing it from a huge stage in front of thousands of people, I think I'll remember it."

"Did you have to remind me?" he asked.

"Are you really nervous?"

"Yes and no. Sometimes I feel a little sick about the scope of the venue; but then other times I am only excited to have an opportunity so many musicians only aspire to."

"You are getting a chance at your dream," Jenna said.

"I am. After tomorrow night I will have a better idea what that really means."

Jenna looked at her watch. "You have a big day tomorrow and you still have to drive me home."

"I like to think I get to drive you home," Boone told her. "It gives me just a little more time in your presence, plus I don't have to worry about some other guy swooping in and changing my plans."

"You have plans?" she smiled.

"I might," he answered, as he stood and reached for her hand.

Jenna gladly took his hand and let him pull her up from the chaise. Neither of them seemed inclined to let go, so they held hands as they walked to the elevator. Jenna looked at their entwined fingers, and wondered at the warmth that spread through her entire body from that small amount of contact. As the elevator doors opened, she looked up at Boone. They entered the elevator together, and as the doors closed, he let go of her hand and put his arms around her waist. When she leaned slightly into him, he dropped his head and gently kissed her. When she responded, he deepened the kiss and she slid her arms around his neck. His body was firm and strong and she felt a protectiveness she didn't remember ever feeling before in a simple embrace. As the kiss lingered, Jenna remembered they were in an elevator and that it did not seem to be moving. She leaned back, looked at the numbers over the doors, and smiled.

"What?" he asked, and then followed her glance at the numbers. Boone laughed and said, "I guess we'll never get home if one of us doesn't press a button."

Jenna only smiled as Boone let go to press '1'. She was thinking that getting home was not really what she wanted to do at the moment. The elevator ride could last the rest of the night as far as she was concerned.

Echoing her thoughts, Boone said, "Although I wouldn't mind spending the night in this elevator."

Just then the elevator stopped on the third floor and a maintenance man entered and nodded to them. No one spoke as they rode to the lobby. Boone found Jenna's hand again as they walked to his car. He programed Sandy's address into his cell phone, and took Jenna back to her mother's condo. The ride resumed their comfortable conversation, although they were both aware of an underlying excitement between them. Boone kissed Jenna again at her mother's door.

"I'll see you tomorrow night," Jenna said.

"I may not have an opportunity to even talk with you guys tomorrow. This is all very new for me and Amber has my time booked solid as I tail Barry. She told me even if I don't get a chance to say much, it will be good exposure and good experience for me to see what's expected of a celebrity," he said with uncertainty. "It's a whole new world."

"You're going do great," she told him. "I believe in you and you're getting a chance to follow you dream."

"When I sing *Dreams* I'll be thinking of you."

Jenna smiled. "I'll be thinking of this," she said as she went up on her toes, touched her lips to his, and disappeared into the condo.

"Whoa!" Boone whispered as he turned to walk back to his car. On the other side of the door, Jenna smiled.

Saturday was an enjoyable day as Sandy showed Jenna, Scout and Jack around Austin. Scout and Sandy pressed Jenna for details of the night before, but she told both of them that she and Boone had a nice time and easy conversation like they did at Christmas. When continually pressed about a repeat of the Christmas kiss, she finally admitted to kissing Boone goodnight, which seemed to make both her mother and her friend's day. Both sent her the pictures they took the night before of Boone on stage.

They got to the concert at the Stubb's Amphitheater not long before the show was to begin. Boone had sent them great seats about six rows back in the middle. As excited as they were, Jenna could not image the nerves Boone must be feeling. She asked Scout for Boone's cell number and sent him a text saying, "Following your dream. You'll be great!"

Jenna couldn't believe how exciting it felt to see Boone on the big stage. She knew Jack and Scout were experiencing the same sensations of wonder and pride as he and his band performed in the lights and smoke with their instruments and voices booming into the night. Again, he started the show with the familiar *Don't Lie.* He spoke often to the audience and appeared confident and comfortable. Boone seemed to receive energy from the enthusiasm of the crowd, as most of them were on their feet, clapping and singing along with the cover songs the band did. For his last song, he announced it was his new single and that Austin was the first to hear it, which produced a loud cheer. He said the song was inspired by a friend who told him everyone needs a dream to follow, even if that dream changes along the way. Then he sang the words that Jenna would have heard at Christmas if she had not run away.

Dreams, Dreams
Dreams, Dreams
No one can live without dreams.
Dreams bring us hope

Hope gives us joy
Joy leads to love
And love makes us dream.

Dreams, Dreams
Dreams, Dreams
No one can live without dreams.

But not all dreams are the same
Unfulfilled dreams bring us pain
But no one can live without dreams.

In life our dreams may change
New people make plans rearrange
But in all of the chaos
We must have a dream
No one can live without dreams.

Throughout life our dreams may change
But no one can live without dreams.
A rainbow gives promise to tomorrow
Our dreams give us hope to go on.
No one can live without dreams.

Dreams, Dreams
Dreams, Dreams
No one can live without Dreams
Dreams, Dreams
Dreams, Dreams
No one can live without dreams.
No one can live without dreams.

Chapter 17

Jenna was at her desk early Monday morning looking at the picture of Boone on her phone. Deborah walked in with her morning coffee and sat down.

"How was your trip to see your mother?" Deborah asked.

"It was great," Jenna responded. "Austin is a beautiful city. Jack and Scout had a room at the Westin with a pool deck on the roof. We ended the evening up there on Friday night and the view was stunning."

"Did you meet the cowboy?" Deborah asked.

"Why would you ask that?"

"You seem all glowy," Deborah said.

"I am not glowy!" Jenna responded.

"Well, I am," Deborah said.

"What?"

"I was out of town this weekend, too," Deborah told her. "Remember me telling you I had gone out with this sweet guy named Scotty? He took me to the mountains; we spent two nights in Asheville."

"Two nights?" Jenna questioned.

"Yes," Deborah smiled, "an adventurous Saturday hiking in the Blue Ridge and then two fabulous nights in Asheville, drinking wine and getting to know one another. Oh, Jenna it was glorious. I think I'm in love!"

"Wow," Jenna said, "that was fast."

"Not really," Deborah said, "I've known Scotty for a while, but we only started seeing each other this year."

"Tell me about him," Jenna said, enjoying the joy on her friend's face.

"He's sweet and attentive and easy-going. He shared with me his dream this weekend to get his master's degree and where he hopes to be in ten years and then in twenty years. I've never had a relationship like this before. It's incredible to really see into the heart of another person."

"Yes," Jenna smiled, "it is."

"Is that what it was like when you first married Drake?" Deborah asked.

Jenna grew more serious. "I'm not sure we ever really knew one another like that," she said. "We were so young and I think I wanted to get married."

Deborah's face fell a bit.

"Oh," Jenna was quick to point out, "I'm not saying that being young was our problem. I don't know exactly what happened with us, but sharing dreams was never part of our relationship, not the way you're describing. I think that means something when you really talk and get to know another person beyond the physical attraction. I'm assuming your Scotty is also cute."

Deborah perked back up. "He's not only cute, he's hot! OMG, Jenna. I can't stop thinking about him.

"Well," Jenna reminded her, "you'd better figure out a way to think about work. I got an email from Arthur this morning already and he needs a spreadsheet from me by tomorrow. I forwarded it to you. If you can send me the necessary info, I'll put together the program information he's looking for. We both had good weekends, but now it's back to work."

"You need a man in your life," Deborah said. "There are things in life much more exciting than spreadsheets, boss."

Deborah smiled as she left the office, but Jenna wondered again about her life. Boone had texted her twice on Sunday. Once to tell her there had been great feedback to her song *Dreams*. Jenna didn't miss the fact that he called it her song. The second text was to bid her a safe trip home.

Jenna thought about Deborah's open excitement over Scotty vs Jenna's secret feelings for Boone. She hadn't even shared much with her mother or Scout, a fact that did not go unnoticed by either. She liked to think that she was just a more private person, but she realized the truth was she was scared of her feelings for Boone. They felt so real, and yet his comments about Amber made her question how much she really knew about him. Boone and Amber argued Friday night, and then he casually mentioned her in a bathtub, and that he would calm her down later. Later—like after he kissed Jenna and left her on her mother's doorstep!

Jenna didn't want to get hurt and she didn't want to be played for a fool. She refused to be just another groupie, and in her skeptical moments she was afraid that might be all she really was. Yet her feelings for Boone were strong. What if she was little more than his sister-in-law's best friend. What if he were just being nice, or worse, just having fun with her? She hated the idea that she might be no more to him than another Amber, or worse, a starry-eyed girl in a tight tee shirt . . . it was too mortifying to even consider. It was best for her to get back to work. After all, Boone was busy chasing his dream, and she had a spreadsheet to complete. After a minute on her computer, she stopped and smiled. She had inspired Boone to write a song. How many people could say the same thing? The reality was, she didn't know. She returned to her spreadsheet.

Chapter 18

April – Easter in Monticello

Over the following month, Jenna found herself feeling more and more lonely. Deborah was all bubbly about her love affair with her Scotty. Jenna was happy for her friend, but tired of hearing about how perfect he was. Brad had not called and the few times she thought about calling him, she didn't. She wasn't sure what she would say to him. She recognized their relationship wasn't really a relationship anymore, and calling only because she was lonely or bored seemed self-serving and pitiful. The fact that he didn't call her probably meant he had found someone else. Drake had moved on. Brad had moved on. Why shouldn't Boone? Jenna tried not to feel sorry for herself, and wished she could say the same, but she had no one to move on to. So, she worked.

Boone had texted her once to say that *Dreams* had been released as a single. He included a very sexy picture that was to be the promotional cover. He was in the same attire he had been in the night at Shady Grove; a black tee shirt, dark jeans, brown boots, belt and cowboy hat, and the buckle she had bought him. He was leaning against a weathered wooden building with a beautiful, but desolate sunset behind him. Over his head was the name of the building. It read,

Dreams   Bed & Breakfast

A Night to Remember

Under the photo he wrote: Amber found this place. The sign made me think of you.

Jenna stared at the photo. Boone had that cute smile that made her smile back, but the mention of Amber kept her grounded in reality. The word dreams may have reminded him of Jenna, but the words bed and breakfast reminded Jenna of his comment about Amber in a bubble bath with a glass of Merlot. That was just too much intimate information for him to know and not be in a relationship with her. He probably sent the same picture to his brother and parents. Jenna was nearly Jack's sister-in-law. Boone probably thought of her as family. Then Jenna remembered the kiss in the elevator. How she wished Boone was nothing more than that guy who lived on his Grandfather's land in a trailer. She knew that guy was one she could fall in love with, maybe she already had. But the country music star? She had no idea if a relationship with him was even possible.

The following weekend was Easter, and the office was traditionally closed on Good Friday. With a three-day weekend looming ahead, Jenna called Scout. If they were free of plans, she'd go hang out with the people she enjoyed so much at Christmas. Boone wouldn't be there, but that might be for the best!

Jenna arrived at Scout's door Thursday evening. Her friend opened the door and gave her a hug.

"I am so glad you called," Scout told her as she pulled her into the foyer. Jack appeared from the kitchen with a smile.

"Hey, Sis!" he said.

Jenna was immediately glad she came. Her loneliness had evaporated as she got closer to Monticello. This simple little town in the flat fields of Illinois was her happy place. It was an odd reality. Most people dreamed of pleasure and peace on a remote beach, not surrounded by fields of corn and soybeans.

As Jenna entered the living room, she saw the bed-and-breakfast picture of Boone framed on the mantle. Scout saw her expression and said, "Did you get one of these?"

"Yes," was all Jenna said.

"Of course, she did," Jack said, "Mom, Dad, Penny, even Uncle Pete got one!"

"He's excited to have Jenna's song on the charts," Scout told Jack. "It's nothing but sibling jealousy," she told Jenna.

"Who sends their picture to everyone they know?" Jack asked.

"He didn't send it to everyone," Scout said, "Only to those who mean something to him. I think it's sexy."

"Of course, you do! It's supposed to be sexy," he said.

"Sibling jealousy," Scout repeated. "Anyway, you should be happy for his success. Not everyone gets the opportunity to have a big-time agent, and tour with a nationally known music group. Boone will be big-time himself one day and I hope when that day comes you'll be happy for him."

"You know I'm happy for him now," Jack said. "I just don't see why we had to frame his bed and breakfast picture and put it on our mantle."

"Your mother did the same thing."

"Exactly, but she's his mother!" Jack said, and then turned to Jenna. "don't mind us. Scout's a little cranky these days."

"I'm not cranky," she said to Jenna, "but I think I'm pregnant. I have a doctor appointment next week, but the HPT came back positive!"

Jenna immediately gasped and hugged her friend. They bounced up and down with their arms around each other.

"I thought we weren't going to tell anyone yet," Jack said.

"Jenna is not anyone!" Scout said, "You really didn't think I could not tell her if she was here for three days, did you?"

"That was silly of me."

"How are you feeling?" Jenna asked.

"A little nauseous now and then, but otherwise fine."

"Can you guess a due date?" Jenna asked.

"December," Scout told her. "I'm pretty sure it happened at the Westin in Austin."

"Is nothing sacred?" Jack asked.

Ignoring him, Scout announced, "If it's a boy, I want to name him Austin!"

"We are NOT naming our son after the place he was conceived!" Jack said over his shoulder as he walked back to the kitchen.

"It could have been worse," Scout called after him. "Boone's concert could have been in El Paso!"

The girls, both smiling, hugged each other again.

The weekend was relaxing and wonderful and again a place and time where Jenna felt accepted and loved. Friday morning Joe called to ask for help at the shop. Beth had another bout with her blood pressure spiking and Joe wanted to stay home with her. Jack, Scout and Jenna got ready and were at the shop to open the doors at 9am. Beth had baked dozens of bunny cookies and had chocolate eggs for customers. They were under plastic wrap in the back room, so the girls got them out and made themselves a pot of coffee. Scout made tea. She said coffee didn't agree with her these days. That was the only sign Jenna saw all weekend of the pregnancy.

Penny had the three of them, along with Joe and Beth over for dinner Sunday before Jenna started for home. As the meal ended, Penny's cell phone and iPad buzzed. She walked over and looked at the screen and smiled. It was Boone on Facetime.

"Hey, bum!" she said. "Wish you were here!"

"Me, too," Boone replied. "Mom said the gang was having dinner at your place today."

Penny turned the iPad toward the table and slowly rotated it. "We're all here," she said.

"Hey, Jenna," Boone smiled, "I didn't know I'd get to see you today."

"Hi, Boone," she said, "Where are you?"

"Miami," Boone replied, "Barry had a big show here last night."

Suddenly Amber in a tiny bikini appeared behind Boone on the screen. "Hey Boonie, do we have any more sunscreen?" she asked, and then saw the screen. Bending forward, so only her face and chest were in the screen, she smiled, "Happy Easter everyone!"

"Happy Easter!" Joe boomed, "You look . . . tan!"

"We're heading to the beach," she said, standing and stepping back so her mostly bare body was visible.

"The suntan lotion is in my truck," Boone told Amber.

"Okay. Don't be long," she said to Boone. Grabbing a lace wrap and tossing it over her shoulder, she turned to walk out the door, her thong suit covering nothing but a narrow strap across her back. Joe continued to smile.

"Sorry for the interruption," Boone said.

"What interruption?" Joe asked, after which Beth slapped the back of his head, and Jack and Boone laughed.

"Thanks for the picture," Penny said.

"You're welcome. I'm pretty happy with the fact that *Dreams* is moving up the charts. I get a good response to it at the shows. I'm working on another song that Amber really likes as well. I may give it to Barry Barns to perform."

"Why would you do that?" Beth asked him.

"I think it's better suited for his voice, plus it will get better coverage if he records it."

"Is he interested in it?" Jack asked.

"I want to finish it before I offer it to him. We are all so busy on tour. Amber gives us little free time, plus we practice daily. She wants to do a beach shoot on our day off this week. Some of the guys are for it, but some of us are threatening to boycott that one."

"I still don't see why you would give a good song away," Beth said.

"I'm a songwriter, Mom. That's what we do," Boone said.

"But now you're a performer, also," she insisted.

"Well, like I said, it isn't finished and I haven't shown it to anyone but Amber. She heard me working on it one night and she thinks it could be another hit. But then again, a lot of decent, even good songs never become hits. It's kind of a crap shoot."

"Not with your looks and voice!" Beth said.

"Spoken like a loving mother," Boone said. "So, Jenna, when did you get in town?"

"Thursday night," she replied, "I'm heading back to Nashville in a little while."

"Well, it was a nice surprise to see you," Boone smiled.

"Boone, let's go!" Amber called from the doorway.

"I guess I have to leave," Boone said. "I wanted to call and wish everyone a Happy Easter. I miss you all. I'm hoping to be there for Mother's Day. We don't have a show that weekend."

"Oh, Boone," Beth said, "that would be wonderful!"

"Will you all be there?" he asked.

"Of course," Penny replied, "and we'll make sure Jenna comes back into town for that weekend, too."

Jenna felt herself blush as Boone replied, "Good," and Amber called again.

"Gotta go," he said. "love you all."

After everyone responded together, the screen went blank.

"Well, that was a nice surprise," Penny said, "How about some dessert before Jenna has to leave?"

Chapter 19

Mother's Day Weekend

Jenna took off the Friday and Monday of Mother's Day weekend. She didn't know if she would stay until Monday, but she wanted to keep the option open. She left Friday morning after rush hour traffic cleared, and drove up to Monticello, both excited and nervous. Boone had texted her a couple times since Easter; just casual texts that she answered. He texted last night to say he was back in Monticello at his trailer, and looking forward to seeing her. She had read the text several times. As simple as it was, it made her heart rate increase and her stomach do flips. She was eager and edgy at the same time. What if she was reading too much into a couple simple text messages? What if she wasn't? They were about to have a few days interacting with his family without a Christmas Faire, a country music concert, or the presence of Amber.

Jenna had been married. She had spent two years dating Brad, but she never remembered feeling such anticipation at the mere thought of spending time with either of them. She was like a kid who couldn't wait to get to Disney World, and then the thought of Amber in bubbles or bikini would creep in and her stomach would roll with dread. Boone, as Jack's brother, would be in and out of her life forever. They would be Aunt and Uncle to the new baby. What if she was making too much out of this relationship? What relationship? They had spent very little actual time together. What if Boone had been acting polite because she was Scout's best friend? She could go there this weekend and make a complete fool of herself if he was just being polite. But then she thought about the kisses; there was nothing polite about those kisses. Boone Archibald was a decent guy. There was no way he would toy with the feelings and emotions of Jack's wife's best friend—was there? Then again, he was Bum—the reckless one; the one at whom girls, young and old, threw themselves. Jenna had a sudden urge to return to Nashville.

Buzzz!

Jenna looked down at her phone. It was a text from Boone. Carefully lifting the phone and letting her eyes dart back and forth between the road and the screen, she read, "Everyone else is busy today. Come straight to the trailer."

Jenna put the phone down and thought about the text. "Come to the trailer" reminded her of "go get a drink." She wondered if everyone else was really busy. Jenna hit the recent calls button and pressed the number for Scout.

"Hi Jenna," Scout answered.

"Hey, where are you?" Jenna asked.

"Jack and I are at the doctor office for my first official OB visit," she answered. "Where are you?"

"I'm almost an hour from Monticello," Jenna said.

"Good. Sunday is not only Mother's Day, but it is our anniversary, so Jack and I are going to have a late lunch and then do a little shopping. I talked to Boone and he's in town already. He said he'd entertain you until we get back."

"Oh," Jenna said.

"Are you okay with that? I thought you'd be happy to have some time with Boone," Scout said.

"He just texted me to come to the trailer," Jenna said. "That will be fine. Let me know when you're home."

"We'll just come by the trailer," Scout said. "Oh, they just called my name. We'll see you later."

Jenna continued her trip to Monticello. Boone said he'd entertain her? She felt like the visiting Aunt Bessy who needed someone to 'entertain' her. Now instead of nervous, she was annoyed. 'Come straight to the trailer!' Did she have a choice?

Jenna's phone buzzed. She picked it up to read the new text from Boone. "Didn't mean to sound bossy. Know you shouldn't text and drive. I have chips and salsa at the trailer if you want to come by. Boone"

Now Jenna felt ridiculous. Why does she make little things into a big deal? She picked up the phone and while watching the road texted, "GPS 45." His response was a thumbs up.

Jenna pulled up near the trailer and watched Yeller pick up her head and thump her tail. The door to the trailer opened and Boone walked out smiling. Yeller stood and loped out to greet her. Taking nothing but her purse and phone, Jenna walked to meet Boone. He said 'hello' as he approached her and then without hesitation, he put an arm around her waist, drew her close, and kissed her.

"I've been waiting to do that since an elevator ride in Austin," he said, and taking her hand, they walked to his trailer. Jenna attempted to find her equilibrium.

He held the door as she entered. Boone walked into the little kitchen and said, "I thought we could sit out back. The crab apple trees are in bloom and there is a nice breeze. I made ice tea, but I have Coke or Ginger Ale if you would rather. I also have wine, but it might be a little early in the day for that. When I went to my Mom's for tea—she always has a great selection of tea and she told me which ones to get and how to make it, I saw a package in the pantry that said tea cookies." He pointed to a plate with cookies on it. "I don't know what they are, but I figured you're supposed to eat them with tea. I tasted one and they're not bad."

Jenna smiled. Was Boone nervous? "Iced Tea would be wonderful," she said. "Do you mind if I use your bathroom to wash up?"

"It's down the hall. You can't miss it," he said.

Jenna disappeared down the short hall and Boone took a deep breath and blew the air out of his cheeks. He put ice in two tall glasses and added the tea. Then he carried them to his back deck and came back in for the plate of cookies and the chip and salsa bowl he had also borrowed from his mother's pantry. After carrying them to the deck, he wondered if he should wait for Jenna on the deck or go back inside. She appeared at the door.

"Do you need anything else to come out?" she asked.

"No, I have everything, I think," he said.

Jenna came out and sat in one of the two chairs positioned by a small round wood table.

"These are cool chairs," she said. "Did you make them?"

"I found them in the back of the barn when I moved here. They needed new springs and the wood was in pretty bad condition, so I fixed them."

"I like them," Jenna told him. "Who picked the color you painted them?"

"They were peeled, dirty white, so I was going to take them back to their original look. My mother suggested I do them in Navy. I think it was a good choice."

"I do too," she said, "Did you also recondition this little table?"

"No," Boone said, "The table is an B A original. I had an idea for the size and shape and just made it out of a piece of barn wood laying around."

"B A?"

"Boone Archibald Originals. That was going to be the name of my furniture company," he said.

"Wow! You can do anything—create songs, create furniture!"

"I couldn't work in an office and do what you do."

Jenna laughed, "Do you even know what I do?"

"Not really, but I'm sure I couldn't do it. How's your job going? Are you enjoying it?"

"That's two different questions," Jenna answered. "My job is going well. My bosses are pleased with both the numbers and my approach to the problems. Am I enjoying my job? To tell you the truth, I enjoyed working your parents' shop on Good Friday more than I like working in my office. I've come to believe I wanted the promotion more than I wanted the job."

"You mean the money part?" Boone asked.

"Well, that's part of it, of course," she smiled, "but I have always been a competitive person, so when there is something to strive for held out in front of me, I go for it. I wanted to prove to myself and others that I could *get* the job more than I actually think I wanted the job. But now it's mine, so I will do my best at making the numbers grow."

"Is there satisfaction in that kind of competition?" Boone asked her.

"What do you mean?"

"It sounds like perpetual frustration to me," Boone said. "I guess when I create something, I find great satisfaction in the finished work. If every step creates for you another level for you to work toward, is there any place where you reach contentment, or is there an excitement in striving for the next goal?"

"I guess I never thought about it," Jenna said. "Maybe in a job like mine the excitement of reaching for a goal is enough. In a way, having a goal could be the excitement. I hate being bored."

"So then finding excitement creates its own type of satisfaction, because that's what you are seeking. That makes sense, I guess."

Jenna smiled thoughtfully, "Taking this full circle, then why do I enjoy working in your parents' shop more than working in my own office?"

"Because its new and different?" he asked, "Because when you do it for a day or two it doesn't feel like work, or maybe you like helping people more than you like motivating people?"

"Huh. You always give me something to think about," Jenna said.

"I do?" he smiled, "well, I'm glad that I can do that for you, although I'm not sure that I really do. I'm a pretty simple guy. Would you like some more Iced Tea?"

"Please," Jenna responded.

Boone took both of their glasses back into the trailer, and Jenna wondered how their small talk had taken such a philosophical turn.

"What are you thinking" Boone asked as he set the glasses down on the table. "You look so serious."

Jenna smiled, "I was thinking you are anything but a simple guy! Knowing you has been one of the most frustrating situations in my life."

"What does that mean?" Boone asked.

"It means let's talk about something else," Jenna said, "What are those trees behind the little crab apples?"

The conversation became actual small talk. Boone told her the names of the bushes and trees in the yard; which ones he had planted and which ones had been planted by his grandfather. He told her the history of the farm and what he knew about his ancestors. He asked about her family and she told him how she had never really known any family. Her father left her mother before Jenna was born, and his family had never cared to know her. Her mother's parents both died young. If she had cousins anywhere, she wasn't aware of them. She said that was why Penny and Scout were so important to her. They might not be blood relatives, but, besides her mother they were the only family she had ever had.

"And now you have my family," he said.

"Joe and Beth are wonderful, and soon the next generation begins," Jenna said. "I am so excited for Scout and Jack. Is Jack nervous about becoming a daddy?"

"I don't think so," Boone said, "Jack will analyze the best way to parent and then go for it. Even as a kid Jack didn't get nervous. He just considered the situation and calculated how to handle it in a way that made sense to him. He'll be a great dad."

"You guys had a good example," Jenna said. "My mom's last husband was a good man. I used to wonder what life would have been like if she had met him long ago."

Boone pretended to strum an air guitar. "If she had met him long ago . . ." he sang.

Jenna laughed. "Is everything a song to you?"

"That's just how my mind works," Boone said.

By the time Jack and Scout arrived, Boone and Jenna were conversing like old friends.

"Where are you guys?" Jack yelled as he walked through the front door.

"Out here," Boone called back.

"I'm getting a beer," Jack called, "Do you want one?"

Boone smiled at Jenna as he stood. "I've got wine. Can I pour you a glass?"

"That would be nice," she said, "can I help?"

"Just sit," Boone said, "We'll be right back out."

Boone disappeared into the trailer. Jenna could hear him and Jack talking in quiet voices. Soon Scout appeared, smiling and carrying a small bag. She leaned down and gave Jenna a small hug as she passed her and sat in the chair Boone had been in.

"How did your appointment go?" Jenna asked.

"The doctor said everything looks good. She gave me prenatal vitamins to take and I go back in two months. Then Jack and I went out for lunch and stopped at a baby shop on the way home. I couldn't help myself," Scout nearly giggled. "Look at what I found!"

From the pink and blue bag on her lap, Scout produced a pair of tiny white booties that were shaped like Western boots.

Jenna laughed and reached out her hand. She caressed the soft material and turned them to inspect each side.

"These are adorable. Austin will look so cute in them," Jenna said.

"We are not naming our kid Austin!" Jack announced as he came out the door juggling drinks.

"Is Austin a consideration?" Boone asked, coming around to the back yard carrying two folding chairs. "That's a great name for a boy or a girl."

"No Austin, Scout," he said, "I'm serious."

"What's wrong with Austin?" Boone asked as he set up two more chairs on the deck.

"Don't ask!" Jack said.

"Look, Boone," Jenna said holding up the booties.

"Austin will love those!" Boone said as he reached for his beer. "What's wrong with the name Austin?"

"Our Austin weekend was when he or she was conceived," Scout announced.

Boone looked to Jack and then said, "You're right. Not Austin."

"Thank you," Jack said, holding his beer up to click Boone's beer in the air.

The rest of the evening was wonderful. Boone had purchased steaks that he and Jack grilled while the girls opened bags of salad and cut up some apples they found. The foursome laughed and talked about everything from politics to the habits of insects when some unknown bug made its way across the deck. As the sun lowered in the sky, the trees became a choir of birds to top off their evening. After yawning several times, Scout announced she was sleeping for two these days, and offered to help clean up the few dishes before they left.

"I'll get those," Boone told her. "Go home and get a good night's sleep. Baby Archibald doesn't want you to overdo."

Scout smiled and looked at Jack who said, "Oh, this is going to be a long nine months!"

Boone and Jenna laughed.

"I'll help Boone and be along soon," Jenna said.

"Take your time," Scout replied, "we'll leave the front door unlocked if we go to bed before you get there." She hugged her friend. "I'm so glad you are here. I know Nashville isn't that far, but talking on the phone just isn't the same."

"Well," Jenna said, "I'm here this weekend."

Boone slapped his brother on the back as he exited the trailer, "Thanks for help on the grill," he said.

"See ya, Boone," Jack said.

Boone and Jenna walked back into the kitchen. Boone put items away as Jenna washed up the few dishes in the sink. As she was about to finish, Boone walked up behind her and put his hands on the counter on either side of her waist. Leaning forward he said in a husky voice, "You look cute doing dishes in my kitchen. I like seeing you here."

"You mean like a maid?" she teased breathlessly.

"I wasn't thinking of you as a maid; you can trust me on that," he said.

Wanting to lighten the situation, she dipped her hand into the suds, and as she slowly turned in his arms, she wiped them on his face. His surprise gave her a chance to move out of his embrace and laughingly get into the living area. Thinking she had defused the tension of being so close, she realized she might have made it worse as Boone approached her with a hand full of suds and the look of revenge in his eyes.

Jenna squealed and ran out the back door with Boone at her heels. She jumped off the deck and continued into the yard, with no destination in mind. Within what seemed like a few giant steps, he caught her. As she twisted to get away, she lost her balance. Turning his body to take the brunt of the fall, Boone went down with Jenna on top of him. Now they were lying in the soft grass, with a nearly dark sky overhead. As Jenna started to get up, Boone tighten his hold and said, "Look at the sky."

"The sky?" she said.

Boone pushed her off him, so that she was now also on her back with her head comfortably on his arm and her body tucked up against his.

"Remember the lights in Austin?" he asked.

Jenna relaxed and smiled. "And the black starless sky," she said.

"Exactly."

"I love it here," Boone said.

"More than the travel and the music and the stage?" Jenna asked.

"It's a hard choice," he said. "I guess at this time of my life I can have both, just not at the same time. I love making music, but in its own way, a moment like this . . ."

Boone turned to look at Jenna. In the darkness of the night, she couldn't see his eyes, but she knew what she would see if she could. At that moment, all she wanted was for Boone to kiss her. He did and she wrapped her arms around his neck. The kiss deepened and Boone suddenly pushed himself to his feet and held his hand out to her. A bit confused, Jenna took his hand.

"You're probably tired from your trip," he said in a husky voice.

"Yeah, I guess I am," Jenna said, dusting the grass off her jeans.

Boone kept hold of her hand as they walked back into the trailer. She let go as she picked up her purse.

"Are you okay getting out of here?" Boone asked. "I could drive you to Jack's and you could pick up your car tomorrow. It's pretty dark."

"I'll be okay," she said.

Together they walked out to her car. Yeller appeared from somewhere and walked with them.

Boone opened her door for her, but stopped her as she started to get in. He leaned toward her and put his forehead on hers.

"Jenna," he said.

Jenna could feel his breath and her own heart's rapid beat. She didn't respond.

"Oh, Jenna," he said, and kissed her forehead and took a step back.

Jenna got into her car. Before Boone pushed the door closed, she said, "Good night, Boone."

"Good night, Jenna."

Jenna backed the car around. As the lights brushed over Boone standing with Yeller, she felt a tear run down her cheek. She wasn't sure what she was feeling, but whatever it was, she didn't think she'd sleep much tonight.

Boone was thinking the exact same thing. He walked around the trailer and sat in the dark with his hand caressing only Yeller.

Chapter 20

Jenna opened her eyes to sunlight, and looked at the big ben style clock on the nightstand. She was surprised to see that it was 9:34. She sat up and listened to a quiet house. There were no hushed voices, no quiet TV or music, no smell of coffee or bacon. She got up, put on a robe and went into the bathroom. A few minutes later, with brushed teeth and her hair pulled back, she walked downstairs. Scout was curled up in an upholstered floral chair, drinking a cup of tea and watching a soft rain falling in the back yard.

"Good morning," she said to Jenna.

"Good morning. I can't believe I slept so late," Jenna replied.

"It's a nice rainy day for sleeping in. I've only been up a short while."

"You have an excuse; you're pregnant."

"Don't need an excuse on a day like today. There's hot tea on the counter or I can put on a pot of coffee if you'd rather."

"Tea will be fine," Jenna said and disappeared into the kitchen. When she returned with a steaming mug and a cookie she'd found in a glass jar, she sat on the end of the sofa across from her friend."

"Is Jack still sleeping?" Jenna asked.

"Heavens no! He can't sleep past 6:30. He has an inspection at some commercial building he sold that he said might take all day. He was meeting the inspector for coffee and breakfast in town. Penny is working the shop today with Karlie. You didn't meet Karlie at Christmas, did you?"

"No. Who is she?"

"She's this sweet, young girl Beth has taken a liking to. When she was only twelve, her mother, who is a friend of Beth's, dropped her off at the shop during an emergency. Karlie loved hanging around the shop and begged Beth to hire her when she turned 16. Beth and Karlie never forgot that promise, so when Karlie turned 16 last fall she started working Saturdays."

"She wasn't around at Christmas," Jenna said.

"No, her family went on a cruise for the holiday, but she is faithfully there if she's in town. She's a hard worker and the customer's love her. She has a natural way with people, kind of like you. People just take to her."

"You think that about me?"

"Of course! You don't see that in yourself?"

"No," Jenna replied thoughtfully.

"Well," Scout said, "we have the day to ourselves. Jack said Boone plans on spending the day in the barn, so what would you like to do? I have to go to the pharmacy, and then make a quick stop at Vintage Nursery for a couple items, but the day is all ours. I figure we'll have a nice lunch out somewhere. It may be raining, but we won't melt running to and from the car."

"What is Boone doing in the barn all day?" Jenna asked.

Scout smiled. "You guys seemed very comfortable together yesterday. Did you stay late? I was asleep as soon as I got home."

"No," Jenna answered. "Boone said yesterday that he considers himself a simple man. Do you see anything simple about Boone Archibald? Everything about him confuses the heck out of me!"

"Well, its different for me," Scout said, "I'm not in love with him."

"What? In love? How could I be in love? We've hardly spent any time together. He travels the country with Amber at his side! I work in a stuffy office, with old men. He has beautiful girls wanting him to autograph inappropriate places!"

Scout laughed, "Oh yeah! You're in love. You just won't let yourself admit it." When Jenna started to protest, Scout amended her statement. "Okay, maybe you haven't had time to actually be in love yet, but you do care for him in more than a brother-in-law way."

Jenna sighed. "I do, Scout, and I don't know what to do about it. When he kisses me it's like everything inside me melts down to hot . . . something! I don't even know how to describe it, but then he just stops!"

"He stops?"

"Yes! He stops!" Jenna stood to pace the room. "What is wrong with him? Or what is wrong with me? Oh, Scout," she moaned, "what if I'm acting like a silly groupie and he is acting like a reasonable adult. When I'm around him, I have no desire to be reasonable. That's not like me! You know that's not like me."

"Love," Scout nodded and repeated, "it's love. I have that same reaction to Jack at times. He can just smile at me or wink and I'm ready to drag him upstairs. It's called love, Jenna."

"But Jack doesn't just stop kissing you when you want him to never stop!"

"He's my husband. It makes a very big difference. You want to know what I think?"

"I'm not sure," Jenna said as she sat back down. "but go on."

"I think Boone may be having the same reaction to you and the same confusion about what to do about it. It's so obvious he's attracted to you."

"It is?"

"Yes," Scout smiled, "but he has the same dilemma you do. He is trying to figure out which dream to follow—the satisfaction he finds in living near family and creating furniture and building a solid life, or the pursuit of his old dream of playing his music on the big stage. He's good at both and he loves both, but it's pretty hard to have both. Then along comes this beautiful, sexy, intelligent woman who lights up his insides. How does he fit you into his chaos?"

"Do you really think he thinks I'm sexy?"

"Of course," Scout laughed at her friend's insecurity. "I've never thought of you that way, but the look on Boone's face when you're around tells me he does."

"What about Amber?"

"What about her?"

"Do you think there is more to their relationship than her being his agent?"

"I guess I can't answer that," Scout said, as she sipped her tea. "You've seen Amber!"

"I know," Jenna moaned deflated, "how does a normal person compare to that?"

"No, what I meant was Amber acts like she's intimately connected to every man in the room. That's what she does and it works for her. Even Joe and Jack act ridiculous when she's around. Beth gets mad, but I just brush it off as stupid."

"Boone doesn't act like that around her," Jenna said.

"Exactly!"

"But maybe that's because he knows what they have together is more than just a show."

"I guess you'd have to talk to him about that," Scout said. "He doesn't act jealous when she flirts with other men."

"But, like you said, that's just how she is." Jenna thought a minute. "Maybe I should try to be a little more like Amber. You said you think Boone may think I'm sexy," she smiled.

"I hope you're kidding," Scout laughed, as she stood and walked toward the kitchen.

"Should I be insulted," Jenna asked, following her to the kitchen.

"Jenna," Scout turned and said, "I can't tell you what is going on inside Boone's head and heart. I can only tell you what I've observed. Boone seems to like you as you are. Don't try to be someone else. Just let things happen naturally."

"But I'm stuck in Nashville and Amber is always at his side."

"Unless you're going to become an actual groupie and follow his tour, there's nothing you can do about that." Scout put her cup on the counter. "I need a piece of toast for my stomach; then let's get dressed and go play in the rain. We haven't had a girls' day in forever. I miss you, my friend."

Jenna smiled. It would be good to just hang out with Scout for the day. She'd try her best to not even think about Boone.

A couple hours later, as the girls were examining items at The Vintage Nursery, Uncle Pete walked in. Everyone looked up as his booming voice came through the door complaining about too much rain this spring. He spotted Scout and Jenna and headed their way.

After bear-hugging each girl, he said, "I hear there is a new Archibald on the way."

"Not till Christmas, but yes" Scout smiled, "Jack and I are thrilled."

"So are Joe and Beth," he said, "I admit I'm a mite thrilled myself to see the family growing. The first time he says Uncle Pete, I'll put a hundred dollars in a saving account for him,"

"Or her," Scout said.

Pete laughed, "Or her!"

"So how are you and my other nephew doing?" Uncle Pete said to Jenna.

Taken a bit off guard, Jenna replied, "Boone? He's working in his barn today according to Jack."

"Ok. Not what I asked, but maybe I'll stop by and see him. You girls having a day out shopping?"

"Just a girl's day," Scout said.

"Well, we guys need those kinds of days once in a while, too. We call it hunting or fishing days—no girls allowed."

Scout patted her flat belly. "What if she likes hunting or fishing?"

"Hum," Uncle Pete put his finger to his chin in mock concentration. "I've got a few months to think on that, I guess."

Scout laughed. "I'd say more like a few years before he or she is big enough that I'd turn 'em loose with a bunch of you guys."

The girls finished their shopping as Pete moved on to converse with others looking over the fresh vegetables and flowers. Scout and Jenna waved goodbye to him as they left. They spent the rest of the day together, just enjoying one another's company. There was no more talk about Boone.

Sunday everyone gathered at Joe and Beth's for Mother's Day dinner. Boone and Jack grilled the tenderloin and fresh vegetables that Beth had marinated. Beth and Jenna had each purchased an Anniversary card for Scout and Jack. Beth also gave Scout a sweet 8"X8" print of a bunny for the some-day nursery. It was Scout's first Mother's Day present. Scout cried. Jack gave her a hug. After the dishes were cleared, Joe, Beth and Penny took coffee to the back porch to watch the drizzle outside. Joe turned on a Cubs game. The younger four pulled out a board game. It was a day of family togetherness that filled Jenna's emotional tank in a way she didn't realize it needed. She was just part of a big family; something she had never been before and it felt good—warm and natural.

Around 6:30, the board game ended, and Beth and Penny emerged from the kitchen with a platter of cold vegetables, two different types of dips, and rolled cold cuts, along with a cheesecake cut into wedges. After everyone ate a little, Penny asked Boone if he brought his guitar. Boone pulled an old guitar out of a closet, and Jack pulled his harmonica from his pocket. Jenna realized everyone expected the day to end this way. The rest of the evening was music. Sometimes Boone sang. Sometimes everyone sang with him. Sometimes Boone and Jack played and the rest of the family listened. Jenna couldn't have enjoyed the day more.

That night in her upstairs bedroom at Scout's she wondered if part of her attraction to Boone was his family and the warmth she experienced when she was with them. Maybe what she loved was that feeling of being accepted and included. Then she remembered the kisses. No, she admitted, it was more than that. Jenna rolled over to face the window through which the moon shined. Tomorrow morning, she and Boone, Jack and Scout were going to breakfast before she headed home and Boone began his drive back to Texas. She wondered when she'd see him again. When she closed her eyes, she dreamed of lying in the grass, wrapped in a strong embrace with a sky full of stars overhead.

Chapter 21

Jack, Scout, and Jenna met Boone for an early breakfast at the Monticello Red Wheel located on the Interstate. Jack and Scout knew the people working there. One of the girls recognized Boone and made a big fuss over getting his autograph.

After the girl left the table, Jack said, "We can't take you anywhere!"

"This is not normal," Boone said. "When we eat out it is usually Amber who draws attention, not me."

"Well, that actually makes more sense," Jack told him, and Boone laughed.

"How long is your drive to Dallas?" Scout asked.

"About 12 hours," Boone responded.

"Will you drive straight through?"

"Probably. The only reason I took two days on the way up was to visit that big Flea Market I stopped at. I'm glad I did because I got a couple pieces that are in the barn."

"Is that what you were working on Saturday?" Jenna asked.

"One of them. It came in pieces, but once I refinish it, I'll put it back together and add some stuff to it. I'm hoping to be able to mimic the detail. It's kind of a new direction for me to try."

The group had easy conversation throughout breakfast. When they got back out into the sunshine, Scout said, "Now the sun comes out! Where was it for our weekend together?"

"I thought it was a pretty nice weekend," Boone smiled at Jenna, "even with the rain."

"So did I," she smiled back.

They started toward their vehicles and Jack gave his brother a pat on the back. "Drive safely," he said, "let us know when you get there."

"Yes, Dad," Boone teased. He then turned to Scout and gave her a hug, "Take care of little Jackie," he said, then raised his eyebrows "good one, huh? Could be a boy or girl!"

"That's an idea," Scout said, but Jack immediately retorted, "We are not going to have a little Jackie Archibald in pink ribbons and ponytails!"

"I think it's a good thing you two have till December to figure this out," Jenna laughed.

Boone turned to her and put his hands on her shoulders. "What time do you think you'll leave?" he asked.

"By noon," she responded, trying to read his expression.

"Drive carefully," he said, and then engulfed her in a bear hug. "Maybe I'll call you from the car."

"I'd like that," she said, with her arms around his waist and her head against his chest.

Letting go, Boone waved and walked around Jack's car toward his truck. The ride back to Jack and Scout's was quiet.

Jenna had been in the car heading home for about an hour when her phone rang.

"Hello," she answered it on speaker.

"Hi," Boone said.

"Hi, yourself," she replied, "where are you?"

"I just got through St. Louis. I have about 3 ½ hours to Springfield. How about you?"

"I'm about half way to Mount Vernon; maybe about 5 hours to go," she said.

Neither spoke for a minute, and then Boone sighed, "I don't know what to do about you."

Jenna smiled. She decided not to help him out and waited for him to continue.

"I care about you, Jenna; I really do, but I don't know what to do about it. My life is complicated right now, so I don't know how to fit you into it."

Jenna wasn't sure if complicated meant his travel, his future stardom, his dreams, or his relationship with Amber, so she didn't respond.

"Am I stepping out of line to say this to you?" he asked when her end of the phone was quiet.

"No," she said, "I am at a bit of a loss in this myself. You called yourself a simple man, Boone, but you are anything but."

"But, what?" he asked.

"But a simple man," she said in exasperation. "One minute you are kissing me breathless and the next minute you are pushing me out the door!"

Jenna could hear the smile in his voice. "So, I kiss you breathless?"

"Oh, you're impossible!" she said. "How is a girl supposed to know how much to trust a man like that?"

Suddenly Boone's voice took on total seriousness. "Jenna, you can trust me. Please believe me I would never do anything to hurt you. In fact, my reaction to you is so frustrating because I don't want to hurt you—or myself, for that matter. You are different than any woman I have ever known. You are just so simple," he finished.

"If that's your best pickup line, you need to work on your technique," Jenna complained.

"I meant it as a complement," Boone said.

"I'm just so simple?" Jenna asked. "Do you mean in comparison to Amber or the women you meet on tour who are exotic and sexy and interesting?"

"Heavens no," he said. "I mean you are real—really beautiful and really sexy and really intelligent, but real. There is nothing phony about you. I can be me when I'm with you, and simple was probably the wrong word. I wish my life was at a point right now that would let me get to know all those layers of you. Looking at you, being with you, makes me want to know you more."

"Really?" she smiled.

"And I can't think about kissing you right now because I'm driving. I'd hate for the headlines to read 'Man thinking about kissing beautiful woman runs his truck off the interstate!'"

Jenna laughed, "Okay. You've redeemed yourself from the 'just so simple' line."

Changing the subject, Boone said, "Hey, as I was driving through St. Louis, I saw the Arch. Have you ever been up in it?"

"Never," she smiled, "but I'm not sure how you segued to that question."

"Safer," he replied, "About the Arch. I remember going up in it once as a kid and thought it was awesome. I was wondering if it seems as cool to an adult. Maybe we can try it sometime."

"Maybe we can," she said. "Are you playing Nashville this summer?"

"Not until Fall," Boone said, "It may be our last concert. I'm not sure. Maybe when this tour is over, I'll move to Nashville and be a songwriter," Boone said.

"What about those pieces of broken furniture in the barn?"

"Dismantled and in need of repair, but not broken!"

"Doesn't 'in need of repair' mean broken?"

"Not in the eyes of a master furniture craftsman," he told her.

"Ah, yes! The simple man; master furniture craftsman, songwriter, country star, among other things. New headline: Simple man kisses girls breathless!"

"First of all, it is not girls with an 's'. Secondly, why do you keep talking about kissing when we are driving in opposite directions?"

"Because about the time I start thinking you are just Jack's brother, I remember how you kissed me, and I don't know what to do with the feelings your kisses generate. Please tell me those were more than casual kisses to you."

"They've kept me awake at night," he said.

Jenna smiled, "Me, too."

"So here we are; I'm heading to Dallas and you're going to Nashville. What should we do?"

"Maybe," Jenna said, "we do what we're doing now."

"Keep moving in opposite directions?"

"No," she said, "we talk on the phone. We get to know each other. When we find out things about one another, we'll eventually care more or less. Maybe we let us, if there is an us, happen naturally."

"I hate it," Boone said.

Feeling suddenly stupid for using the word 'us', Jenna said, "Really?"

"Well, not what you said, but that we have to do it from a distance. What about if while I'm telling you all about my wonderful self over the phone, some hot Nashville guy is singing country music to you in person. What if he gets to kiss you and all I get are fantasies of kissing you?"

"Hmm," she teased, "that could be a problem."

"Oh," he moaned, "you were supposed to assure me that would never happen."

Jenna refused to mention Amber in their playful conversation, but she liked knowing that maybe the jealousy went both ways.

"Hmm," she repeated, "there is something awfully sexy about a singing cowboy, and we do have a lot of them in Nashville. Since we're starting this new relationship thing."

"A relationship thing?" he asked.

"Well, whatever you want to call it, as we get to know each other, if I meet any sexy singing cowboys, I'll be sure to let you know."

"You're killing me, Jenna," he exaggerated.

"This," she said, "is coming from the guy who autographs body parts?"

"Tee shirts!" he exclaimed. "I autographed her tee shirt!"

"Uh-huh," was all she said.

"Hey," he said, "do you like ice cream?"

"Why?"

"I just passed a billboard for ice cream and I realized I don't know if you like ice cream or not."

"I like ice cream," she said, "Who doesn't like ice cream?"

"Uncle Pete!"

"Really?"

"That's what he's always said," Boone told her.

"Umph! He seems like an ice cream kind of guy to me," Jenna said.

"I know. Go figure!" Boone replied.

Their conversation continued for about an hour or so until Jenna was approaching Carbondale.

"I think I'll pull off at this next exit," she told Boone. "I need a water and I might as well get gas."

"Ok," Boone told her. "If you want to talk later, you know where to find me."

Jenna called Boone again about an hour outside of Nashville.

"I'm almost on my last leg of the trip," she told him.

"That's good," he said, "I'm almost to Oklahoma, but Texas is a big state. I'm still a long way from home."

"What does home in Dallas look like?" she asked him.

"Amber owns a large house in Dallas that most of us live in when we aren't on the road."

"Wow!" was all Jenna could say.

"Yeah, I guess her parents owned the home originally. They were killed in a small airplane accident, so Amber inherited the property and a very large bank account."

"So, she's not only gorgeous, she's wealthy?"

"Pretty much," he said.

"What does a big house mean in Texas?" Jenna asked.

"About the same as it means anywhere, except it sits on hundreds of acres. There are eight bedrooms and baths in the guest wing. The master suite is nearly 3,000 square feet on the opposite side of the house. I think the shower is half the size of my trailer. It is ridiculously huge. The center of the bathroom has an eight-foot round pedestal table with a five-foot tall flower arrangement on it. Why, you ask? I have no idea."

"Wow!" Jenna repeated.

"That's probably what makes Amber so good at what she does," Boone stated.

At the moment Jenna was thinking of bubble baths and a massive pink wardrobe.

"What she does?" she asked.

"Yeah. It's pretty hard to intimidate someone who doesn't need the money. If someone calls her bluff, she can just walk away."

"But she's negotiating someone else's job!" Jenna reminded him.

"Well, there is that," he laughed. "I'm sure there have been times her own client was sweating more than Amber's opponent. She's good at it, though. She rarely loses."

"But when she does, it isn't Amber that loses; it's whoever she is negotiating for," Jenna argued.

"Like I said, Amber almost always gets her way. It's a thing of beauty to watch her in action. She comes across as just a hot body, but there are a lot of brains in that beautiful package. We have been together a long time. She still amazes me."

"Does she date?" Jenna asked, hesitantly, almost afraid for the answer.

"I'm not sure what she does is what you would call dating," Boone said. "Like I said, Amber always gets things her way. When Amber decides she wants something from you, you find you are giving it to her before you know what happened. It's kind of hard to explain. Hey, do you like hotdogs?"

"Why, did you pass a hotdog billboard?" she smiled, glad the conversation had turned from Amber.

"Yep. So, do you?" he asked.

"I'm not really a hotdog person," Jenna told him. "Is Uncle Pete?"

"Uncle Pete loves hotdogs, especially at a ball game. Even at a ball game you don't eat hotdogs?"

"Well, I might be persuaded to have one at a ball game," she said, "after all, it's almost un-American to refuse a hotdog at a ball game, isn't it?"

"It might even be a crime in some states," he agreed.

The conversation continued until Jenna was pulling into her neighborhood.

"I'm only a couple blocks from home," she told Boone.

"I'll miss our conversation, but it has been fun to take you with me on this trip—figuratively speaking, of course," he said.

"Of course," she replied. "Boone?"

"Yes?"

"I'm glad we're going to get to know one another," she said.

"I'm glad, too," he said, "I have to warn you, though, that my schedules are sometimes crazy and open to change on a whim of Amber. There will be times I cannot answer my phone, even a text, so be forewarned."

"I understand," she said, although she wasn't sure she did. "I feel this weekend changed things for us."

"It feels that way," he replied, "I don't know when I'll be able to call again, though. I know tomorrow I'll be out of contact. I was on the phone with Amber in Missouri. She was not happy with me taking this week off, so she is monopolizing my time for the next couple days and then we are on the road for next week's concert. Barry will probably be glad to have me back," he laughed, "When Amber gets mad at me, she takes it out on him."

"Well, drive safely," she told him. "I'm home now."

"Bye, Jenna," he said, softly.

"Goodbye, Boone," she responded.

Jenna was in bed at 10:26 when her phone buzzed. She looked at the text and read: Made it home. Sweet Dreams

Chapter 22

The following morning as she walked into her office, Jenna's phone buzzed. As she greeted Deborah, she set her coffee on her desk, and pulled her phone from her purse. We r back to real life. Let's make 'us' work.

"Well," Deborah grinned, "that's a special smile. Does it have anything to do with your long weekend?"

Jenna looked up at her assistant and friend. "It does," she smiled.

Coffee in hand, Deborah dropped into one of the chairs before Jenna's desk and said, "Tell me everything! I haven't seen you smile like that in . . . ever! Who is he and I want details."

Jenna sat. A part of her wanted to keep Boone all to herself, but a part of her wanted to shout to the world how she felt. She opted for reserve.

"It's just a text from Scout's brother-in-law," she said, lowering herself into her chair and picking up her coffee. "We kind of connected this weekend."

"The Rock Star?" Deborah asked.

Jenna smiled. "He's a country music singer, and yes, that's the one."

"So, what does 'kind of connected' mean?"

"We enjoyed one another's company. Most of the time we were with Jack and Scout and family, but there was a connection. Actually, we talked more as we both drove back to our real lives than we had a chance to talk alone in Monticello."

"Doesn't he have a song on the radio?" Deborah asked, visibly excited.

"Yes, and he's touring this year with Barry Barns. It's his big break into the industry."

"Did he kiss you?" Deborah wanted to know.

"What are we? Junior High?"

"Is that a yes?"

Jenna smiled and became busy putting her purse away and starting up her computer. "Yes, we kissed," she said.

"And?"

"And nothing," she stated. "We live different lives. He travels around the country singing on big and little stages, while I'm stuck here with you." Jenna smiled. "What did I miss the two days I was gone?"

"Are we really going to talk about business now?" Deborah asked.

"That's what we're here for," Jenna reminded her.

"Okay, but before we start, I met Scotty's parents this weekend," she said, eyes sparkling.

"Met them, like MET them?" Jenna asked.

"They came into town, and I think they liked me," Deborah said. "I want him to go with me to Florida soon and meet my parents."

"Wow! This is serious."

"Yeah, he's amazing," Deborah said.

"So, when do I get to meet him?" Jenna asked.

"When the time is right," Deborah said, "and I am so glad you now have your singing cowboy!"

Jenna laughed. "He's not MY singing cowboy, but I'm looking forward to getting to know him better. However, being back at work, I have to wonder how we could ever work out a real relationship living in two different worlds. For now, I guess I'll just enjoy the journey."

"As you should!" Deborah stated.

"Now, about work," Jenna said.

Jenna felt confined in the office, so she decided to walk her lunch hour. She found a place to sit near the river, and drank a smoothie she had purchased on her way. A girl sat near her with a to-go bag from a Japanese restaurant. Jenna pulled her phone from her purse and texted: Looking at a lunch to-go bag. Do you like sushi? The girl eating the egg roll, smiled back at Jenna as Jenna rose to go back to work. Jenna wondered if she could think of Boone without smiling.

That afternoon as Jenna walked toward the conference room for a meeting her phone buzzed: Prefer steak – with you – at a trailer. Jenna smiled and put her phone on mute. This 'us' thing was kind of fun.

Late that night Jenna was propped up in bed in a worn, old tee shirt that she had confiscated from Drake when they split up. She was reading a Nora Roberts book she had read before, when her phone buzzed: u awake? She responded that she was and then the phone rang. Facetime? She ran her hand through her hair and wished she went to bed wearing makeup.

"Hi," she smiled.

"Hey," Boone smiled back. "I've only got a minute, but you look cute and comfy."

"I was just reading," she said, running her hand through her hair and pulling the blanket up higher. "This is a little too comfy for the beginning of a relationship."

"What does your nightshirt say?" he asked.

"It's just an old shirt of Drake's," she responded. "It says 'Got Milk?'"

"Original," he responded, "I'm not sure I like thinking of you in Drake's old shirt."

"It's just a shirt," she said.

"I'll send you a new one," Boone announced.

"This one is old and long and soft," she said. "It's the only thing I kept from Drake because I like it."

"Okay. How was your day?"

"Normal work day. How about yours?" she asked.

"Same. Amber had it packed with interviews and promo recordings, and then the band practiced a new song."

"One you wrote?" she asked.

"No, but it's a good one."

Jenna yawned.

"I should let you get to sleep," Boone said.

"I am a little tired," Jenna said.

"Well, good night," Boone said. "I'll dream about you curled up in that blue and white bedroom tonight."

Jenna smiled, as she ran her hand through her hair again, "It's not polite to drop in on a girl unexpected, you know. We like to look our best when we're trying to impress a guy."

"You already did that. Sweet dreams."

The call ended before Jenna could say goodbye.

An odd call, she thought. This long distance 'us' thing might be a little harder than she thought.

The week proceeded with random, short text messages each way, but no more calls. Jenna thought about calling a couple times, but knew he was busy, so she didn't.

Saturday, as she was giving her little apartment a good cleaning, the door bell rang. She accepted a large padded bag from the postman, and looked at the return address. It was an unfamiliar address in Dallas, Texas. Something from Boone?

Jenna tore open the manila packaging to find a note card and a shirt. The shirt was a pale blue in a plastic bag. She opened the card and read; I had the laundry lady wash it a dozen times this week so it would be softer. Now I will dream of a soft blue shirt being where I'd like to be. Your singing cowboy.

Jenna removed the shirt from the bag. It was similar to the one Amber wore in Austin. It said 'BOONE' in vertical letters down the side of the front and had his picture and the words, 'I'm with him" on the back. Jenna had a second to wonder if Amber slept in one like it, but then pushed that thought out of her mind. Amber's was one-quarter the size of this one. She laughed and hugged it to her body. As she did, she realized it smelled like Boone's cologne. "Oh, he's good!" she said out loud. Then she rushed into her room and donned the new shirt to finish vacuuming. It wasn't as soft as Drakes, but with time it would get there. She wondered what time would do to their crazy kind of relationship. All she knew was it was starting out just fine!

The next two months continued with both of them working and looking forward to texts and short phone calls, and longer facetime calls. It became a game to watch for billboards (bb) and ask a question. One such text from Boone read; bb – what kind of cars do you like? She answered, 2seat convertible Once in a while there would be time when they both could talk. Those calls were usually late at night on a work day, because Boone's weekends were promotional events and late-night concerts. Jenna was busy all day during the week.

Jenna's office closed four days for Independence Day, so she had made plans to spend the weekend with Jack and Scout. The weekend before, she got a call from Scout that Beth had suffered a mild heart attack. Scout said she was doing fine, but the doctor had said it would be a while before she could work. She said Beth was a little scared by the episode, but she was recovering well. As she hung up from Scout, her phone rang. It was Boone.

"Hi," she said, "I just got off the phone with Scout. How are you doing?"

"I'm a wreck," Boone told her. "I have a flight up to see her Tuesday morning. It's the soonest I can get away."

"Scout said she's stable and that your dad is hovering over her like a mother hen," Jenna told him.

"I know," he said, "she probably doesn't need me, but I need to see her. I have to fly to Birmingham Wednesday to catch up with the band."

"I know your mother will love that you are there," Jenna said.

"Can you come?" Boone asked.

"What?"

"Can you come to Monticello on Tuesday? I know you are planning on being there for the 4th of July, but I hate to think we are so close and don't get to see each other. Plus, well, this scared me a little. I'd like you to be there."

Jenna thought for a moment. How could she manage a six hour drive up to Monticello for a Tuesday to Wednesday and then drive back on Thursday night for the long weekend. It would make more sense to go and stay, but could she really take a week off unscheduled? Her bosses would not be happy.

"I'll try," she said. How could she not go when Boone so sincerely wanted her there?

"Yes!" he said. "I know it's a lot to ask, but I'm getting tired of the phone being the only thing that connects us."

She was too, she realized. "I'll be there," she told him, "and don't worry about your mother. Scout says the doctors are confident that this was just a warning. They will adjust her blood pressure meds and she'll be fine."

"Thank you, Jenna," he said.

Jenna heard someone call Boone's name in the background. "Go back to work," she said. "I'll see you Tuesday."

"I like the sound of that," he said, and the call ended.

Later that day she got a text: bring the blue shirt. Jenna laughed. "Men!" she thought, but she'd bring the blue shirt.

Jenna got up at 3am on Tuesday so she could meet Boone's flight into the Charleston, IL airport. She parked in short-term parking so their first encounter would not be at the curb with cars honking for them to keep moving. She was watching for him, as she saw him heading toward the outside door.

"Boone!" she called.

He turned her direction, and a huge grin covered his face. As he quickened his gait toward her, she ran into his arms, and was welcomed with one of those kisses that melted her heart. When he didn't let go, she pushed against him laughing.

"People are going to think you've been off to war," she laughed.

"Do I look like I care?" He started to pull her back into an embrace, but she stepped back and took his hand.

"Let's go before someone tells us to 'get a room'," she said.

Boone wiggled his eyebrows, and squeezed her hand. He picked up his duffle bag from the floor and they walked to the parking lot. Boone drove her car to the hospital. As they drove they talked about his mother, her departure from work, the band going to Alabama without him, and anything else that came to mind. Jenna realized that after all their phone and text time, they we completely comfortable together. It felt like they had known each other forever.

When they entered Beth's hospital room still holding hands, their posture was not lost on his mother for a minute.

"Well, look at you two," she exclaimed.

"I told you they were both coming," Joe told her.

"I know what you said," Beth responded, "but I didn't realize they'd be coming together."

"How are you, Mom?" Boone leaned down and kissed his mother's cheek. "You know how much you scared all of us?"

"Your father has been telling me daily," she sighed, "Hello, Jenna." Beth reached her hand out for Jenna to take it.

Avoiding the IV line, Jenna took Beth's hand and leaned down to also kiss her cheek.

"You look good," Jenna told her.

"I look old and tired, but I'm much better now that I see you two," she said.

"I picked Boone up at the airport," Jenna told her. "I know Penny, Scout and Jack have been manning the shop until you are up and running again."

"She won't be working for a long while, if I have anything to say about it," Joe offered as he rose from the chair next to her bed.

"Hey, Dad," Boone said, giving his father a hug.

"Hi, Joe," Jenna said, "I know how worried you must have been."

"Okay," Beth admitted, "Saturday was scary, but I've been fine since then. I made him go home and get some sleep last night. Look at him, Boone, he looks worse than I do."

Getting choked up, Joe said, "I couldn't lose you. What would I do?"

"You're not losing me unless you drive me crazy with your hovering," Beth said.

Boone laughed. "Well, you two seem fine, but you both look tired."

"Why don't you take him to breakfast and let me get a nap," Beth said.

"We can do that," Boone said. "Jenna got up at 3am to get to the airport on time. I'm sure she'd like something to eat."

"Oh my goodness!" Beth said. "You guys go! I'll be right here when you get back."

Boone dropped his father back at the hospital after breakfast. Then he and Jenna drove to the shop.

"Look who's here!" Penny called as they walked in the front door. "Bum," she said, "I know your mother appreciated you coming all this way to see that she was okay. She fussed that it wasn't necessary, but she was scared Saturday."

"So was I," Boone replied as he hugged her.

After greeting all around, the shop had a break in customers, so they all sat in one of the upholstered furniture settings.

"I know it is still early and Dad is reeling from Saturday, but he's talking about giving up the shop," Jack told Boone.

"Really?" Boone said, "to do what?"

"I don't know," Jack replied, "travel, hang out with Mom. He was really scared."

"Your mom won't agree to that," Penny said.

"She might if she's concerned about worrying Dad," Scout said.

"Maybe Mom should back off from so many hours at the shop," Boone said.

"We can run it," Penny said, "Between Scout, Karlie and I, with Jack's help when he's available, the schedule is very doable. Karlie can go fulltime until school starts. Most days Karlie and one adult is sufficient."

"I was thinking," Jack said, "maybe we buy the shop from Dad and Mom."

"We, like in you and me?" Boone asked.

"Sure. I checked into what a fair price would be to buy them out. We're both in the financial position to afford the mortgage, and then the shop stays in the family, at least for now."

"How would that change things?" Scout asked.

"Well, Mom could still work occasionally once the doctor okays it, but she wouldn't feel responsible to be here all the time. If Dad gets an itch to go somewhere, they can just pick up and go. I don't think she'd let it go to strangers, but I think she might sell it to us. We'll present it as an opportunity for us and as a legacy for the future," Jack said and patted Scout's slightly rounded belly.

"I like it," Scout smiled.

"I knew you would," he said.

"Who would do the purchasing?" Penny asked.

"There would be details to work out, but whoever wants the job could be trained by Mom and Dad until they were secure doing it on their own."

"Too bad Jenna has a job," Boone said, "she'd be great at that. She has great decorating skills. You should see her bedroom!"

"He's only seen it on facetime," Jenna was quick to assure the group, as she gave Boone a look.

He laughed. "She's right. I've only seen it on her phone, but she has skills.," he bragged.

"She also has a job in Nashville," Penny reminded him.

"Well, there is that," Boone agreed.

Since Boone had another morning flight to Birmingham, it was agreed he'd stay at his parents' home since the trailer was closed up. Jenna was staying at Scout's, who invited them all to her house for pizza. Joe wanted to stay at the hospital until Beth fell asleep for the night. Penny said she was tired from her hours at the shop, and Boone and Jenna excused themselves to have an evening alone. No one objected to this seemingly new direction of their relationship.

Picking up to-go meals from Bennie's Pub and a bottle of wine, Boone drove Jenna out to the trailer. It was quiet although warm, but there was a breeze on the back deck. Boone retrieved his two reconditioned chairs from the barn. He opened the stuffy trailer to retrieve a bucket for the bag of ice he had purchased. That also gave them access to a very hot bathroom.

"I hope you don't mind, but I dream about spending time with you on this deck," he said.

"That's sweet," she said, "why would I mind?"

"Well, it would be cooler if we had eaten at Bennie's."

"I like this better," she said, as he handed her a glass of wine.

She took a sip, but Boone didn't move to the other chair. Instead, he reached his hand out to her. When she took it, he pulled her to her feet, and wrapped his arms around her, bringing her close.

"What am I going to do about you?" he whispered in her hair.

Jenna couldn't speak. She had never felt so treasured. She believed she could spend the rest of her life on this deck in this embrace. Then she remembered their different lifestyles.

"We're a mess," she smiled.

"I want you," he said, still holding her against him. "I want you like this, where I can hold you and talk to you about life and decisions and hurts and joys. How do we do this?"

"I don't know," Jenna said.

She looked up at him and he kissed her.

There it was. That kiss that made everything else in life pale. When Boone kissed her, she believed nothing else mattered.

Boone released her, and she instantly felt the loss.

"There has to be a way," she said.

They spent the evening, until after midnight, holding hands, kissing and discussing options for the future. By the time she dropped him at his parents' house, they had come up with no conclusions, but it had been a great night trying to find one.

The next morning, Jenna pulled up in front of the Archibald's house. Boone was watching for her and came out as she exited the car.

Laughing he dropped his bag and lifted her off her feet to twirl her in a circle that ended with a kiss.

"Wow!" she laughed. "Is that how you say good morning?"

"It is when I see my girl wearing my shirt in the morning sunlight." He held both of her hands and pushed her back. "Let me get a mental picture to carry with me," he smiled.

"I did have to put leggings on under it to wear it in public, but let me take this moment to say thank you." She leaned up on her toes to kiss him. He released her hands and gave her another hug.

"You're welcome," he said. "Did you throw away Drake's?"

"You're so bad," she said, "are you driving, or am I?"

"I'll drive, but you didn't answer my question," he said as he walked to the passenger door and opened it for her.

"I'm wearing your shirt, aren't I?" she teased, turning to where it said 'I'm with him.'

"I'll take that as a yes, or at least believe you will burn it when you get home if you haven't already."

"Would making it a cleaning rag work for you?" she asked as he got in the driver's seat.

"Is it ripped into small pieces that clean the toilet?" he asked.

"Oh brother!" was all she replied.

He grinned at her and winked.

She hated that she was taking him to the airport, not knowing when they'd be together again.

Chapter 23

Jenna spent the following week enjoying her 'family' in Monticello. She helped at the shop, hung out with Scout, and spent time visiting with Beth who was now resting at home. She was surprised when the holiday was over how much she didn't want to return to Nashville, but how could she not? Monticello was a nice retreat for her, but she didn't really have a life there. She had worked hard for the job she had in Nashville and she was good at it. She also had Boone on the phone or texting her daily now. Jenna determined to be satisfied with the good life she had and not long for more.

The next two months progressed with the routine of working hard and watching for texts, calls, and facetime with Boone. Jack had made his proposal to Joe and Beth that he and Boone buy them out and was surprised at the little resistance he received. He told Boone he doubts their mother feels quite as strong as she pretends. Boone called Jenna concerned that maybe his mother was really sick and not telling them. Jenna assured him Beth would be honest with her family, because that's who she was. Maybe, she suggested, it was a perfect way for Beth to back away without walking away from something she and Joe had built together. Even without the heart attack, Jenna reminded Boone, his parents weren't getting younger. Working so many hours had to be harder than it used to be. After all, a lot of singing cowboys didn't still tour when they were his parents' age.

Boone gave his new song, *You're Better Than This*, to Barry Barns and after showcasing it at a few shows, he cut it as a single. It instantly started up the charts, a fact that thrilled both Barry and Boone. Jenna heard it on the radio one day and wondered how Boone could write such different lyrics and melodies. She listened to Barry sing:

Remember that day?
It seems so long ago
You didn't want to stay
You didn't want to go
There is another way
You have a choice to make
A different path to take
Be real or be fake
But there is another way

So, Baby don't cry.
You're better than this
Oh, hear what I say
You're better than this

Don't let darkness abide
Deep down inside
You're better than this

It's not who you want to be
Where's the girl I used to see?
She's still there
Oh, Baby, she's still there

Oh, hear what I say
You're better than this
Baby don't cry
You're better than this
You're better than this
So much better than this

You can do it
Be Courageous
Take the first step
Don't look back
Don't be frightened
I'll be with you
You can do it
Don't look back
You're better than this
So much better than this
So, Baby don't cry
Baby, don't cry

You don't have to stay
There's never just one way

So, Baby don't cry
You're better than this

You're better than this
So much better than this
Baby, don't cry
You're better than this.

As Jenna listened to the song, she knew Boone had been right about Barry singing it. Barry had those high notes that Boone didn't, although in the lower registry (a term she had learned from Boone) his voice had a mellow sound that Barry's was missing. Jenna loved Boone's voice. She believed she could sit forever just listening to him sing.

She wondered as the song grew in popularity if Amber had forgiven Boone for giving it to Barry. He had done it without her blessing. If Jenna could see the wisdom in the decision, she assumed Amber now could. She was sure, however, that Amber was concerned about Boone. He didn't say that, but reading between the lines of what he did say, Jenna knew Amber was concerned. She had invested in Boone and even Jenna wasn't sure what Boone was planning for next year. She could hear the indecision in his voice at times and worried that he was choosing her over his career. If he had a future as a full-fledged country artist, would it be right to walk away because of her? If he did, would he resent her later in life? That would break her heart.

Boone had an upcoming week in Myrtle Beach, South Carolina. Amber had rented a beach house for the bands to occupy for the week. After getting there, Boone went to Beach Realty and rented a smaller beach house for the following week. He called Jack first and suggested he check into the idea of Penny and Karlie working the shop for a week so Jack and Scout, Joe and Beth could join him and Jenna at the beach. It would be a last trip before the baby for Jack and Scout, and an ocean get-away for Joe and Beth. Plus, he confided in Jack, he didn't think Jenna would come spend a week with him at the beach alone. He sounded very proud of himself when he announced it was a win-win for everyone!

Under the conditions, Jenna had enthusiastically accepted the invitation to the beach. Nothing sounded more romantic nor safer than a week of ocean breezes and time alone with Boone, with his family all right there. She and Scout had never had a beach vacation, so the two of them excitedly planned for it. Scout wished she weren't six months pregnant for her first beach trip, but she was still thrilled.

The day after Labor Day, Jenna got a surprising call. The head of one of the big recording studios in Nashville said he had heard good things about her and wondered if she would be willing to come in for an interview. They had a position opening up that she might be interested in. The challenge came out of nowhere, but Jenna could not let it pass. She didn't even tell Boone about it, since she had no idea what the job was about or if she would actually qualify. In fact, she was a little curious that she had been called. She had not been thinking about a job change; at least, not one in Nashville. Still, there was no way she could ignore the request to interview.

The following Saturday, Jenna was still reeling with the offer that had come to her computer just before she left work the day before. She had met with two people from the recording company who said they were looking for a new face to promote and sell their artists, and someone to oversee the handling of events. It was an incredible opportunity to get back into more of a people job. Instead of a numbers and paperwork, Jenna would be meeting people and traveling. She knew she could do the job and would enjoy growing into the challenge of something as exciting as this job sounded. They were also willing to pay her more than twice what she was making now. She had emailed back that she was heading out of town and would get back to him next week.

At the Myrtle Beach Airport, Boone stood at the curb grinning over his rental car, a Lexus SC convertible with the top down. Jenna laughed as she walked up and kissed him.

"When I texted convertible, I wasn't thinking quite this classy. What color do you call this?" she asked as she ran her hand over the side of the door that he opened for her.

Boone put her bag in the backseat, and walked around to his side. Still grinning like a boy who just got a pony for Christmas, he said, "Chardonnay Pearl."

"Excuse me?" she said.

"The color; it's called Chardonnay Pearl."

"Perfect! The name matches the car."

After buckling his seat belt, Boone pulled out onto Harrelson Blvd, and Jenna threw both arms straight up into the air and squealed. Boone couldn't stop grinning. So far, his plan was working. He was doing something to make Jenna happy. He wanted this to be a special week for her. As the wind blew her hair, she reached up and somehow tied it back, and then smiling reached for his hand. Boone felt like he had handed her the world and he knew he wanted to spend a lifetime feeling that way.

After about 20 minutes of driving past beach shops and restaurants, Boone turned toward the ocean on Atlantic Avenue. They drove several blocks and then crossed an area of marsh with tall grasses and standing water. A heron swooped over them and Jenna was delighted. A couple blocks later she spotted the ocean.

"Oh, can we stop?" she asked.

"Sure," he said as he turned right onto Waccamaw Drive, "but why?"

"I want to walk out to the water," she told him.

"We're almost to the house," he said. A few moments later, Boone turned the car into a drive that led up to a tall yellow house with small, shuttered windows facing the street.

As he shut off the engine, Jenna pointed and exclaimed, "Boone, there's the beach!"

She was out of the car and running toward the water. Boone pulled her bag from the back and dropped it at the bottom of the stairs, then followed Jenna out toward the sand. She was carrying her shoes and walking toward the water. She turned back toward him and called, "Boone, Come on!"

Boone set his shoes on the back deck and followed Jenna to the water. He was amazed at her delight.

"I know I'm being silly," she said, "but I've never seen the ocean before. Drake and I talked about making a trip here, but now I'm glad we didn't." Walking over to take his hand, she said, "I'm glad I'm experiencing this for the first time with you."

Boone was overcome with a desire to show her the world and protect her from harm. She had not been here an hour and he knew this had been a good decision.

"Jenna," he said.

She looked up at him expectantly, "Yes?"

"I love you."

Jenna caught her breath, and then threw both arms around Boone. "And you said it at the ocean! Could it be more perfect than that?" She kissed him, knowing she would always remember this moment, with the warm, salty breeze blowing over them.

The house had four bedrooms. Boone gave the first-floor room to his parents, and gave Jenna her pick of the other three. She left one of the oceanfront rooms for Jack and Scout, and took the other for herself. "Is that okay?" she asked Boone.

"Anything you want," he said, "I'm just trying to figure out where this girl came from."

"What do you mean?" she asked and then squealed again when she found a hot tub on the upper story balcony, oceanside.

Boone laughed. "I was just remembering that stiff, cautious woman who looked ready to bite my head off that first day when I told her to go get a root beer from the garage. I would never have guessed that inside was this delightful, warm woman who squeals at the sight of a hot tub!"

"But look, Boone," she pointed out, "it's on the ocean!"

"I can see that," he smiled.

"You know what I think the difference is?" she asked with a twinkle in her eye.

"What?"

"I hadn't yet met a guy who could kiss me breathless."

"If I'd only known my powers," he said and kissed her again.

They were still enjoying each other in the warm salt air of the porch, when a horn began honking below them.

"Scout's here!" Jenna cried and took off for the stairs.

It was a great reunion, as Jenna drug Scout out to stand in the shallow waves of the Atlantic Ocean. Boone showed his parents their room, and Beth announced she wanted to rest for a bit. The father and sons walked out to the lower porch and found chairs. The girls were sitting shoulder to shoulder in the sand.

"Is Mom okay?" Boone asked his father.

"Just tired," Joe replied.

"Well, thanks for coming, both of you," Boone said.

"Thank you," Jack said, "you're the one who paid for this week. I didn't get to talk to Jenna yet, but she looks happy. Anything we should know?"

Boone smiled. "She's never seen the ocean before," he said.

"No kidding?" Joe said.

"She does know it isn't going anywhere, doesn't she?" Jack asked.

"She knows," Boone said, as he stood. "I stocked the refrigerator with drinks. Can I get you guys anything?"

The weather at the beach could not have been more perfect. The three couples spent time alone and time together, walking the beach, sitting in the sun, splashing in the water. They ate a big lunch each day at local establishments. Evenings were spent at the beach house with a light meal they fixed for themselves. The days were bright and warm; everyone got plenty of sun.

Chapter 24

Thursday night Boone arranged for his father and brother to take their wives to an early dinner and a movie. He told Jack and Joe he wanted some time alone with Jenna, and they were happy to oblige. Beth and Scout took afternoon naps. The guys found a ballgame on the TV. Jenna took the car to do some shopping.

Joe and Jack had fallen asleep watching the game when Boone's cell phone rang. He looked down and saw Amber's number. Not wanting to wake anyone, he walked out the door toward the ocean. As he closed the door, he looked up and saw Amber standing out near the water, with her phone by her ear.

"What are you doing?" he asked, instead of saying hello.

"I need to talk to you," she said into her phone.

"I'm listening," Boone replied.

"Come down here, Boone," she said, "we have to talk."

"I can hear you just fine," he said.

"Boone, please," she said.

Since Amber never said 'please,' Boone disconnected the call and walked toward the beach. Amber was barefoot, wearing a bikini top with a low-riding, long, flowing skirt blowing around her legs. As he got closer, he could tell something was wrong. He was sure she had flown home last weekend when the band left, so he wondered what she was doing back in Myrtle Beach.

"What's wrong?" he asked, when he was close enough for her to hear him.

"Can we walk?" she reached for his hand.

"No," he said, "why are you here? I thought you had an important appointment in Texas."

She took his hand, and looking down at her fingers entwined with his, she said, "I did. I'm sick."

"What?"

"I'm sick," she said, looking up at him, "I thought I was pregnant, but I'm not. I had a doctor appointment and I'm sick."

Everything in Boone softened. "What kind of sick?" he asked.

Without letting go of his hand, Amber began to walk along the water's edge. Boone walked with her. He waited for her to talk.

"The doctor thinks from the tests they did, that I might have cancer," she finally said.

"But they don't know?"

"I have to have more tests," she told him, and then gave a short, pathetic laugh. "I thought I was pregnant and that seemed bad, but this is worse. Boone, I'm sorry to interrupt your vacation, but I didn't know who else to turn to. You have been the one I could turn to for so long. Even when we didn't see each other, I always knew I could count on you if I needed anything. I didn't know where else to turn. Boone," she cried, "I don't want to die!"

Amber turned in his arms and sobbed. Boone held her. He realized over the years he had always held her when something went wrong. They had been lovers; they had been friends; they had been agent and client. Yet when anything upset Amber, she turned to Boone. Since her parents died, she was pretty much alone in the world. Men ogled and desired her. Women hated and/or envied her. She was independent and confident in her ability to get what she wanted, but she was alone. At the end of the day, Amber had her ambition and her dreams and her memories of adoring parents, but she lived in a mansion that was quiet unless she filled it with band members and people who wanted or needed something from her. Boone's heart went out to her.

"Amber," he whispered, as he lifted her chin with his finger, "Did the doctor tell you that you were going to die?"

"He said it didn't look good," she sniffled.

"But they don't know what is wrong yet?"

Amber didn't answer, but put her head against his chest, and tightened her arms around his waist.

"You need to be positive," he said, "you may be over-reacting. It could turn out to be nothing."

"But what if it's something bad?" she sighed.

"Then I'll be there for you," he said.

"Promise?" She looked up at him.

"Haven't I always been?"

Amber leaned up and kissed Boone. Because it had once been a natural response between them, and because she was hurting, he returned the kiss.

When it ended, he draped his arm around her shoulders and they walked back toward the beach house.

"How did you get here?" he asked her.

"I rented a car," she said.

"From Dallas?"

"No, from the airport. When I got the news, I needed you to tell me everything will be okay."

"Everything will be okay," he smiled down at her. "Where are you staying?"

"I'm flying back," she said. "I have to see Jason Hurt's attorney tomorrow, so I can't stay."

Boone laughed, "You're crazy, girl!" he said. "You are a one of a kind, Amber."

"So are you, Boone," she said, "when will you be home"

"Sunday," he replied, "where is your car?"

"I parked on the street," she said, "my shoes and shirt are there, too."

Boone laughed again.

Amber went up on her toes, and gave Boone a quick kiss, "I love you," she called as she ran to her car.

"I know," he whispered as he watched her run up toward the street.

A few minutes earlier, Scout had entered Beth's bedroom to see how she was feeling. Beth was looking out the window toward the beach, and motioned for Scout to join her. Together they watched the interaction between Amber and Boone.

As Amber ran called "I love you," and ran off, they watched Boone walk back toward the house.

"What should we do?" Scout asked.

"I'm not sure," Beth said. "I usually stay out of my boys love lives, but maybe I should talk to Boone."

"I could tell Jack and have him talk to Boone," Scout said.

"Or maybe we should let them be adults and work it out on their own?" Beth wondered.

"But Jenna is my sister," Scout said, "I can't not tell her what I saw, can I?"

"Let's not say anything yet," Beth said, "Maybe it was not what it seemed, and Boone will tell Jenna about Amber being here."

"Well, if he doesn't, I think I'll have to," Scout said, "if it were Jack and an old girlfriend, I'd want to know."

"You're right," Beth said, "but let's give them time to take care of it on their own."

"Why aren't we going with them?" Jenna wanted to know as the others left for dinner without Boone and Jenna.

"I asked them to give us time alone," Boone said.

"So, they just left?"

"Yes."

"We could have left, instead of making them leave," Jenna said.

"Jenna," Boone said, "they didn't mind."

"Are you sure? Beth and Scout acted kind of funny."

He took her hand and said, "Let's sit on the porch and talk. Would you like a glass of wine?"

"I think I would," she said, and sat on the counter stool as Boone picked a bottle and opened it for them.

At the same time, they both said, "I have something I wanted to talk to you about."

"You first," Jenna said.

"No, ladies first," Boone said as he handed her a glass.

They took their drinks outdoors and sat in the porch chairs facing the ocean.

"I got a job offer," Jenna blurted out.

"What? When?" he asked.

"Just before I came here."

"Why didn't you say anything?" Boone wanted to know.

"I guess I almost forgot about it. Nashville seems so far away from here."

"I didn't know you were looking for a new job," Boone said. "You didn't tell me."

"I wasn't," Jenna said, "It just came out of the blue. The president of this recording company called me to come in for an interview. I didn't mention it because I really wasn't looking for a job and I had no idea what the job was. Well, it turns out that it's a job I think I would love and the pay is more than twice what I make now. What do you think about that?"

"I think it sounds like an unbelievable offer. Who did you interview with?"

Jenna told him the names of the two men. "Do you know them?" she asked.

"No," he said, but he knew the one was a good friend of Amber. Something felt very manipulative about this, but Jenna seemed so pleased.

"So, what did you tell him?"

"I told him I'd get back to him this week."

"Did you?" he asked.

"No, I wanted to talk to you first."

"Really?" he asked, sounding surprised and pleased.

"Well, Boone," she took his hand, "We're working on this thing called 'us' and you did tell me you loved me, so how could I make a decision like that without considering you?"

"Was it a job you would like?" he asked.

"I'd probably love it, but I haven't decided to take it. I'd be working with people more than paper, and it would involve travel. I'd be good at it, but, well, I'm just unsure. Now what were you going to tell me?"

Boone took a sip of his wine and hesitated.

"I'm not sure I should say it now that you have this great offer in Nashville," he said.

"Boone," Jenna said, really hurt, "don't do that. I grew up without an example of how couples are supposed to behave, but I've watched your parents and Jack and Scout. They talk about things and they don't shield one another from the hard stuff. My job offer is just that—a job offer! Please tell me what you sent your family away to say to me."

Boone knew he had no choice.

"I already told you I love you, which by the way, you haven't responded to in kind," he said.

Jenna smiled and put down her glass of wine. She stood and moved onto his lap. Putting her hands on each side of his head, she said, "I thought it was obvious."

"What was obvious was that you loved the ocean," he said.

Jenna smiled, "Not as much as I think I love you."

She kissed him and he pulled her close to extend the kiss.

"You think you love me?"

"Well, this 'us' thing is still kind of new, but . . ."

"But what?"

"But how could I not love a guy who kisses me breathless; a guy who is always on my mind."

"I think that song's already been written," he smiled and then turned serious.

Boone, took her hand and rubbed his thumb back and forth over her palm. "What if I had hated the idea of you taking that job for some reason?" he asked, looking only at her hand in his.

"Boone."

He looked up at her.

"If you had told me you hated that job for me, then we'd talk about it. What you think is important to me."

"What if I didn't hate the job, but I just wanted you to be with me?" he asked.

"I don't think I understand," Jenna said.

"Jenna, I love you. You complete something in me that I didn't even know was missing. I have this all-encompassing need to be with you, to protect you, to share my life with you, but my problem is I don't know where my life is heading."

"What are you asking me, Boone?"

"I guess I'm asking you if you love me enough to follow my dreams with me?"

"You mean like a groupie?" she asked, cautiously leaning away from him.

"No," he smiled, "more like a life partner. Do you love me enough to have a life on the road if that's what I choose? Go with me into a life where you spend more time away from home than at home? Some weeks spending more time with me and the band, than me alone? If I chase my dream of a music career, can you live with that?"

When she started to answer, he put a finger over her lips.

"But," he continued, "what if I decide to be a furniture maker in a barn in the cornfields of Illinois? Could you see yourself happy in that life? I know it's not fair to even bring this up when I haven't figured it out, but how you answer may help me know what I want to do."

Jenna stood. She walked out to look at the ocean as the sun lowered in the sky behind her. Boone held his breath.

"I'm not sure how to answer your questions, Boone," she said and turned to face him. "Are you asking me as a career counselor, or somewhere in all of that was there a proposal?"

They starred at one another for a few seconds, and then Boone slipped from the chair on to one knee and reached into his pocket.

"If you have to ask that question," he smiled, "I really made a mess of my ocean view pitch."

"Pitch?" she laughed, "Boone, for a songwriter, you have a terrible vocabulary. I don't care which job you're pitching."

Boone pulled the ring from his pocket, and Jenna's smile became a look of total joy. "If that was a proposal," she said, "the answer to being the wife of a singer, a songwriter, a carpenter, or whatever dream you pursue is yes! Yes! Yes! Yes!"

His relief was so palpable, she laughed again as she threw herself into his arms, nearly knocking the ring from his hand.

"Whoa," he laughed, "I may have botched the proposal, but could you put this on your finger before I lose it through these deck boards into the sand."

For the first time, Jenna looked at the ring. "Oh my gosh! Boone! It's beautiful! I love it! I love you more, but I love it, too!"

She began kissing his face and laughing at the same time.

"Can we get in the hot tub?" she asked.

"Now? With our clothes on?"

"No. Of course not!" she laughed.

"Without our clothes on?" Boone began to unbutton his shirt.

"Let's go get our suits on," Jenna smiled. "I want to watch the sky grow dark in the hot tub with you. I want to drink my wine and tell you how much I love you. Can we do that?"

"Absolutely," he smiled, and then sobered, "Jenna, I do love you."

"I know, Boone. And I love you, too."

The family came back a while later. Jack and Scout walked up to the second floor and walked out on the porch where the outside light was on. Boone and Jenna sat with towels wrapped around their wet suits, and their bare feet resting up on the porch railing. There was a plate of cheese and crackers half eaten between them. They turned when the inside door opened.

"Well, you two look cozy," Jack said.

"Oh, and you were in the hot tub," Scout sighed, "I'm so jealous. I can't do it pregnant."

"Did you have a nice evening?" Jenna asked.

"The restaurant was great" Scout told her friend, "how was your evening.?"

"It was lovely," Jenna said, smiling and waving her left hand in front of Scout.

"Okay," Scout said, and then she saw the ring. "Is that what I think it is?" she squealed.

"Yes," Jenna jumped up and hugged her friend.

"Oh my gosh! Oh my gosh! Jack! Boone! Oh my gosh!" Scout didn't know who to turn to or who to hug.

"Congratulations, Bro," Jack said, hitting his brother on the back. "You could have told us why you wanted us out of the house tonight."

"I could have," Boone said, "but how embarrassing if she had said no."

"Like that was going to happen," Scout said. "We have to go downstairs. We have to tell your parents before they go to bed!"

The celebration only lasted for a while. Scout was tired and so was Beth. There was a night game on TV which the guys decided to watch. Boone and Jenna got dressed and took a walk along the beach.

Holding his hand, Jenna looked up to Boone's face in the moonlight.

"You've become awfully serious since we left the beach house," she said.

He smiled and squeezed her hand. "Just thinking," he replied.

"About . . . ?"

"I don't know what the future holds," he said.

"No one knows what the future holds," she replied.

"Most people at least have a path, a definite direction," Boone sighed.

"I think you might be wrong about that," Jenna said, "We can't live our life counting on absolutes. Life is messy."

"But there are so many unknowns with us," he said, "What if I stay with the band and you hate life on the road? What if you look back with regret at not taking this big job opportunity? You're the one that told me to follow my dream. What about your dreams? Most people have more of a foundation. Look at Jack and Scout. They are so happy because they are grounded in Monticello and having a baby. Maybe the life I am offering you isn't fair. Maybe I'm taking advantage of ..."

Jenna put her fingers over his lips. "Where is all this uncertainty coming from?" she asked.

"My life is just complicated," he said, "but I really do love you, Jenna."

"Boone, you're the guy who took a risk after high school and followed his dream. The man who can write a hit song, charm an audience big or small, build unique pieces of furniture, or figure out how to drop a safe in the floor because his father needed it. You buy buildings and build mangers."

"This is different," he told her, "This is important."

"What's important, Boone?"

"Us. I don't want to mess it up."

"You're afraid," she said. "So am I."

"Of us?"

"Not in the way you think," she said. "I never had a dream to make it big in the Nashville recording industry. I don't even know where that offer came from, so I'm not afraid of losing what I never sought in the first place. I'm afraid of losing us, not to the outside world, but from within. I've taken this step before. I know I never loved Drake like I love you, but I know people who care about each other one day can hurt each other down the road. Because we care so much, we are risking so much. Risk has reward, but it is still . . . risk."

When Boone didn't respond, she continued, "What if I'm the one that's not enough? You are surrounded by beautiful, talented women every day. We have known each other such a short time and . . ."

Before Jenna could continue, Boone turned her and crushed his mouth to hers.

"Jenna," he said, as he held her tight. "I'm sorry I said anything. We have nothing to fear. We have each other and we always will."

"I know, Boone. I love you. We won't let anything come between us . . . ever!"

As they continued their walk, she said, "Sing to me."

"Sing what?"

"Anything."

It was a perfect ending to a very special night; the sound of the waves, the scent of the salt water, and a full moon. Boone softly sang *Dreams* as they walked the beach. It was a night they both wanted to remember forever.

Chapter 25

October in Nashville

Jenna got home late Saturday night. Boone called her when she was in the car to make sure her flight got in alright. He called her again after she was in bed.

"Yes," she answered the facetime call with a smile. "Didn't I just spend a week with you?"

"If you're tired of my face after just one week, I'm in trouble," he mocked a frown.

Jenna smiled more at his antics. "You are so pathetic," she told him, "and by the way, I will never get tired of that face—my own singing cowboy."

"Or maybe your own songwriting carpenter," he said.

"I told you it doesn't matter to me," she reminded him.

After several rounds of 'I love you,' 'I miss you already,' and 'good-night,' they ended the call. Jenna was still smiling when she fell asleep.

Monday morning, Jenna went to work with a new spring in her step and a fresh manicure to show off her new diamond ring. It didn't take long for Deborah to notice it and gush!

"I am so jealous!" she said. "How long have you been dating your cowboy and you don't even live in the same city! Scotty and I talk about long term plans, but he has never popped the question! How did he do it? Was it a romantic beach scene? Oh, I can picture it in my mind!"

Jenna laughed. "It was pretty romantic, but I think I'll keep the details to myself for a while."

"You are so secretive," Deborah challenged, "So will you guys travel around the country in a big trailer/van? You'll be back stage when he sings to all those screaming girls, knowing he is yours alone! Never mind the romantic proposal, you're going to have the whole package—a romantic life. Jenna, you'll probably be at the CMA awards and meet people like Luke Bryant and Keith Urban! Now, I'm really jealous!"

Jenna started to say that Boone might not continue on tour, but decided against it. Deborah was having too much fun living in Jenna's presumed fantasy. Once Deborah left her office, she endured a morning of people poking their heads in to see the ring and offer congratulations.

Most of them were familiar with Boone's songs. A few asked for tickets to his concert next month in Nashville.

Next month! Jenna was thrilled that she would see Boone again in only a few weeks. She was so used to their long-distance relationship, but that had all changed. She thought about seeing him every day; waking up to his unshaven face, sleeping in his arms. Jenna shook her head and looked at her computer screen. Thoughts like that would keep her from accomplishing any work today. Stop thinking about Boone, she told herself. As her screensaver lit up, her phone buzzed: 20 days to Nashville! Jenna smiled. She would have to learn how to work and think about Boone at the same time.

Jenna hit the button on her office phone to play whatever message the blinking light indicated. The message was from Friday afternoon, and she was pleased and surprised to hear;

"Jenna, this is Tom Anderson from Apex. I just got your message that you are turning down our offer. I realize it's a big job, but we believed we offered you a substantial compensation in accordance to the workload. As I explained when you interviewed, the position is a new one that won't actually start until sometime in late November. We would like you to keep the option open, but we will have to look for another candidate. I think you would love working here and we would love having you, so if you change your mind in the next few weeks, let us know. Both Paula and I enjoyed meeting you."

Chapter 26

Boone and his band were booked in Nashville without Barry Barns. Barry had requested time off before his holiday season began. Boone was only opening for him through this month. Barry had created a special Christmas Show that included others and didn't need a warm up act. He had offered Boone a spot, but Boone had graciously declined. He loved the holidays at home and was looking forward to a break. He liked to think that Monticello would miss him at the Christmas Faire. Since it was located in his barn, he figured he should be there. Amber had created a scene last summer when Barry announced he was planning his Christmas show and wouldn't need an opening band. She said Boone didn't understand how important timing was and that he needed to stay and be part of the show. She had argued to no avail; it had not been a pretty scene.

Boone flew to Nashville with his band. They were booked for Thursday, Friday and Saturday concerts. Most of them were staying in town till Monday. You just couldn't come into Nashville and not extend your stay. A couple of the guys had family living nearby. Boone was the only one not going straight to the hotel. He looked around for Jenna's little car. He spotted it as she cut off another vehicle, slammed on the brakes and jumped out. Running around the back of the car, she flew into his arms, almost knocking him off balance.

"Wow!" he laughed, "I'm glad to see you, too."

They kissed until the honking horns made it difficult.

"I'll drive," Jenna said, so Boone put his bag in the back seat, and got in the passenger side.

They had a quick lunch at a little place Jenna knew about. Then she dropped him at the entrance to his hotel and headed back to work. If only Boone had a local job, she thought, we could do this often. Then she realized that Boone was a musician and a star, and that the singing cowboy was part of what she loved about him. Smiling, she shrugged; they'd figure it out. At least this weekend, she'd be a part of his other life.

After three days and nights of working, Sunday was a beautiful day to experience Nashville. Jenna and Boone had gone out after his Friday night concert, and then met for a late breakfast together before he had to rehearse for Saturday night. But Sunday was all theirs. They went out for a traditional breakfast at the famous Loveless Cafe. They drove down to the town of Franklin, where they walked in and out of shops and then opted for The Coffee House at Second and Bridge. Because they planned an early dinner at Josephine, they each ordered a latte and split a Funky Monkey bagel.

That evening as they were leaving Josephine, they halted between tables to allow a small group to be seated. As the hostess walked away, Jenna recognized it was Deborah being seated.

"Deborah! Hi!" Jenna exclaimed, "What a nice surprise. These must be your parents."

"Yes," Deborah said, hesitantly, "Mom, Dad, this is my boss and friend, Jenna Atherton. Jenna, these are my parents, Rick and Nancy Hurley."

Rick Hurley stood as Jenna reached across the table to shake both of their hands.

"It is so nice to finally meet you," Jenna said, "I couldn't do my job without Deborah. We have been friends for a long time. And this," she added as she turned toward him, "is Boone Archibald, my fiancé.'"

Boone shook hands and smiled as he greeted them.

"We finally meet," he said to Deborah, and then to her parents he said, "I have heard so many good things about your daughter, and we have sort of met on speaker phone."

A familiar voice behind Jenna stated, "I had to park way across . . . Jenna?"

"Brad," Jenna said, and then realized he was talking to Deborah's table. She turned to Deborah with eyes filled with questions.

"Boone Archibald," Deborah said, "Bradley Scott . . . sometimes known as Scotty."

The men eyed one another non-committedly.

"We met once," Scotty said.

Boone put out his hand. "Yes, at Jack and Scout's wedding. It's nice to see you again."

They shook hands, and Scotty walked around Boone and Jenna to put his hand on the back of Deborah's chair.

"It appears you two have finished your meal," Rick said, unaware of the conflict, "any suggestions on what we should order?"

Scotty sat next to Deborah. Boone looked at Jenna's expression and answered for them. "We had seafood, but everything on the menu looked wonderful."

"Yes," Deborah told her father, "everything here is good."

Jenna came out of her surprise to graciously say, "You can't go wrong at Josephine. We should be going. It was nice meeting you," she said to the Hurley's, and then added, "it's nice to see you again, Brad."

She walked toward the front of the restaurant. Boone smiled, said his goodbyes, and followed her.

"Are you upset?" he asked her as they walked to her car.

"I'm surprised. No, I'd say I'm shocked, but I'm not upset."

"You seem upset."

"Well, wouldn't I have a right to be"

"Because?"

"Because I've been deceived!" she said as she got to the driver's door.

"Should I drive?" Boone asked over the top of the car.

"Why?"

"Because you seem upset."

"I'm not upset!" she shouted, as she got into the car and slammed the door.

Boone got into the passenger seat and reached across to put his hand on Jenna's arm.

"Take a deep breath and tell me what's wrong. Let's just sit here for a minute."

"Don't tell me what to do!" she snapped.

Boone put his hand into the air. "Okay," he said and leaned back to fasten his seat belt.

Jenna tugged hers into place and started the car. She then hit the steering wheel with the base of her palm and fell back into the seat.

"She's dating Brad," Jenna sighed.

"You're upset about seeing Brad with Deborah?" Boone asked.

"Of course I'm upset about her dating Brad!"

"You're upset because you still have feelings for him."

"No."

"No that's not why you're upset or no you don't still have feelings for him," Boone asked.

When she didn't answer immediately, Boone prompted her, "Jenna?"

"What?"

"I don't get it. Are you so upset because it hurts to see Brad with someone else?" Boone asked.

Jenna exhaled deeply. "Don't you get it, Boone?" she asked.

"I don't think I do," he answered.

"I don't care if Brad is dating Deborah. Actually, they probably make a cute couple. I think they have been together since Valentine's Day, and Deborah has not been shy in telling me all the details about their relationship."

"So, you did know?"

"No, I didn't know. That's the point. I spend five days a week with her and she purposefully never told me that the Scotty she's in love with is the Brad I used to date. Why did she lie to me? Why not just tell me the truth? That's what hurts. I thought she was my friend."

"So, you're not still in love with Brad?" Boone smiled.

"I wasn't in love with Brad when I was in love with Brad," she assured him. "I never had with him what I have with you."

"Really?" his smile grew.

"Really!" she assured him.

"No breathless kisses?" he smiled

"Never!" she said and added, "Plus, the guy can't sing a note on key!"

"Well, there ya go!" Boone exclaimed. "Let's go meet the guys and listen to some good Nashville music! They're going to love you, and you'll have a whole table of singing cowboys!"

"Who could ask for anything more?" she said and pulled out of the parking lot.

Boone's flight to Dallas was not until Monday afternoon, so he took a cab to the airport, because Jenna had to work. She was sitting in her office when she recognized the sound of silence in the main office area. She looked up, and was surprised to see Amber Golden turning heads as she determinedly approached. She reached Jenna's office and without waiting for an invitation, walked in and closed the door.

"Amber," Jenna said, "please sit down. I didn't know you were in town."

"I'm in and out of Nashville often," she said. Looking around Jenna's office she spotted the picture of Boone under the Dreams sign, and she rolled her eyes.

"Did you want something?" Jenna asked when Amber remained standing.

"I'm concerned about Boone," Amber said.

"Did something happen?" Jenna asked, alarmed.

"Yes. You!" Amber stated.

Realizing Boone was the same as she'd left him last night, Jenna stiffened her back and indicated the chair in front of her desk.

"Please sit down, Amber, and you can tell me your concerns, although it seems to me you should be having this conversation with Boone."

"I've had this conversation with Boone!" she stated and dropped into the chair. "He won't listen to reason, so I thought you might. Boone doesn't want to hurt you, but he's making a big mistake."

Recognizing drama for what it was, Jenna said, "Boone seems like a reasonable grownup who can make decisions for himself."

"You have not known Boone as long as I have," Amber said, "he's a man and easily swayed by what seems too good to be true."

"Why don't you tell him your concerns," Jenna said. This was her turf, and she was determined to keep control of the conversation. She glanced at the sparkling diamond on her finger, and then looked up, waiting to hear what Amber had to say.

"Let me start at the beginning," Amber said, crossing her legs and also sitting up straighter. "I first met Boone years ago when he was living out of the back of an old camper truck and playing whatever gigs he could get in Dallas. He was very good, but he was a nobody with a big dream. That was what drew me to him as much as his talent; his dream." Amber smiled in remembrance, "You should have seen him in those days. He was all fire and passion about making it big. He would play a two-bit bar with a dozen people in it as though it was a stage before thousands. We were more of an item then, and I went to all his shows. I would watch the reaction from the patrons, and I just knew he had what it took if he could just get a break. He told me once, in the middle of the night, that when he closed his eyes, he could see himself performing at the CMA awards. Obviously, I was a little hurt at the time that his dreams were of the big stage and not my . . . well, you know."

Amber paused for effect to let what she had just said sink in.

"Over the years, he kept fighting. It was all about the dream for him, and I loved his passion and perseverance. Then just about the time I worked myself into a position to be able to help him, he left. I never understood why. How could he be content living in a barn? When he lived out of the old truck he was determined, but living in a barn? I was there if you remember. I saw his audience. He still commanded their attention and devotion, but Boone was meant for greatness. My god, Jenna! You should see him command an entire football stadium. He lights up and I see the old Boone, the guy with the fire and passion come alive. When I got him this opportunity to open for Barry, it was his step into the big ring. He can make it in this business. People love him, on stage and off. Other artists respect his work.

"I know Boone gave you a ring last month, and now he is thinking about not touring next year. That's just not right! You have known Boone what? A number of months and most of those you were not even in the same state! I have known Boone for years. I know the man and I know what his dreams were before you distracted him. *Don't Lie* sung by Boone is being played more than the original. *Dreams* just made it to the top twenty. All he needs is more exposure and he's getting it. It just takes time. But you come along and what does he do? This summer he gave *You're Better Than This* to Barry who is taking it to the top of the charts. I'm happy for Barry, of course, but that should be Boone's hit! I may also be Barry's agent, but I really care about Boone. With another year of touring and promotion, I'll be able to make Boone a name in country music. He has worked hard. He deserves his chance, because he has the God-given talent to be a star. I'm in the business, Jenna, so you can believe me when I say most people don't! Even the ones that do, don't often get the opportunity I've given Boone!"

Jenna just looked at Amber. She knew she should take back control of this meeting, but what if the things Amber said were true? She told Boone she would be whatever he needed in a life partner, but was she somehow distracting him from a big career that he deserved. She loved him and wanted the best for him.

"Why are you here, Amber?" Jenna asked. "This still seems like a conversation you should be having with Boone and not with me."

"Jenna, I implore you," Amber's voice softened to a manipulative pleading, "I'm not asking you not to love Boone. Everyone loves Boone. I know I do and that's why I want the best for him. I don't want him to settle."

"And being with me is settling?" Jenna couldn't hide her resentment.

"No, dear, that's not what I'm saying at all," Amber cooed. "Boone sincerely cares for you, even loves you. All I'm asking is that you put his needs ahead of yours for just one year. Encourage him to continue his dream. Let your love continue to grow even stronger. Travel with him if you want, meet his needs and see what I'm talking about. Come stay with him at my place in Dallas; I'm fine with that. I'm only looking out for what is best for him!"

Jenna felt her face heating up with indignation at what Amber was suggesting.

"I'm not a groupie!" she told Amber.

"Of course not," Amber said, "you really love him, but you haven't had enough time to really know him. You know what I'm saying is true. He makes you feel loved and sexy and wonderful. I know, Boone can do that to a girl. I've seen it. I've experienced it. But you haven't lived with him. You don't know his dream like I do. You don't know what he can become if given a little more time."

"Amber," Jenna said, "I have not asked Boone to stop singing. I would never do that. I love his singing. If he made that decision, he made it for himself."

"Don't you see, Jenna," Amber continued, "he's thinking of walking away to be with you. What if it doesn't work? What if he gives up his dream and then a few years down the road, your marriage isn't what either of you expected it to be. I know you understand that can happen," she added. "By then it will be too late for Boone. His time is now. He is on track to do great things. I'm not judging your feelings for each other. I'm just saying you could test them for longevity and at the same time give Boone a shot at his dream!"

Jenna felt herself wavering and the look on Amber's face meant she recognized she might be winning.

"Jenna," Amber said, "I know you have been offered a great opportunity yourself with Apex Recordings. That's a job hundreds of people would die for. Take it for a year. You two could become the new power couple of country music, with you behind the scenes and Boone on stage. Give yourself a chance to reach for stars of your own, rather than just riding along on Boone's star. If your love is real, it will surely last! In the big scheme of a lifetime, what's a year? You can be together as often as your schedules permit, but neither of you will be standing in the other's way. It will give you time to be sure—both of you, that this passion you feel is the kind to stand the test of time. I know how amazing Boone is both as a performer and as a man. If you really love him, you'll give him his time, without any ties."

Jenna stood.

Amber gave one last plea, "Love him all you want, Jenna, but don't limit his potential with unspoken demands that aren't fair. I know you wouldn't intentionally hurt him. I can see you love him, and at this moment in time all he can see is you. Let him have his shot. Is that really too much to ask?"

"As I said at the beginning, this is a conversation you should be having with Boone," Jenna said, "I am engaged to a man who can make a decision for himself. He doesn't need you or me telling him what to do."

"He can," Amber said as she stood, "but love clouds a man's thinking. He's not thinking with his mind these days. You could help him reach his dreams by giving him space. Love him and support him as he reaches for his star. This is his time, Jenna. Don't deprive him of this opportunity. If what you two have is real, you'll both benefit from his success one day. It's never a bad idea to be sure what you have will stand the test of time and space. The world is full of loving starts that end with disillusionment and tears, especially in the entertainment world. I'm just asking you to be absolutely sure."

"I have a job here, Amber, and I need to get back to it." Jenna said, wondering how Amber knew about Apex.

"For the sake of your relationship with Boone," Amber said as she walked to the door, "I suggest you not mention our conversation. Think about what I've said. True love wins out naturally in the end, Jenna. Don't force it. You two may have a lifetime together; so why rush it?"

Without a goodbye, Amber left the office, getting the same amount of attention leaving as she had coming.

Jenna dropped into her chair. How much of what Amber had told her was true? Was Boone's love for her damaging his chance to fulfill a life-long dream. He said his song *Dreams* was inspired by her. Was that just a line? Had it actually been a part of him all along? Jenna shook her head to try and put her jumbled thoughts back in order. One visit from Amber and she was doubting Boone and their relationship. Wasn't that exactly what Amber wanted? Amber told her not to talk to Boone about this. How could she not? However, if Amber was right in what she said, then telling him about her visit could make him angry and determined to prove Amber wrong. What if he chose her over his dream to spite Amber?

Jenna tried to get some work done. She had a lot to figure out before she mentioned the conversation to Boone, although at some point she knew she would.

Jenna had two meetings that afternoon. During one she got a text from Boone: Back home. Still miss you.

As she was leaving the office, a bouquet of flowers was delivered with a note that read, 'To my fiancé, Take these home and dream of me!'

Jenna wished Amber had never walked into her office. As she drove home, she had the pictures in her mind that Amber had planted of her and Boone together. She would not let that bother her. Jenna had been married to Drake, and Boone's relationship with Amber had been a long time ago. Hadn't it? Could it be Amber wanted Boone and was jealous of their new status? Jenna turned a corner too fast and forced herself to slow down. She thought of her time with Boone on the patio, in the hot tub, on the beach, talking about a future together. She would not let Amber Golden intimidate her about Boone. Boone loved her and she loved him! Maybe Amber wanted Boone for herself, or maybe Amber really was looking out for her client, or maybe she was thinking of all the money and prestige that would come to her if Boone made it big.

Jenna had waffled back and forth a dozen times by the time she pulled up to her condo. She took the flowers and walked up the stairs. As she put the vase on her counter, she realized one thing Amber was right about. Jenna had not known Boone as long, or as closely it seemed, as Amber had.

Jenna wasn't hungry. She put on a pot of tea, and looking at the beautiful bouquet, sent a thank-you text to Boone with a picture. She waited for a reply, but it didn't come. Figuring he was busy, she called someone who knew Boone even better than Amber. She called Scout. After all, she and Boone were family.

"Hey, how was your week" Scout asked.

"It was good," Jenna said. "I got to see Boone perform Thursday, Friday and Saturday nights. Sunday we just hung out together and had a nice dinner, after which I got to hang out with him and his band."

"Boone says they're good guys," Scout said.

"They are," Jenna told her, "I liked them. We listened to live music. I enjoyed listening to the guys comments about what they liked and didn't like about the other bands."

"Did you guys have any time alone?"

"We did on Sunday, and oh, you'll never guess who we saw as we were leaving the restaurant."

"Garth Brooks?"

"No, Brad!"

"Paisley?" Scout asked.

"No, my old Brad," Jenna said.

"Oh. Was he with a date?"

"Yes," Jenna exclaimed, "Deborah, my assistant!"

"I thought she was all gooey in love with some guy?" Scout said.

"She is—Brad!"

"No way! And she never told you?"

"Well, she's told me everything else about him, like how he makes her break out in goose bumps when he just touches her neck!"

"Ewww! She told you stuff like that about your Brad?"

"I'm glad you understand why walking into them made me crazy! Boone thought I was upset because I still care about Brad. No! I was thinking of all the little personal comments she had gushed about him!"

"Ewww! I might have just thrown up right there and then," Scout laughed. "I hope you convinced Boone that Brad wasn't a threat."

"I did," Jenna said, "but I do have something else I need to talk to you about. You can talk to Jack about it if you're sure he won't say anything to Boone."

"Jack?" she said, "He's the most tight-lipped guy I know. What's up?"

"Amber came to my office today to tell me I should convince Boone to tour another year. She said he was giving up too much to move back to Monticello, and that he was only doing it because of me."

Jenna proceeded to tell Scout as much of the conversation with Amber as she could recall.

"She has a lot of nerve!" Scout said. "I'd have punched her out!"

"No, you wouldn't have!" Jenna laughed, "but do you think she might be right?"

"About what, Jenna? You aren't second-guessing Boone, are you?"

"NO! I don't know! No.," Jenna moaned, "she put pictures in my head of her and Boone that I can't get out."

"That was one of her intentions. You know that, don't you?"

"Yeah. I know, but do you think I'm holding Boone back from stardom?"

"I have to tell you something, Jenna," Scout said.

"What?"

The night you got engaged, did Boone tell you that he met Amber on the beach that afternoon?"

"What do you mean?"

"Remember when Beth and I decided to take naps and the guys decided to watch TV, you went shopping," Scout reminded her.

"Okay," Jenna said.

"Well, I woke up and went to Beth's room to see how she was feeling and she was watching out her window. She was watching Boone and Amber on the beach."

"You mean like talking? I thought Amber had gone back to Dallas with the band," Jenna said.

"That's what we all thought, but she was there on the beach with Boone."

"What do you mean 'with Boone'?" Jenna asked.

"They were in serious conversation," Scout said, "and then they hugged, and..."

"And what?"

"They kissed."

"They kissed like a peck on the cheek kissed?"

"Listen, Jenna, we didn't know what they were doing there or what they were talking about, but when we came home that night and you were engaged, and both so happy, well, Beth and I figured either you knew about Amber or it wasn't anything to worry about."

"Scout, I asked you if it was a peck on the cheek or a real kiss," Jenna said.

"It looked like a real kiss, but we weren't that close and then she left and you got engaged," Scout said.

"Why didn't you tell me? Why are you telling me now?"

"Oh, Jenna," Scout said, "Beth and I didn't know what to do, but when we got home and you two were so happy, we decided that what we saw meant nothing. Boone is so over-the-moon in love with you, and he would never play with your affection. Beth and I were sure of that."

"So, why tell me now?"

"Because I think Amber plays games, and is trying to keep you out of Boone's life."

"Scout, I love Boone, but this doesn't make what she said today better, it makes it all worse. How could he kiss her and propose to me within hours of each other, and not mention being with Amber on the beach? Maybe Amber is right. Maybe I don't know Boone as well as I thought I did!"

"Now you're sounding as dramatic as Amber," Scout said. "Jenna, Boone loves you. I may not know him in the music world like Amber does, but I know Boone. Think back to last Christmas. Did Boone seem unhappy living in Monticello? I think he was content and would have stayed that way if Amber had not shown up. Forget about the beach for a moment, and think about the Boone that you know and love."

"But she kept talking about how his music and passion were so real before I distracted him."

"Did you tell Boone he had to choose between you and his music?" Scout asked.

"No."

"Did you trick or manipulate Boone into proposing?"

"No," Jenna laughed, "if you had heard his proposal you would know it was all him."

"Yeah, some day I'd like to hear that story, but what I'm saying is this is Boone's decision. Of course, you are a part of it, because he loves you; but he has to choose which dream he wants to follow. Isn't that what his song says? Dreams may change."

"Amber implied that his lyrics had nothing to do with me; that they had been in him back when he was with her," Jenna said.

"Of course, she did!" Scout said. "Maybe Amber still wants Boone and thought with their closeness on this tour that they would be a couple by now, and then Boone goes and falls in love with you. Maybe with all her talk about Boone's dreams, it was really her dreams that were broken."

"Maybe, but why didn't he tell me he saw her that day?" Jenna said.

"I don't know, maybe he didn't want it to ruin his evening plans with you. Maybe it wasn't important enough for him to even mention it," Scout said.

"But he kissed her," Jenna sighed.

"You should talk to Boone about all this," Scout told her.

"I can't yet."

"You have to," Scout insisted.

"I will, but not yet," Jenna said. "I want to think about it some more. Maybe we do need to know each other better. I mean she's only suggesting I give him time."

"Time for who?" Scout asked. "You can think about it, but don't let Amber Golden's words outweigh Boone's words in your head. I know Boone. He's not a cheater. I'm sure if you ask, he has a simple explanation for the scene on the beach. As far as his career goes, he may be on cloud nine in love with you, but he's still a grounded guy. If he wants to be a star, I see him just taking you along for the ride. But maybe it's a ride he's decided not to take. Talk to him, and remember that Amber has an agenda coming to you. We just don't know what it is."

"Thanks," Jenna said.

"That's what sisters are for," Scout returned.

"Oh, I got flowers today and several text messages," Jenna said, smiling.

"Sweet Bum! A true romantic, at heart," Scout said. "I'm glad you guys found one another."

"Me, too, I think," Jenna said, hesitantly.

"Hey, don't let Amber come between you two. Talk to Boone!"

"I will," Jenna assured her, but she knew it wouldn't be right away.

Chapter 27

Amber walked onto the patio of her home glad to see Boone alone. The place would be quiet once all the guys left for the holidays. She listened to the song Boone sang and recognized its potential to be another hit. The guy was on a roll as far as his music went. If she could only convince him to come back next year. There would always be another Jenna to come along. Maybe she could make him look at her that way again. Either way, he had a career in music, and he was about to throw it away.

Amber quietly walked up behind Boone as he was strumming and singing the new song he had written for Jenna. He hadn't played it for anyone, because he was going to sing it for the first time at their wedding.

Amber waited until Boone was finished singing and then she grabbed him from behind, hugged him and turned his head to plant a big kiss on his mouth.

"OMG!" she squealed, "That is the best one you have ever written!"

His lack of response or enthusiasm didn't faze her. She pushed the guitar off his lap and sat down, determined to be persuasive about what she had just heard.

"Every woman in America will want to hear that song from the guy she loves," Amber gushed, kissing his cheeks and his temples, "and until then, she'll be hearing you and dreaming about you singing it to her. Your fans will go wild over it!"

Boone gently moved her off his lab, and stood up. "I haven't decided what to do with it," he told her, and that's when the confrontation began. It was nothing she hadn't said before, but this time she pulled out all the stops. Amber was in full combat mode and was determined to win. He was ruining his life, she shouted, and giving up a career that thousands of young musicians would give their right arm for, she wailed.

Amber stepped over the line, however, when she called Jenna a dime-a-dozen gold-digger. Boone was as close to decking a woman as he had ever been in his life. Realizing she had taken it too far, Amber immediately turned on the charm and apologized, saying she was only thinking of his career. When he didn't soften toward her, she began to cry, a tactic Boone hadn't seen since the beach.

"Did you ever get the results from your medical tests?" he asked, as he put distance between them.

Amber smiled. "It turned out to be nothing," she said.

Boone looked at her for a moment, and then said, "Amber, I'm through playing games. I appreciate all you have done for me, and I will always be grateful to you, but just I'm a songwriter."

"Don't say that!" she shouted, "you are so much more! You have the voice, and the talent to be both. You command a crowd and they love you. Please, Boone," she begged, "don't limit yourself when you have so much to offer. This is your time! This is your dream!"

"My dreams have changed," he quietly said.

Amber dropped to the floor in anguish. "You're doing this because of her!" she screamed. "I can't bear watching you walk away from everything. Boone, don't do this! Don't give up on yourself! I can make you a star! Don't leave me, Boone! I love you, Boone. Don't walk away!"

Boone sadly walked back into the house. He moved to a hotel in Dallas the next morning.

Boone had his last opening for Barry the first of November. He called Jenna after the final concert, and was a bit surprised at her lack of enthusiasm that he was coming home.

"Is something wrong?" he asked.

"We can talk about it at Thanksgiving," she said.

"I think we should maybe talk about it now," he replied, wondering what was wrong.

"No, I'm okay," she said.

"Jenna, if something is bothering you, please, let's talk about it. If you're upset, I want to help."

"I think it's something we need to talk about in person," she said.

"Jenna, let's not keep things from one another," he began, "I'll worry about what's bothering you, and I don't want to have secrets from one another."

"Oh, that's interesting, coming from you," she said.

"What's that supposed to mean?"

"Let's just wait until we are together," she said.

"That's not fair," he responded, "I don't keep things from you. Why won't you trust me and just say what you're thinking."

"You don't keep things from me?" she asked.

"No, Jenna, I don't," he was getting agitated.

"How about kissing Amber on the beach before proposing to me the same evening?"

"Oh."

"That's all you have to say? Oh?"

"How did you know? Have you known all along?"

"That's all you've got to say?"

"No, of course not, but why didn't you ask me about it at the time? I'm just wondering why you didn't ask me then?"

"And I'm wondering why you didn't tell me then," she said.

"Because there was nothing to tell," he defended, "she thought she was sick, but it turned out to be nothing. Why are you bringing it up now?"

"Scout just told me about it. She and your mom saw you and Amber in an embrace and kissing on the beach. They thought when we got engaged, that you had told me about it and that it was nothing."

"It was nothing," he said.

"Then why not tell me?" she sighed.

"I should have, but I was wanting the evening to be special, so why would I want to talk about Amber?"

"I don't understand, Boone," she said, "Amber said she was sick, so you hugged and kissed her? That doesn't make sense to me."

Boone sighed deeply. "It was stupid. She was dramatic and upset, and it just happened. I don't know how or why. It was stupid. I'm sorry."

"How would you feel if it had been me and Drake, and I didn't think it was worth telling you? The difference is, I wouldn't fall into Drakes arms and kiss him because he said he was sick. I would say, 'sorry to hear that!' Why did you kiss her?"

"I don't know. It just happened, but I promise you it will never happen again—not with Amber, not with anyone. I should have told you, but we were so excited about being engaged that night, I really didn't even think about it. It was nothing, but you're right. I shouldn't have kissed her. I hope you trust me that it will never happen again."

"I'm working on it," she said.

"Jenna, I love you and I've hurt you," Boone said. "I never meant to do that. Please forgive me."

"I love you, too, Boone. I have to go, but we'll talk later."

"Jenna..."

"I'm okay, Boone. We'll talk later."

The Wednesday before Thanksgiving, Boone was covered in sawdust in his barn. He had music blasting on speakers, as he ran a buzz saw down a long piece of lumber. Yeller was sleeping on an old horse blanket off to the side.

Jenna walked unnoticed through a side door. She stood and watched her fiancé absorbed in his task. Suddenly she was overwhelmed by the realization that this was her man; the carpenter, the songwriter, the singing cowboy and the love of her life. How could she have doubted him and their love all these weeks? She watched the muscles in his arms as he maneuvered the heavy board, and knew that his strength was more than physical. He had inner strength that she could depend on for life. Some day the muscles might be gone, but the man of character would always be there for her and her for him. The noise from the saw stopped leaving only Blake Shelton singing *Honey Bee* over the speakers, with her cowboy singing along. He looked up and saw her. His smile for her reached his beautiful eyes. He walked to the wooden shelf and turned off the speakers.

"Hi," he said, as he approached her, "Blake and I were just singing about you!"

"I heard," she smiled, "he's not bad—for a backup."

Boone laughed. "If I ever meet him, I'll won't tell him you said that. I didn't know for sure what time you were coming, so I decided to work out here," Boone told her, brushing sawdust off his pants. "I'll go in and shower."

He took her hand. "Are we okay?" he asked.

Jenna smiled. They had talked many times since their conversation about Amber on the beach, but this was the first time they had been face to face.

"Yeah," she said, "we're okay."

"Good," he smiled, and squeezed her hand, "Come with me. I bought some of that fancy water you like to drink."

"Ok," Jenna said, "when you're done, we need to talk."

Boone stopped and dropped his head to his chest. "Please tell me we aren't going to talk about Amber on the beach or me touring again."

"No," Jenna told him, "I have something to explain, and then a suggestion to make."

"Oh, boy," Boone said, as they walked toward the trailer, "I don't know if I want to take a fast shower or step in the shower and not come out."

"Make it fast," she said. "I think you're going to like my suggestion."

Still looking skeptical, he opened the trailer door for her, kissed her lightly, and headed down the little hall. "Make yourself at home," he said over his shoulder.

Jenna looked around the trailer. "I could make this my home," she said to no one. She pictured them eating at the little table or sitting at the counter. She could imagine evenings listening to the incredible audio system he had installed, or watching The Voice on TV as they discussed song choices and vocal skills. She helped herself to a drink from the refrigerator and looked out the back window. It was too cold to be out on the deck, but the view was still pretty with the blue sky showing through the bare trees. Boone had told her at dusk and dawn deer wandered out of the woods at the back of the property.

Jenna heard the shower go on and Boone started humming a tune she didn't recognize. It was pretty. She wondered if it was something he was working on. He was a complicated man, her singing cowboy. He had looked so content in his barn, all dirty and sawing a big hunk of a tree, picturing in his mind what he would create. The song he gave Barry had become Barry's signature hit, and although most people didn't know Boone wrote it, Boone knew; and that seemed to be enough for him. Plus, he got royalties on it. He owned property, he made people laugh, and he was trustworthy. She was grateful for such a man. She silently vowed to be a worthy life partner to him.

Boone appeared, bare feet and damp hair. She noticed he wore his black tee, tucked into jeans with his 'tour' belt.

She reached over and touched the belt buckle. "Touring today?" she asked him.

"Not with a beautiful woman in my trailer! Do you think I'm crazy?"

"I was just thinking about all the things you are, and crazy was definitely not one of them," she said.

Boone put his arms around her and they kissed a kiss that said so much. When it ended, they both smiled.

"You want to build up my ego and tell me the good stuff you were thinking?" he asked, holding her hand and walking her to the sofa.

"No," she said, "I want to explain the last few weeks to you."

Hearing the serious tone of her voice, he said, "Okay," and waited.

"I know we've had a few arguments lately about stupid stuff," she began.

"Hey," he said, "I can be stupid."

"I know," she smiled, "and bullheaded, and difficult, and stubborn."

"I hope this isn't the good stuff," he said.

"No, I wasn't thinking of any of that when you walked in. I was thinking about the great guy I'm going to marry and what a wonderful life we have ahead of us."

"I like that," he said.

"But I've doubted you. I've doubted us lately, and I want to apologize for that and for being difficult and unreadable."

"Okay," he said, "what else did I do?"

"Nothing, but I had a visit a few weeks ago from Amber," she told him.

"Oh, boy," Boone moaned, "when?"

"The day you left Nashville."

"And you waited this long to tell me about it?" Boone asked, obviously annoyed.

"I know, but I had to think about what she said," Jenna told him.

"I can imagine what she said. In fact, I can probably tell you exactly what she said."

"Maybe," she said, "but some of it made sense, so I had to sort it out for myself."

"Like what?"

"Well, she reminded me that we hadn't spent nearly as much time together as you and she had, and that she knew you much better and in ways that I didn't."

"Oh," Boone moaned, "I should have decked her that day."

"What?"

"Never mind. What else did she say?"

"She said that if it weren't for me you could fulfill your dreams; that you'd be a big success. She said you told her in the middle of the night about your dream of being on the CMA awards."

Boone reached over and pulled Jenna to him. "I am so sorry she did that to you," he said. "I wish I could erase it all from your head, but maybe over time I can. I was with Amber a long, long time ago, and she will pull anything out of her bag of tricks to get her way. She has no shame. Believe me, Jenna, I love you and only you."

Jenna pushed herself away from him. "I know that," she told him. "After my visit from Amber, I had moments of doubt, not about our feeling for one another, but whether or not I was good for you."

He started to reach for her again, but she stood up.

"No. Let me finish," she said. "I told her you could make decisions on your own, and that I had never asked you to choose between me and your music, but over time I began to question that ability in you. I began to wonder if what we have is enough, and if your desire for me now would be something you would regret in the future. I came here today to ask you to forgive me for ever doubting you; for ever doubting us.

"Scout told me to allow your words to drown out Amber's and it took me a while to let that happen. I want you to know that I will never doubt you again. I may argue with you, or even question a decision, but never will I doubt you. You are as solid and as good as a person can be, and I am excited to spend the rest of my life with you, Boone Archibald."

"What about bull-headed and stubborn, which I think are both the same characteristic?" he asked.

"Well, since I have a bit of both in me too, I guess I'll have to overlook that quality."

"It can come in handy," he said. "All the arguments that Amber used on you, she tried on me; probably more, but I held my ground," he took hold of her hand. "Jenna, if I had really wanted the limelight, I would have just taken you along with me. I love music. I love singing country music, but what I have come to realize is that there are a lot of things I love. I love hearing a song I wrote on the radio, but I don't have to be the one singing it. And I love thinking of us having a family and growing old together in this trailer."

"You're kidding about the trailer, right?"

"You don't love my trailer?" he teased.

"I do. I really do. It was the family and growing old here part I questioned."

"I'm seeing a new side to you," Boone feigned surprise.

"I have a lot of sides you haven't seen yet," she smiled.

"I'm counting on that," he said, and he stood.

"Wait," she said, "sit back down."

He sat and said, "There's more?" he moaned.

"Yes, but this is the good part."

"Okay."

"Let's get married."

"I thought we'd already decided that part," he said.

"I mean let's get married this Christmas, in the barn, with all the lights, and the flying angels, and candles, and just our families there. Can we do that?'

Boone's smile lit up his face. He stood and took her in his arms, and said, "I think we can do that. In fact, I'm sure of it, but I thought girls needed lots of time to plan a wedding."

"I don't want a big wedding," she said, "I just want us and family. What do you think?"

"I think I want to do that breathless kissing thing."

Wrapping her arms around his neck, she said, "I'm all yours."

After a minute of kissing, he said, "Oh, I just thought of something."

"In the middle of breathless kissing?" she asked.

"I wrote you a song," he said.

"When do I get to hear it?"

"At the wedding," he said, then resumed what they were doing.

Chapter 28

Jenna was convinced that she was needed at the shop in Monticello for the month of December since baby Archibald was due the 15th. Long work days were hard on both Scout and Beth. Karlie only worked Saturdays during the school year.

Jenna gave notice to leave her job the end of November. Deborah was going to be promoted to Jenna's job, much of which she was familiar with. She and Jenna had lost the closeness of their friendship. Deborah was expecting an engagement ring for Christmas. Brad was talking about buying a house.

The end of Thanksgiving weekend Boone drove his truck to Nashville to take Jenna's personal items and a few pieces of furniture to store in the barn. Jenna was selling the condo with the rest of its furnishings.

"This is a nice piece," Boone commented on a small antique console that Jenna had emptied.

"My mom got it from her mom. It's the only heritage I'm bringing to this marriage," she said.

The tinge of sadness in her voice prompted Boone to but down the box he was carrying, and walk to her.

"Hey," he said. "We're going to make our own history. It's already started in fact."

"How's that?" she smiled.

"We've got heart, Kid," he took her hand and patted his heart, "right in here. We're going to build a legacy by teaching our kids to work hard and care about the important things in life; you know, prioritize your needs!"

"We both just gave up high-paying jobs," she reminded him.

"So we can pursue new dreams," he reminded her.

Jenna hugged him.

"I think I should add 'visionary' to your list of special qualities that I love. I'm good with the idea of new dreams—and the idea of kids," she softly told him, "I love you."

"Me too you," he replied, "how many?"

"How many what?" she asked, snuggled against his chest.

Boone's phone rang. He took it from the holster and answered it.

"Whoa!" he stepped back from Jenna, "we're just finishing up here and we'll be on our way. Good luck, Man, or whatever you're supposed to say at times like this."

"Scout?" Jenna asked.

"Yeah," Boone said, moving to pick up a big box. "Let's get the last of this packed. They're on their way to the hospital."

"Is she okay?" Jenna frowned,

"I think she's great," Boone smiled. "She's having a baby!"

Baby Colt waited for Boone and Jenna. In fact, he took his time, not making an appearance until 4:42 am. Scout looked exhausted, but smiling when Boone, Jenna, Joe and Beth poked their tired heads in to greet him before everyone went home to sleep.

The month of December went by quickly. Jenna lived at Scout's and helped with the baby evenings so Scout could be up at night. Jack lectured his son about his sleeping schedule to no avail. Jenna and Penny held down the busy shop, with Jack, Karlie and even Boone filling in.

The Christmas Faire was planned as usual, so Boone also stayed busy getting the barn ready. This year the barn needed to be perfect, because it was also going to be the venue for his wedding. Plus, he and Jack had been busy getting documents and paperwork done for the sale of Grandpa's farm to Boone. He hadn't told Jenna yet, but he wanted her help in designing a real home to sit up on the hill behind the barn. Word had spread that Boone was back and would be available for woodworking projects. He wondered if his status as a 'famous' county singer in the eyes of Monticello increased his popularity, since very few of those requesting his service had actually seen anything he had made.

One Saturday night, as the two couples sat in Jack and Scout's living room, looking at Colt sleeping in Jenna's arms, Jack said, "Can't you pinch him or something?"

"No!" Jenna said, "Aunties don't pinch babies."

"If he'd wake up now, he might sleep tonight like a normal person," Jack complained.

"He's not a person yet," Jenna said. "How can you be mad at that sweet face?" she asked him.

"I'm not mad. I just don't understand. When it's light he wants to sleep. When it's dark he wants to cry."

"Maybe he's afraid of the dark," Boone offered.

"Then stay awake when its light and sleep through the dark!" Jack offered.

"He'll be on schedule by New Year's," Scout assured him.

"Ohhh!" moaned Jack. "Will I survive?"

"You'd better," Jenna smiled. "You have best man duties this month. Did you guys decide on what to wear for the wedding?"

"Oh, Jenna," Scout said, "Boone picked out the coolest suits. They are western style and they both will look so handsome!"

"We're always handsome. We're Archibald's!" looking at his son, he added, "all three of us!"

"Western style, huh?" Jenna looked at Boone.

"Well, the suit had to match my buckle," Boone smiled.

She returned his smile as little Colt stretched and yawned.

"Oh, he's waking up," Jack said, "let me have him. We need to have another talk."

The other three laughed as Jack took his tiny son and began explaining the beginning facts of life to him. Colt opened his eyes to watch his father for a while and then started to go back to sleep.

"I'll change him," Scout said. "That might help wake him up for a while. He hates it."

"Make sure that wipe cloth is really cold," Jack said, as he kissed his son's head and handed him to Scout.

It was after 11pm when Scout fed Colt, and she and Jack took him to their room, hoping for at least four hours of uninterrupted sleep.

Boone and Jenna sat together on the sofa enjoying the Christmas tree and the fireplace.

"Do you miss Nashville?" he asked her?

"No, I love working at the shop, especially now that it belongs to the four of us. Your mother has been teaching me how to anticipate needed stock and I found a vendor she didn't know about. I think we're going to put in an order with them after the first of the year. It's pretty cool stuff."

"I know Mom and Dad are pleased that you have jumped right into this new role."

"I like the idea of running a business," she told him.

"Good," he replied. "We'll make a good team. I can make furniture and write music, but the business paperwork makes me crazy."

"Jack handles most of the shop paperwork," Jenna said, "but if you need me to learn how to manage B A Originals, I'm up for the challenge."

"That's my girl!" he said. "I have some other details for which you need to become familiar."

Putting her hand over her mouth to yawn, Jenna said, "Sorry."

"I'd better go," Boone said as he stood. "Get a good night's sleep. I have somewhere for us to go tomorrow afternoon. I'll pick you up at 1 pm. Wear a warm jacket and boots."

"Ok," Jenna yawned as she stood.

Boone laughed. "Goodnight," he said as he kissed her nose and turned her toward the stairs. With a gentle push, he added, "I'll lock the door as I leave."

The following day was sunny and cold. Boone picked Jenna up at the appointed time and drove her back to the farm. Thinking he must have forgotten something, she was going to wait in the car, but he walked around and opened her door. Putting a hand out to her, he smiled.

"What are we doing here?" she asked.

Boone didn't answer. He pulled a large canvas bag from the bed of his truck. Taking her hand, he began walking toward the woods.

"Where are we going?" Jenna asked.

"I want to show you something," he said.

Boone and Jenna walked onto a path that wove through the trees. He pointed out small things to her as they went. The walk seemed to be taking them up an incline. All of a sudden, they reached a clearing. The grass that stuck through the snow on the ground was scruffy and unkept. It wasn't exactly a clearing, but the trees were less dense. In front of them was a wooden picnic table and benches.

"Where are we?" Jenna asked.

Boone walked to the table and opened the bag. He pulled out a large blanket and spread it over the table. Then he put a smaller one on one of the benches, and indicated she should sit, which she did.

"I brought us coffee," Boone said, pulling a thermos and two mugs from the bag.

"What else do you have in there?" Jenna laughed. "I'm waiting to see if a guitar comes out."

Hitting his forehead with the palm of his hand, he said, "I should have thought of that!"

"You're crazy," she told him, "Is this going to be our special place to get away from the world?"

"In a way, yes," Boone said. He poured them each a steaming coffee, and then sat beside her.

"If I had stayed on the career path I was once on, I might have been able to give you a mansion one day in Texas or Nashville or where ever you wanted one," he said. "But what I discovered was that the big stage with the lights and screaming crowds was not the life I really wanted. By walking away from that, I walked away from the potential of really big money, but it would have come at a cost. I don't think I would have been happy long-term, and it would have defined our relationship by the travel and demands of a performer. What I also discovered is that what I really love is writing music. You know I don't care who sings my songs; I just love the idea that people connect to them. However, that means my songwriting and woodworking income will have to satisfy us."

"Boone, you know I was not looking at you as a country music star," Jenna said. "If that was the life you chose, we would have figured a way to make it work. The thing is, I am satisfied with us. I am actually excited to see what our future holds, and I know with you it will never be boring or dull. Right now, you are a songwriter, woodworker, business owner, property manager, Christmas Faire director, singer, and soon-to-be husband, just to name a few of your current titles."

"I'm tired just listening to you," he laughed, "but I brought you here to tell you about my latest challenge."

Jenna smiled at the man she loved, realizing just how much of a dreamer he was.

"You are sitting in the middle of our farm," he said.

"How big is your Grandfather's property?" she asked.

"80 acres," he answered.

"Wow!" she exclaimed, "I have no idea how much that is, but it sounds big!"

"It's a good size," he said, "but it's no longer my Grandfather's farm. I bought it from the family. It's our farm, Jenna."

"Our farm?"

"Yes. I hope I'm not overstepping my role, but I wanted to offer you more than a trailer. It will be a while before we can build anything, but I'm thinking that this spot would be perfect. We will make a road through the trees that comes up from the barn."

Jenna didn't react immediately. Boone worried that he had fallen into that "bossy" mode she hated. When the silence began to stretch, he didn't know what to say. Before he could decide, Jenna began to smile.

"We could plant a garden," she said, as a tear slipped down her cheek. "As a girl in the apartments I always wanted a garden. I never had a garden, but I'm sure Uncle Pete could teach me."

Boone put both arms around her and drew her close. He had given her her first time at the ocean, and one day he would give her a garden. Layer by layer, she was so simple to love.

"For a second I was afraid you hated the idea," he said.

"I guess I'm not used to surprises yet, but I have the feeling I need to expect them doing life with you."

"So, you're happy?" he asked.

"Yes, Boone! I love the idea of building a house here with you. Just think of how exciting it will be to plan it together! It will be our own little place to escape from the world."

"Don't forget all my family is here. They drop in often," he said.

"I will love having family dropping in! It will be our own little house on the prairie."

"With running water," he said.

Ignoring him, she asked, "Do you have an idea of what it will look like?" Jenna asked.

"That's totally up to you," he told her, "although I'm sure all my family will have ideas. Jenna, this will be our house—however you design it!"

Looking into his eyes, she quietly said, "Thank you, Boone, for the life we are going to have. I love it already."

The sun disappeared behind some clouds and the air became cooler. Boone and Jenna packed up the blankets and coffee and walked back down to the trailer, where a large box had been delivered to the front door.

"I didn't order anything on a pallet," Boone said.

"Maybe it's a Christmas or wedding present," Jenna speculated, "Do you have out-of-town relatives?"

"Maybe," he replied.

Boone started to move the box and discovered it was very heavy. With a shrug, he pulled a small knife from his pocket and slit the packaging tape. Inside was a card from Amber. Boone handed the card to Jenna.

"What's this?" she asked.

"I saw who sent it and I don't want any secrets or misunderstandings. Whatever it says, it says to both of us."

Jenna opened the envelope to find a flowery wedding card. Inside Amber had written: "Because the wedding is only family, you are excused for not inviting me. I hope this gift for your new home together will remind you of our friendship."

Boone and Jenna exchanged a look that said, "Here we go!" Boone continued to open the box. For a second, they looked inside with open mouths, and then they both started to laugh. Boone cut the sides of the box to expose a round glass-topped end table with a concrete pedestal base in the form of a pink cactus.

"I'm not sure what to say," Jenna said, "or, for that matter, where we could put it."

"I'm thinking out in the barn," Bone said.

"Is this a joke?" Jenna asked.

"She has one like it by her pool," Boone told her.

"Hmm," was all Jenna could reply.

"The barn?" Boone asked.

"Perfect!" Jenna said, "Although it is a conversation piece."

Without further word, Boone walked to the barn and returned with a wheelbarrow. As he pulled the bright pink cactus table away, Jenna smiled. For her it was a symbol that Amber was out of their lives.

Chapter 29

The Christmas Faire was another big success. Joe and Beth were less tired this year, because they had been working only part time at the shop. Christmas Day was low-keyed, with a lot of the attention on baby Colt, who was beginning to be awake a little more during the day. Sandy arrived Christmas Eve and stayed at Penny's house. The two old friends enjoyed their time of catching up on the past twenty years. Jenna realized the two of them together could mean trouble.

December 26th was busy. As the guys changed the barn from a Christmas Faire to a country chapel, the girls prepared for the wedding. Sandy, Penny, Beth and her sister-in-law, Dorothy all had their hair done in the morning, and then met the younger generations at the nail salon as scheduled. Jenna, Scout, Ally and Kelly were finished with their manicures and pedicures, but the younger girls, Brooke, Anna and Maddie were just finishing pedicures and starting manicures when the grandmas arrived. Baby Colt had been fed and was asleep wrapped on Scout's chest. It was a silly, noisy occasion that Jenna loved. She smiled as she realized all these women were her family! When everyone was finished, they headed to lunch at a place where Beth had made reservations. Jenna was having too good a time to even be nervous about her upcoming ceremony.

By 4:00, it was just dusk outside the barn. Inside, there were heaters and a myriad of tiny lights and rows of seats. Along the aisle, near the back, middle and front rows were white candle stands with holly sprays under white candles in glass globes. Behind the rows of chairs, stood tables with white cloths and red candles encircled with fresh, red and white flowers where dinner would be catered.

Off to the side was Brooke at a keyboard and Anna with her flute. Behind them were the guys Boone had traveled with the past year. The platform which a few days ago held Santa and Mrs. Claus now served as an altar and held more flowers and candelabra. Boone, looking happy, but nervous, stood next to his brother. In the rows of chairs sat Boone's immediate and extended family. Penny sat next to Sandy on one side of the row, with Dorothy who held Colt. Uncle Pete, the self-appointed usher, had seated the guests. He was dressed in all black--jeans, shirt, and jacket. He also wore a silver-colored string tie that he let Scout pick out to match her dress.

When all the guitars quit playing, the keyboard and flute began. Uncle Pete opened the back doors of the barn to allow Scout to begin her walk in ahead of Jenna. Scout, who swore she would never forgive Jenna for getting married so soon after she gave birth, was all smiles in a becoming, long silver/blue dress. A short distance behind her, Jenna entered in a cream-colored, long dress that was plain and fitted in the front, but was bare to the waist in back except for some skinny crisscross straps. As the girls walked toward the brothers, music softly played.

Boone was all smiles as Jenna approached. As she reached him, Scout took her flowers. Boone took her left hand with his right hand, and put his left hand behind her back. When he touched bare skin, he stood straighter, his eyebrows went up, and he leaned back to check out the back of her dress. Looking back at her, his grin widened.

"Plan for a life of surprises," Jenna said to him, as the congregation chuckled.

After the vows were said, the minister announced that Boone had a gift for his bride. Boone walked over and picked up his guitar. As his band softly played, he sang what became his next hit, *She Completes Me.*

I want a girl who completes me
Takes all my guff and still needs me
Smiles when I frown
Won't let me down
Her strength and her heart,
She completes me

The girl of my dreams is not perfect
She gets mad, she hurts and she fails
But she doesn't give up
When life isn't fair
She'll reach for the stars
Believing they are there

I want a girl who completes me
Takes all my guff and still needs me
Smiles when I frown
Won't let me down
Her strength and her heart,

She completes me

Her cool eyes challenge
Her embrace hot as fire
Her mind drives me crazy
Her body's my desire
I found a girl who is both soft and strong
I found the girl who completes me.
Oh yes, Forever,
She completes me.

When the song ended, Boone put down his guitar and walked back to where Jenna's eyes sparkled with tears.

"That was beautiful," she softly told him.

"So are you," he answered.

"May I now introduce for the very first time, Mr. and Mrs. Boone Archibald!" the minister announced.

Boone's eyes shone as he looked into the trusting eyes of his new life partner.

"Breathless," he whispered, and then ignoring the applause, he kissed the bride.

B. J. Swanson lives in Murrells Inlet, South Carolina with her husband and little, white dog.